QUITTER

Kevin Hicks

ISBN 978-1-63575-179-6 (Paperback)
ISBN 978-1-63575-180-2 (Digital)

Christian Faith Publishing, Inc.
296 Chestnut Street
Meadville, PA 16335
www.christianfaithpublishing.com

Printed in the United States of America

PROLOGUE

"So was he like that when they found him?"

"When the boy found him, yeah. Called 911 right away. May have saved his life. Sort of ironic, if you know what I mean."

"Ironic?"

A pause. "I'm sorry. I may have spoken out of turn. It wasn't that long ago, so I thought you knew. You and Mr. Bertollini were close, right?"

"More colleagues than friends. Bert didn't let too many get close."

Another pause. "Well, you've been a big help, Mr. Chambers. And as soon as you can contact...Who did you say it was? His sister?"

"His niece."

"Yes. The sooner you can contact his niece, the better. We hope for the best, but in cases like these, decisions sometimes need to be made."

"But I thought you said he was stable? The paramedics said he responded well to the CPR."

"Yes, his heart responded well. But for now, his heart is the least of our worries. When he fell, he hit his head. That blow has caused substantial bleeding in the frontal lobe of his brain. Given his age and...other complicating issues, I think it best that we have family on hand as quickly as possible."

"This just doesn't seem like it can be happening. I mean, Bert... he's always been such a big...I don't know...*Presence*, I guess."

"Here's a card with my cell number. Please call me if you are able to locate his niece."

"I'll see what I can do. But like I told you, it's been years since she's been home. Last I heard, she was out in the Phoenix area. I'll make some calls and see what I can find out."

"I'm sure you will do your best, Mr. Chambers. Like I said, we always hope for the best. But if decisions need to be made…"

The voices burbled and droned just beyond the reach of the old man's consciousness. They were fuzzy far-away things, like shapes of rescuers above the surface of a pool. Is that what was happening? Was he drowning? No, not drowning, he decided. And he wasn't dead either, at least he'd better not be. He had too much to do today. Too much good work ahead. Most of it involving something important too. A final thing, an ultimate thing it seemed, though what exactly it was lingered just beyond him. It felt like it involved children. It didn't matter. There was too much to do. And he was only…how old? Not old enough to die to be sure, even though he suddenly felt very old. Besides, he had been reading up a bit on the subject, and there was supposed to be a light or angels' voices singing. Yes, that's something he did remember. He'd read quite a bit about heaven lately, and even some about hell. Now he was no expert on either subject, even though in his past he'd sworn liberally by both. He regretted that. That might have been what led him to read so much about heaven.

Anyway, this wasn't either place. This place was wooly, warm, comfortable. Even a little sleepy. But most of all, it was empty. Empty except for those queer voices murmuring in the distance.

He forced his dull thoughts toward them. It was distressing labor, for as he drew closer, the soft comfort began to slip away and cold ache pressed in. The first voice was familiar to him. A man's voice. Kind, concerned, one that could be mistaken for slow-witted if not listened to closely. And it was a voice that could be taken advantage of if care was not given. He trusted the man. There was a past between them, or something akin to it, and it summoned a mild comfort amid the growing cold and ache. It annoyed him when the man's voice paused and the second voice whistled in. This second voice was harsh and clinical. A woman's voice. He didn't know it. He didn't really care to, he decided, even if she was talking about him. Now that was strange. He liked to be the center of conversation, especially if an intelligent woman was speaking. But this place was just too cold. He was too tired. The voices throbbed in his head.

The sleepy comfort of silence tugged at him. It seemed right to drift back. But then a word spoken by the man blasted like a trumpet blare through the flimsy membrane of consciousness.

"I'll let you know, Doc, as soon as I make contact with Sarah."

Sarah. Now that was a name that spoke of both heaven and hell. And it was more than a name. It was a love, a hope, a fear, a regret, all framed in those two soft, sweet syllables. He pried at the shell of memory to reveal more. *Sarah*. Dear lord, but there was a burden in that small word. What was it? Something too long hidden. Yes, he began to remember the sweet torment of it all. But as he did, the old secret grew larger by one. There was another name that needed to be added to the ledger. A man's name. One that he hadn't spoken in years and for good reason.

He fought to swim closer to the voice. Speak her name again. The warm fuzzy sleep now lay far beneath him. He was near the surface now. It lay cruel and cold just above his reach. Pain pounded in his temples as he reached for it. *Throw it to me, and I'll grab on like a buoy.*

But it was a different name that shattered the elusive surface and brought reality crashing in on his suffering head. It was that name he hadn't spoken in many, many years.

"Wasn't she married?" the woman's voice grated. "To the actor. What was his name? Sawyer?"

"Kent," came the terse reply. "Sawyer Kent."

Edward Bertollini's frail body convulsed, and his eyes sputtered open. Raw light poured in, dragging behind it darting figures, insistent voices, and the cloying stink of etherized instruments.

"Bert? Bert? Can you hear me?" It was the familiar man's voice—Artie Chambers. "Squeeze my hand if you can hear what I am saying."

Waves of pain broke against the old man's forehead as Ed Bertollini considered the preposterous request. His left hand had always been one of his greatest assets and an uncommon ally. It had worked a brush across countless canvases, extracting beauty from lumps of oil. It had maneuvered the bird-thin waists of eager dancing girls about endless waltzing floors. Perhaps more importantly, that hand had signed the contract that granted him the job he so desperately loved. But now it lay slack at his side like a disinterested spectator.

"Don't worry," Artie continued, but his words were glazed with just that. "I'm going to contact Sarah. She'll be here before you know it. And don't worry about your classroom. I've got plenty of good subs to cover your classes. And as for the show…" He hesitated, and Bert found this pause more troubling than all the others. "Well, I guess Donna can take that over."

No! Bert wanted to scream, but his voice was as useless as his numb hand. Donna is lovely but incapable. She won't have time to learn it all. There isn't time. And as the pain continued to gyrate against his gray brow, he understood that there might not be time for many things. Nausea stole into his guts. Lifeless cold webbed down half of his body. No, there may not be time. All the while, his head clanged like a clapper in a bell.

With a focus born of desperate determination, Edward Bertollini challenged his right hand to move.

It wriggled with surprising alacrity, and Artie was right there with the answer. "You want a pen? Sure, Ed. Here's a pen. If you want me to bring someone else in, just write it down. Heck, I'll call in Spielberg if that'll set your mind at ease."

No. Only one person could set his mind at ease. Sarah would be coming. But she was only part of what he needed. It was time to finally let go of the burden. But to do so would require digging up old bones, just now before his own would require a place to lie. He had made the plan for this some time ago. Now it was time to set it into motion. Yes, they both needed to know. He could rest at peace with that.

The pen quavered as he carved out the letters on the pad of paper that Artie held. They looked as though they had been scrawled by a kindergartener, but to Bert, they curled with the grace of a poignant epitaph.

Artie looked down at the scribble with dismay, even a little disgust. "Please, Bert. You can't mean him. Anyone but him. Think of Sarah."

But the old man was thinking of Sarah. But he was also thinking of heaven and what he wanted to proclaim generously at those magnificent gates. He couldn't bear to think of greeting his Savior without it so. And he was tired, so very tired.

As Edward Bertollini let the pen tumble from his exhausted hand, the soft, warm darkness returned, wrapping comfortably around him. And as his eyes slid gently closed, he could almost swear that he heard the faint voices of angels singing.

ONE

T he afternoon usually went bad when Rodriguez came over. It got even worse if he brought Canadian whiskey. But since the day had already begun miserably, I didn't exactly shoo him away when his small frame came scampering up to my apartment door. There's a certain harmony in a day going from bad to worse. I was sort of in the mood for it, especially if it involved Canadian whiskey.

"Happy birthday, Shakespeare," Rodriguez rattled a plastic jug between the door and jamb. "Two busted crates at the dock today. Lucky me, I was in charge of returns. I even got a movie for later. Open the door, man."

It wasn't really my birthday, but it was something he liked to say any time he scored some hooch from his job at the distillery. "This isn't a good idea, Rodriguez," I protested faintly. "It's not even four o'clock. Oprah's still on for cryin' out loud."

"Like I always say, it's five o'clock somewhere." he grinned like a jack-o-lantern. I really think Rodriguez thought he had invented that expression. I was always going to correct him but could never bring myself to hurt his feelings. A man has to feel he's accomplished something noteworthy in life after all. "Come on." He slapped the neck of the bottle against the security chain. "Open up. I don't want old lady Schultz to see me out here in the hallway. My wife said she was knocking on the door this morning looking for the rent. Let me in, man. Let's get this party started."

I pulled back the security lock, and Rodriguez slithered in. He was wearing faded jeans and an old Mets jersey with his name written in magic marker across the back. "Got ice?"

"Probably," I said, knowing it didn't really matter.

He thrust the jug up above his head like a trophy and did what looked like a two-step over to my refrigerator. The only thing Rodriguez liked better than ducking our German landlady was celebrating with free booze. And to be fair, so did I.

But that was where the differences began to show themselves. These evenings had polar effects on us. For Rodriguez, they ushered him up a quick escalator to sleepy euphoria. He would start talking about weddings, Christmases, or things he was going to say to his boss in front of the rest of the guys. He would laugh and want to bump fists. He would make preposterous promises about things we were going to do some day. But for me, the booze only made me think of what I hadn't done—or worse, things I had done that I couldn't take back. And if there was a nostalgic video to watch while we drank, it inevitably meant that the pistol would come out.

Today, I had borrowed rent money from a man who didn't believe in late fees. A few hours later, I received a letter declining my appeal for extended worker's comp. Like I said, it was a day that had begun miserably. So Rodriguez's bottle and his VHS copy of *Field of Dreams* coaxed the gun out from between the mattresses by seven thirty.

"Man, put that thing away." Rodriguez lay slumped on the futon like a tiny Jabba the Hutt. "We're almost to the part where the guys come out of the cornfield." He shook the ice in his plastic cup and took another rancid sip.

"I'm serious, Ernesto. This is real. I'm not joking." And he knew that I wasn't. Nobody ever called him by his first name, including himself, unless that person meant business. His cup stopped rattling, and I think I saw him wriggle erect. "One of these days, you're gonna hear this baby go off." I leveled the pistol sideways like a gangbanger and then pointed at my head. "Bang!" I snapped off the TV at the same time for effect. "And I'm counting on you to know what to do with all my stuff."

Rodriguez slowly scanned the room like an appraiser at an estate sale. There wasn't much to appraise.

10

In my thirty-eight years, I had managed to amass the following items of consequence: a K-mart TV/VCR combo left behind by an old roommate who got married, a Presto pizza maker, a drawer full of old programs signed by fellow actors I'd long forgotten, a clock made out of a saw blade with mountains painted on it (a wedding gift that I failed to give to the roommate), a set of stained hot-pan holders (they went with the clock, sort of), a desktop computer on a card table, and the futon Rodriguez was sitting on. Admittedly, there wasn't much left of my once-proud empire.

Rodriguez looked disappointed. But he took another drink and quickly rallied. "Ah, come on, Shakespeare. Why you gotta talk like that all the time? You ain't never gonna pull the trigger on that gun. You got too much to live for. You're gonna get one of those movie parts any time now, I know it. And until then, you got old Rodriguez here to pass the time. You know what you need to do?" He cocked his head as though the idea had just taken him. "You need to call my sister. She could put a smile back on that face."

"You've mentioned that before, Rodriguez." I rubbed my fingers over the smooth bore of the pistol. "And I've seen your sister. Unfortunately, she bears a family resemblance." I handed him the crumpled letter from the insurance company. "Take a look at this. The worker's comp department says that I have been 'medically cleared to resume vocational activities.' You know what that means?"

"Vacation's over, huh."

"No. The vacation's permanent. There isn't a theater within a hundred miles of this city that will hire me now. Nobody loves to gossip more than directors and producers, except for actors, maybe. The word is out that I've been milking this bad back." I wanted to say something snide about actors and directors but I only muttered, "I can hardly blame 'em."

Rodriguez brushed it aside. "Ah, who needs those stinkin' theaters. You'll get a movie part maybe, or what about that TV show you were tellin' me about?"

He was referring to a pilot for A&E that I had auditioned for well over a year ago, just before my accident actually. I had read for the part of an introverted librarian that helps a New York detective research cases. The relationship was to be sort of a "Sam and Quincy" kind of deal. The casting agent liked my read. She said I had a "shallow, vacant quality that worked well against the vibrant warmth of the detective." I never let on that I wasn't trying for "shallow vacancy;" it's just what came out. Anyway, the project was dead, as far as I knew. My agent finally told me not to call him about it anymore. He'd e-mail me if he heard anything new. That was easy because Verizon shut down my number not long after because I hadn't paid the bill.

"That's a dead end," I confessed. "I haven't heard from my agent in months." I peered into the bottom of my empty cup and thought that I should be able to serve up a clever metaphor. Instead, I just stared at the withered ice cubes. "I'm in trouble, Rodriguez," I finally said, and my voice rolled out as cold and bleak as a December funeral.

A sharp knock at the door and the shrill call of our landlord sent us both into motion. I hastily shoved the pistol into my back pocket while Rodriguez sprang for the fire escape. Quick as a monkey, he was out the back door, a burst of late January wind the only evidence he had been there.

"Sawyer, it's me. Frau Schultz." She started to knock again, but I pulled the door open, and her bandy fist punched nothing but air. "Ah, good," she said in her husky German accent. She smoothed the jacket of her jogging suit and smiled.

Most of the tenants of Beekman Apartments lived in fear of Ruthie Schultz. Left an orphan after WWII, she learned the hard way how to be Gestapo-tough and get what she needed. Several of the tenants used to joke that she didn't so much collect the rent as extort it. That seemed to apply to everyone in the building except me. I think she told me once that I reminded her of one of her favorite cousins or something. But whatever the reason, when it came to me, she was all smiles and edelweiss.

"Is there a problem?" I leaned against the jamb, blocking her view of the room.

"No, Sawyer. No problem vit you. I vas looking for Ernesto."

"Well, he's not here." I stood back so she could see in the room. He was gone, and I was glad I didn't have to lie.

"Vell, if you see him, tell him he better have his rent. I am too old to keep chasing him down. Next time, I just hire a man." She pantomimed shooting a Tommy gun. "Bang, bang, bang, go Rodriguez."

"I'll tell him."

"I don't know vy you two are friends. This Rodriguez"—she plucked out a cigarette from her jacket pocket and lit it up—"he's a nothing. He is a go no-vere sort of man." I couldn't help but watch the cigarette bounce on her thin lips and wonder how bad I'd look smoking. Somehow, Ruthie pulled it off artfully. "But you…" The smile was back in her eyes, and she let out a plume of blue smoke. "You are a good boy. You are going places. Someday, I vill see you even in the movies, ya? And I vill tell people that I knew you here at the Beekman. I vill tell them that you were a good boy."

I never knew that kind words could hack like a machete.

I shut the door and slumped into the chair in front of my computer. The dark screen was like a dismal mirror reflecting my aging face and the meager appointments about my apartment. I tugged out the pistol and admired it in the screen. Like so many things in my life, it, too, was broken. I had bought it at a flea market several years ago when my life really was going somewhere and life seemed easy. Out of pride, I didn't ask enough questions. I wanted to look like an expert. The vendor saw right through me. He unloaded a pistol with a defective firing pin, and I never bothered to make him correct my mistake. Like I said, I was too proud and, well, life seemed easy, and it was headed somewhere.

The gun was heavy, smooth, and cold. I watched the reflection with odd detachment as I dragged the bore along my temple, down my jaw, and into my mouth. I knew the face in the mirror too well. There were no secrets between us. He wasn't a man whose life was going places, whose face would someday be on a movie screen. No. He had played that hand poorly and lost. Now he was just waiting for the rest of the chips to play out. He was tired and resigned. His days all went the same. And his nights always tasted like cheap whiskey with a gun-metal finish.

I had owned several titles in life. I had been a son, a star, even once a lover and husband. But now the only title that truly defined me was "quitter." And it wasn't the whiskey talking. It was the uncaged truth that sometimes only comes out after a glass or two.

I was only good at one thing. Quitting.

In junior high school, I had played football. But when it got too tough, I moved on to golf. When golf didn't draw enough crowds, I moved on to acting. Granted, I stuck with that for a while. But after a few disappointments, I quit that too. And after all those years on the stage, when I fell off that rehearsal platform and heard the crunching sound of vertebrae, I could only think one thing. *Finally. Now, how long can I make this injury last?*

There was no fire in my belly. No passion. Just resignation. Time to move on to something else. This gig is just too hard.

Now, to my defense, I'm good at quitting. I'm good because I know the secret. See, many people *want* to quit. They want to quit their jobs or their wives or some other miserable situation they have wandered into. The problem is, they don't have the guts to really quit. They leave behind an opening or a doorway. They give a forwarding e-mail address or phone number. And that mars the quitting with the possibility of a reunion.

I don't do that.

Call it a blessing or a curse of the acting trade, but when I quit, I control the feelings. I shut off emotionally. I compartmentalize. I walk away and command my heart to never look back.

I learned it from my dad.

My only problem was that as life stumbled on, there was a diminishing life to quit. It was like working down a ladder. Eventually, the only move was to step off the rungs.

That's how I felt with that gun in my mouth. It's why I wished the gun wasn't broken, why I wished it were loaded. But the only thing in that room that was loaded was me.

I slammed the pistol down hard on the card table. The force jiggled the computer mouse, and my black mirror vanished. A scene of white-capped mountains took its place, and a small tab popped into the top left corner. "1 New Mail," it gleamed cheerily, and I pushed back from the table.

I didn't usually get new e-mail. I usually didn't get anything new. I had tried Facebook for a while but decided that it was just a phony platform for narcissistic youths. I quickly grew sick of it. The truth was, I didn't have anything to say and got annoyed with those who did. I quit Facebook years ago.

That cheery pop-up continued beaming happily back at me. I felt a faint twinge of excitement and silently cursed myself. But I couldn't stifle the silly notion of what might lay behind that digital door. I stuffed the pistol back between the mattresses. If my agent was really contacting me about a job, it didn't seem right to have a gun in my mouth.

I took a deep breath and tapped the link to my e-mail. It read, "Achambers@hanover.k12.il.us. Re: Director's position."

The address looked like gibberish, but pieces of it were familiar. Thoughts of my agent calling evaporated and dread hovered in its place.

Hanover, Illinois, was my hometown—a place I was glad to be rid of. And Achambers might be Arthur Chambers. He used to teach in the vocational tech department at the high school there, and still did as far as I knew. As for the rest, I wasn't sure I wanted to know. The old director was Ed Bertollini. Bert, or Mr. B as I usually called him, was a man who gave me far more than I ever gave back. He took me in like a son when I desperately needed a father. He went out of his way to teach me more than just stagecraft. He tried to teach lessons about being a good man. I only listened to half of what he had to say. The story gets far more complicated after that, but the sum of it is this: of all the people I quit, Ed Bertollini was the one I regretted the most.

When I was working routinely on Broadway, I used to fantasize about running into him on the streets of New York City and having a beer together, you know, patching things up. Every now and again, I'd even dream I was back in high school rehearsing for a show. He'd be there, pacing the boards, leaning forward and listening with one arm tucked behind his back. He'd correct a mistake but all the while let me know that he still believed in me. Sometimes, even Sarah was there, sitting on the bleachers, smiling.

But if there was a director's position now open at the school, it meant that there would never be a chance to reconcile.

As far as I know, Mr. B didn't believe in retirement.

I steeled myself and clicked open the e-mail.

> Mr. Kent. Your mother thought I might be able to find you at this e-mail address. Ed Bertollini left a written request that you resume his position as director of shows at Hanover Township High School. This is a paid position. Please contact me ASAP if you have any interest in this job.
>
> Arthur Chambers
> Principal
> Hanover Township High School

He left his cell number at the bottom, but my stunned eyes slid from the screen. I'd like to tell you that I felt the warm flicker of hope kindle in my heart, or something dramatic like that. But the truth is, I didn't feel anything. In fact, I just sat there thinking, *Sawyer, how do you feel about this? What are you going to do? This isn't an antiseptic article in a newspaper. This is about Mr. B. This is about you.*

Slowly then, the glacial plates that sealed the diseased emotions of that past began to grind open. And like a midnight assassin, shame crept in.

Before I dropped out of college, I took a class that was supposed to teach us about acting, characterization, and plot movement. Two things I remember. One was that my buddy I sat next to liked to speculate that the professor was probably a hot-looking woman back in her prime, back in the '60s. I would then reply, "What do you mean, the 1860s?" The second thing I remember is that the old gal was pretty sharp. She insisted that a character in a good script would continue to act in a certain manner until something happens that makes his situation intolerable. Only then will the character change.

I used to compare that logic to my own life and found it only partly true. I had made plenty of changes, but not every time was it because I found myself in an intolerable situation. I might have been uncomfortable, but nothing as bad as "intolerable." Heck, sometimes, I changed things out of pure fancy. But as I stared at those six lines on my computer screen, the midnight assassin made my situation intolerable.

The notion of returning to the scene of my greatest humiliation and regret was utter anathema. Aside from my mother's funeral, I vowed never to step foot in Hanover again. But the hideous prospect of disappointing Ed Bertollini one last time was something I hadn't considered. And now, as I threw it all onto the scale, having nothing to live for afforded little dignity to lose. My own pride was inconsequential. Shame was what drove me from home. And shame would be the crook to yank me back.

I staggered down to Ruthie's apartment and pounded on the door before I could change my mind. "Mrs. Shultz? May I use your phone?"

The first call was easy to make. Mr. Chambers was curt and efficient on the phone. He simply instructed me to be in his office Monday morning if I was serious about the job. The conversation was frosty but short. I'm not sure he even said good-bye.

The second call was to my mom. It had been so long I barely remembered the number.

"Hello, Mom?"

"Sawyer? My goodness! Honey, how are you?"

She could have asked, "*Where* are you?" or "Where have *you* been?" Or she could have scolded me, "You haven't called in over a year! You've missed every Christmas and holiday for over a decade! Any call from you must mean you're in trouble. The prodigal's father had a better son." Any of those would have been as deserved as they were true. But instead, she purred, "Oh, sweetheart, it's so good to hear your voice."

My mother is a beautiful woman with a pure faith in God that I often envied and sometimes mocked. I'm not proud of that, but it's the truth. During my teen years, I came close to making it my own.

I traveled with a passel of kids who went to Bible study, prayed regularly for one another, and seemed to have more fun than anyone else I knew. I hovered just at the edge of their warmth and commitment. I guess I was afraid that if I got too close to the fire, it might expose things I didn't want seen. My mom fanned what little flame limped inside me, but when I left home, it wasn't enough. She never gave up though. I could hear that now in her unashamed affection.

"I was just thinking about you this morning and praying that you had a wonderful Christmas." Her warm grace poured like lava over my ears. My chin crumbled. I struggled to move my lips so that words came out and not a tsunami of sudden tears.

"I need to come home, Mom," I think I said. "There's a job. It's Mr. B's. I'm in trouble. I'm sorry."

"Sawyer, honey, it's okay. Just tell me what I can do."

More unbearable grace. I thought I might break to my knees. My next words leaked out with a trickle of tears. "I need a bus ticket. I don't have any money." I pulled the phone away, ashamed and surprised at the ferocity of sadness inside me. I took in several deep breaths while I heard my mother's reassuring voice try to calm me.

"Sawyer. Settle down, sweetheart. It's all going to be fine. Just tell me what I need to do. Where I can send you a ticket?"

One last sobering sniff and the wall of tears abated. I cleared my throat. "Actually, Mom, do you have a credit card?"

I managed to end the call without slipping maudlin and without too many questions from Ruthie. I needed to get out of there. I was jangly with nameless nerves. I felt like a kid at the top of a sled run—scared but excited as the sled tipped downward. I just wanted to be off with it. Too much more thinking and I might dig in my heels.

It was time to leave this town and the wreck I had made here. It was time to quit again.

I burst into my apartment and snagged the only coat I owned, a smart-looking wool overcoat I'd had for years. The rest could stay, with the exception of Rodriguez's whiskey. It tucked so nicely beneath the folds of my large coat it'd be a shame to leave it behind. Besides, it was cold outside.

There was a Fast Cash station that stayed open late just a few blocks away. Over the last few months, I'd gotten chummy with the owner there, a short middle-aged Pakistani guy named Zareef, who everyone called Pak-man. He had been helpful advancing me funds against my unemployment and insurance checks. I knew he'd be able to convert Mom's credit card numbers into enough cash to get me home.

"How much I make this for?" he asked, his hand poised over a keypad.

"I don't know. How much do you think a bus ticket from here to Chicago and then down to Peoria will cost?"

Pak-man looked pained. "Too much, I tell you that right now. Better make for three, four hundred. You need to eat and maybe get cab." Then he stopped and eyed me. "You can pay your mother back, yes?"

"I'll pay her back, Pak-man," I told him, and I meant it.

He finished the transaction, and I was back out in the bracing cold. It was crisp and exhilarating in my dusty lungs. The bus station was at least four miles away, and even though I had ready cash in my pocket, I began hiking my way uptown. I had the whiskey to keep me company.

I never minded walking the city, even in the winter. I loved the way the tall buildings stood stark against the pink city glow and black sky above. A friend once said they looked like "dark urns full of diamonds." I liked that. The city hadn't been romantic for me in some time, but tonight, it was magical. It was like an elegant but mysterious lady wearing black, with the stars done up in her hair. I just hoped that the spells she cast would be favorable.

It was well after midnight when I arrived at the station. I was lucky. A Greyhound was leaving at 6:00 a.m. and traveling a route that ran west along the Great Lakes to Chicago. I bought a ticket and sat down on the end of a bank of blue plastic seats. An old lady bundled in woven blanket sat a few chairs down, eating scrambled eggs out of a Tupperware dish. She thoughtfully chewed each spoonful and mooned her eyes up at the ceiling, and as I watched her, I wondered if she knew my dad or had ever seen him.

I know that's a stupid thought to have. But it was at a bus terminal that I last saw my dad, or at least the last time I saw him when he meant something to me. So every time I'm in a station, I find myself glancing around, wondering if I'll see him again. I don't really know why. Like I said, stupid, right?

Yeah, I guess it's probably time to unpack that crate of memories. It's not one of my favorite topics, but I suppose I should probably talk about my dad and me.

When I was a kid, my folks used to fight all the time. But I was little and just figured it was normal. In the back of my mind though, I wondered if some of it was my fault. See, my dad was a big man, six foot three, with shoulders as wide as an axe handle. And he wasn't just big, he was a tremendous sportsman. He even played first base for a little while in the Tiger's minor leagues. I think he hoped I'd inherit his affinity and skill.

But I was a pudgy kid with little ability and even less interest. I'd much rather have played with my Legos or make believe I was Han Solo in the backyard than put on a mitt and toss a ball. By the time I was nine, I still couldn't play catch, and I knew that it bothered my dad.

About that time, things had been getting pretty bad at home. The fights were turning physical, and we were buying new lamps nearly every week. My older sister (yes, I have a sibling, a successful dentist whose story will have to wait) understood the gravity of it all and tried to protect me. But I was nine, and I had a great idea that even Han Solo would have appreciated.

I was going to finally learn to play catch. And to show my dad that I meant it, I was going to buy him a brand new glove for his birthday so we could play catch together. I even had a scheme to raise the money. It was going to be epic.

I remember it was cold, probably February or March, when I first hatched the idea and put it into action. My teacher at school always would walk us down as a class to use the bathrooms before heading on to the gym, where lunch was served. Now, all of us fourth graders had recess right after lunch. That meant most of us clever kids gobbled down our lunches like convicts getting shot at sunrise because it meant more time on the playground. Our teacher was a nice old lady with cotton-white hair and rosy varicose veins in her cheeks. But she wasn't particularly attentive, especially at lunchtime. So I would linger in one of the bathroom stalls until I heard my classmates reform the line and march on down to the gymnasium. Then I'd grab my coat and duck out to the playground with a nifty seventy-five cents of lunch money clinking in my pocket.

It was a terrific plan. Sure, I was ravenous by the time the school bus deposited me back at home, but my growing nest egg easily stemmed the hunger pangs. I had it all worked out. I could pocket three and a half bucks a week. My dad's birthday was in late May. By the time that rolled around, I would easily have the $28.97 that I needed for the leather Spalding Tom Seaver model mitt at Jacobsin's Hardware.

I was so proud. In early May, I bought the glove on the sly, even making Mr. Jacobsin promise not to tell anyone. I darted home and stashed the gift in the back of my closet, all the while dreaming of Han Solo and secret missions.

But my dad never got the glove. It wouldn't have mattered. At the time, I didn't realize that a leather baseball mitt couldn't cure alcoholism. And it certainly wouldn't have fixed the infidelity. My sister could have told me, but she didn't know either.

All we knew is that one heart-gutting weekend, Dad packed the big Samsonite suitcase, and we drove him to the bus station. It would have been even more terrible had it not been so surreal. We took him in the station wagon and just said good-bye. Come to think of it, he didn't even say that. He just kissed me on top of my head and said, "Be good." It was like we were dropping him off at the hospital for a procedure of some sort, except we all knew that he wasn't going to ever come back. He and Mom just politely exchanged good-byes, and he was gone. Nothing was left behind but bus fumes and butchered hearts.

I know that I cried. I cried my shirt wet. But that's not what I remember most. What clings in my memory like a tumor is that Mom took us to see the movie *The Princess Bride* right afterward. All my friends had been raving about it, but I couldn't even look at the screen, let alone concentrate. All I could think of was that I didn't give Dad his baseball glove.

I held on to that mitt for a couple of years. I kept it buried under my toys in the back of my closet. I know I was hoping that Dad would come back. Someday, we'd finally have that birthday party. He'd blow out the candles, and I'd hand him the glove. His face would light up far brighter than the candle-lit cake, and Mom and Dad would hug. Then we'd go outside, and I'd catch and throw the ball like Willie Mays.

But after a while, resentment curdled that white, milky hope. Just the sight of the glove made me angry. I was mad at Dad for leaving, and I was mad at myself for holding on.

There was a set of railroad tracks that cut through a field not far from our house. When I turned eleven, I decided that if I was old enough to have two digits in my age, I was old enough to start acting like a man. And as far as I knew, men didn't hold on to silly dreams. Men made hard choices and did things that were tough. So I plucked the mitt from under a pile of Hot Wheels tracks and lost Legos and headed out for the field.

Around sundown, the train finally appeared. It was one of those long piggyback trains with a string of boxes, open cars, and flatbeds. I waited until most of them had passed by me. But when a rusty boxcar with graffiti lacing its sides came rumbling by, I pitched that glove up onto its roof and let it bear the wretched thing away.

I stood there for the longest time—I'm sure until after I was late for supper—watching that train trundle away. It got smaller and smaller, just like my childish hopes, until it disappeared into the dark line of the horizon.

My father did try to reenter my life several years later, when I was a senior in high school. He had been living in Northern Indiana with a new wife and her son from a previous marriage. My father had done well for himself. He and a partner had opened a company that made chair lifts for staircases in old people's homes. From what I understand, they hit it rich. The plant was in Indiana, but he got a tax break to sell in the Chicago area as long as he maintained an office in Illinois. So he opened a central office just down the state highway in Carlock, only thirty miles or so from Hanover. He wanted to see me, but I refused to let him come to the house. He didn't belong there anymore. So I met him in his office in Carlock. He knew that I had won an acting scholarship to Illinois State University and that I intended to study drama. He told me he was proud of me for going to college but wanted me to pick up a business minor to fall back on. He said that he could find me a job in his company when I graduated if I couldn't find work on the stage.

I responded with a number of uncharitable statements about his company, his offer, and himself.

I didn't see him again until my wedding day. I wasn't even going to invite him, but Sarah insisted. I finally yielded, but only with the promise that he not be my guest but hers. I even went so far as to instruct the ushers to seat him on the side of the bride. If anyone was going to play the part of my father, it would be Mr. B.

It was a triumphal day. My father was parked humbly in a back row on the left side, and I refused to shake his hand. The only words we shared came when he approached Sarah during the dollar dance. As soon as I saw him, I cut in. I remember thinking of Michael Corleone in the *Godfather* telling his brother Fredo that he was "nothing to him anymore." I was channeling my inner Corleone when I looked my father dead in the eyes and said, "This is where I step in. And this is where you step out." Nothing could have been more definitive.

What gave me the strength to be so bold was that day in the field by the railroad tracks. It was the first time I was genuinely glad for it. I used to tell people that, that day was the day I became a man. It was the day that I made a good decision even though I knew the consequence would be hard.

I felt just like that sitting in the station, watching that old woman eat eggs and holding a bus ticket for home in my trembling hands.

TWO

The bus trip took much longer than I expected. We made stops in Buffalo, Erie, Cleveland, and South Bend all before finally chugging to a halt at the depot in Chicago. I was glad for the breaks. The rumbling seat sent nasty twinges up my gimpy back, and consequently, both it and Rodriguez's whiskey gave out somewhere outside of Rochester. So I stretched one and reloaded the other at nearly every stop.

By the time I hit Chicago, I knew I had to dump the bottle. I wasn't sure what hold drinking had claimed on me in the last few years, but I wasn't about to greet my mother half drunk. I bought two water bottles and a pack of Big Red chewing gum at the Chicago depot and clambered aboard my final transfer, which would roll me south down Interstate 55, into Peoria, and to the past that awaited me.

Hanover, Illinois, is a town where very little happens. But what does happen is never forgotten. That's why Sammy Deets, who stripped the football and recovered it in the end zone, giving the Hanover Falcons its only state championship, still can't pay for dessert or appetizers in either of the two cafes or at the Casey's General Store. It's the same reason every child over the age of five can point to the bullet mark in the masonry of the bank facade and tell you the name of the gangster that Bugs Moran had bumped off after the traitor fled south to link up with one of Capone's men.

And it's that same capacity to remember, for better or worse, that elicited my vow to never return home.

Now, I'm no Bugs Moran to be sure. I've been a thief, yes. But there are those in Hanover that would accuse me of murder, or attempted murder anyway. That's not fair, but Sarah has scars on her neck and wrists to support their fable. I still don't know exactly how much guilt I have to bear in that ugly business. It's more than a little though, I'm sure.

Sarah Gibson was the darling of Hanover. Everyone in town knew her and loved her. She possessed an exotic beauty, but one that was belied by Midwestern practicality and kindness. The first time I saw her, a freshman chorus girl in Brigadoon, I remember thinking that she didn't belong in Hanover. She looked like a girl from one of those foreign films with subtitles that Mr. Bertollini insisted on showing us. Small-framed and athletic, Sarah smoldered with dark tangly hair and pebble-smooth olive skin. Only her blue tender eyes placed her back in Illinois. The eyes were a family trait—one that was claimed by her uncle, Ed Bertollini, and her mother, Joanna Gibson, the school secretary and sometimes nurse.

Hanover loved its own. And if its own was a sweet, tender-hearted girl with a suffered past, it embraced her even more.

Sarah fit the bill.

Everyone knew her uncle, and everyone adored her mom. Her father, though, was a bit of a tragic mystery. He had been killed one sun-splashed April morning while cycling the streets of Peoria. It was early in the day, before church, and a drunk driver came racing down Abingdon Hill and never saw him. Sarah was eight at the time, certainly old enough to understand what she had lost but far too young to know where that loss might lead her.

As it turned out, it led her to me. Neither of us had a dad, and that gave us a common point of reference as we began talking and later dating. That was during Brigadoon, Sarah's freshman year and my sophomore year. It was a magical time. I had never had a girlfriend before. I even gave her my class ring, and she wore it proudly on a necklace. It seemed so perfect, that is, until the next year when a second tragedy struck. Her effervescent mother, Johanna, was diagnosed with cancer. Brain cancer. Late stage. It was ugly. Bless her, she battled courageously, but the cancer was insidious. The tumors took her hair, then her spirit, and within eighteen months, her life.

It was the winter of Sarah's junior year, and like all of Hanover, that's when I really fell in love with her. And it wasn't pity. Like I said, she and I had dated prior to her mom's illness. But Sarah suddenly coaxed out a noble desire in me that I had never experienced before. I wanted to save her, sacrifice for her. Sarah made me feel like a hero. And it wasn't some stupid kid's fantasy, like Han Solo rescuing Princess Leah or something. It was a deep, penetrating magnetism that pulled me to her. Having her uncle, Mr. B, looking on and approving all the while only confirmed the deal. Sarah and I were married the summer after she graduated high school.

But I didn't expect the ferocity by which she clung to me. I was only twenty, but I became her most immediate family. I wasn't prepared for it. Sure, she had her uncle to remember birthday parties and such, but I was the one she counted on to lift her up emotionally, to lean on for most everything. I thought my shoulders (my dad's shoulders as it turned out) were wide enough to bear it all, but they weren't.

One thing about being a hero is it can get suffocating under all that armor. For me, I began to feel stifled by her need for me. I couldn't push it away. So after a while, I pushed *her* away. I knew it was selfish and wrong. But I had another lover by then. The stage had bewitched me. I tried for a while to create a world in which I could love them both. I couldn't make it work. Towards the end, I didn't even try. Sarah and I were divorced within two years.

I got up to stretch my back and use the Spartan bathroom before hobbling back to my seat. The bus was only half full, and I could take liberties. I sprawled my six-foot frame out over the pair of velour seats in my row and laid my forehead against the cold window. I looked out and watched as the snowy field rows flickered by.

I had forgotten how vast and vacantly beautiful an Illinois winter could be. In the city, the horizon is no more than a street corner away. But here, the flat prairie stretched out like a magician's white-gloved hand, promising much more than met the eye. For me, it conjured the sweaty anxiousness of being young in a world still full of undiscovered possibilities. Occasionally, we rolled past a familiar landmark, an old barn with a weathered Meramec Caverns sign painted on its planks or the abandoned strip mine outside of Kankakee, and that youthful excitement bubbled inside me even more. I was falling back into my past. It was horrible and wonderful all at the same time.

And looking back, I wish at that moment I would've remembered one other thing: I'd left a gun, a gun registered in my name, between the mattresses in my abandoned apartment.

THREE

Mom was waiting for me at the bus station when I arrived, nearly a full twenty-four hours after I had left. She was wearing a pair of stylish corduroy slacks tucked into fur-lined leather boots and a green hooded cloak that fell past her knees. Mom always looked young. Some of it had to do with her gracious smile, and some of it could be accounted for by tricks she learned during her years as a beautician. At sixty-five, her hair was still the color of strong tea, shot with highlights of honey. Most of her youthfulness, however, stemmed from her fierce reluctance to act old. My friends used to marvel that she attended concerts of our favorite artists and that she routinely kept up with the latest fashions. Standing in the parking lot of the Peoria bus terminal, her green cloak flapping in the January breeze, she reminded me of a wise elf right out of one of Tolkein's novels.

She didn't say a word when she saw me. Instead, she wrapped me up in those small arms and rocked me side to side.

I think a few flakes of snow began falling before she finally said, "Oh, sweetheart, it is so good to have you home."

"Well, you might be the only one that feels that way," I answered, but returned her strong hug threefold.

"Let's grab your bags and get out of here."

"I don't have any."

"No luggage?"

"I didn't have anything worth lugging," I explained, and she laughed at that.

My mom and I shared the same sense of humor. Even in the rough days of my youth, even when Dad left, I was able to make her laugh. It warmed me to see I still could do it.

"Oh, Sawyer." She playfully slapped at my shoulder before ushering me over to her white Nissan Murano. But then her face turned serious. She stopped before unlocking the door. "Before we go any further, I probably should tell you something."

"What, Mom?"

"I don't live alone anymore."

"Really?" I couldn't have been more stunned if she had told me that she was responsible for the Kennedy assassination, but all I could think to say was, "Really?"

"I know that surprises you, but don't let yourself worry. I've told him all about you, and I think he understands. It's just that…"

"What, Mom?"

"It's just that he can be pretty jealous at times. You might call him a little *territorial*."

"Territorial?" I was beginning to think Mom did have something to do with Kennedy's death.

"I just hope that you'll give him a chance. He's very particular about who he likes. He doesn't have many friends. But, Sawyer, he absolutely loves me."

I know my head must have slumped in disbelief, but I heard the chirp of the door opener and was thankful that the conversation was over. I tugged open the door.

Sitting inside on the passenger seat was a footstool-sized black dog. He gave me a suspicious glare.

I think the word *footstool-sized* came to mind because that's sort of what he looked like. His body was solid and blocky, supported by short, stubby legs. But his head was proud and regal, the head of a golden retriever, only black. Given his feathery curled tail, which stood stock-still, he looked a dog that God had assembled with a bunch of spare parts.

"His name's Noah." I heard Mom say as she climbed into the driver's seat. "Like I told you, he's particular about friends. But he absolutely loves me. Noah, get down. Noah? Down."

I sputtered out a chuckle that was more relief than laugh and watched as the dog sullenly stepped down into the foot-well at the front of my seat. Mom gunned the car to life, and that's how we rode the thirty-five miles back to her house. Mom cheerily manned the wheel, all the while nattering about improvements to the house she'd made and people in the neighborhood who either moved in, moved away, or died. Meanwhile, Noah sat between my feet in the shadows of the foot-well and stared up at me between my knees. His eyes were Sheol-black with the exception of tiny white rims that looked like fingernails against his black fur. He studied me the entire journey like a hit man summing up his prey.

The talk of neighbors dying brought up the unenviable topic of Mr. Bertollini, so I reluctantly broached the subject. "So did you go to the service for Mr. B? The visitation or whatever?"

Mom nearly stopped the car. "Visitation? For Edward? Honey, he's in the ICU at St. Sebastian. He's not dead."

My misassumption slammed me in the chest like a sledge-hammer, blasting out my wind and denting my words. "I guess I thought...From the way Chambers's e-mail read...I just assumed..."

Mom must have realized that I was processing a new revelation. Her tone softened. "He's not doing well, Sawyer, but he's hanging on. One of the gals in my Bible study is a nurse on the floor there. She's not allowed to say much, but Ed's been on our prayer-chain list since he fell. But he's a tough old bird, you know that. And sometimes, God chooses to perform miracles. So we'll keep praying."

"So he fell. Was that it?" I was vaguely nodding as I tried to put it all together visually in my head. "I didn't know how it happened. Chamber's didn't tell me much."

"He had a stroke, honey. At least that's what I understand. He was home working, and when he fell, his head hit the corner of his desk. He hasn't been conscious since then, as far as I know. I figured you'd want to go up and see him sometime anyway." She flicked on the turn signal and began slowing for a stop sign. "But that's your choice, of course."

My choice? Hardly. Conscious or unconscious, I would have to go visit. But I wasn't prepared for Mr. B in either state. I wasn't even sure which one I preferred. Of course, I was happy that Mr. B was still alive, but these last several hours, I had been preparing to visit a grave. Mom's words felt like a spade digging his corpse back out of my heart.

"Do you think they'd even let me up on the ICU floor? I'm not family…Well, not anymore. And there are a lot of people that would rather not see me anywhere."

"Sawyer, Edward personally requested that you come and take over his position. From what I heard, he had it written down or something." She cringed with a show of sudden guilt. "Okay. You got me. Yes, after you called, I did some snooping. Call it the prerogative of a curious mother. Anyway, it all adds up the same. Edward wanted you back. How could the hospital not respect his wishes?"

Even Noah must have seen my face go pale. He placed a fuzzy paw on the seat near my thigh and pushed his head forward. He shoved his wet black nose against my forearm and rested the side of his head there.

"You can think about all that later, sweetheart," Mom said as she angled the car into the narrow lane that led to her driveway. "I bet you're hungry. At least I hope you are because I've got dinner ready."

I glanced at the clock on her dashboard and said without thinking, "Dinner at 9:06 in the morning?"

"We're Kents. When did timing ever get in the way of a good meal? And besides, it's Christmas."

Like I said, Mom and I shared the same quirky sense of humor, so I didn't bother asking about the Christmas reference. I would find out in due time. She was doing an admirable job of keeping the tone light, and I didn't want to spoil it for her.

Our old house was a small ranch-style home with a detached garage and large backyard that backed up to a wooded gully and farm fields beyond. Despite the family chaos, it was a wonderful place to grow up in, with room for my young imagination to wander. As we turned into the gravel driveway, I couldn't help but think that the yard and woods didn't seem nearly as big as they once did.

The house had a side door adjacent to the garage that led down a flight of stairs to Mom's beauty shop in the basement or up to a landing that opened into the kitchen. As a kid, we always entered the house from that door, but today, Mom jostled me up the uneven walk to the porch and front door. Noah led the way.

When she flung open the door, an aroma from my childhood nearly flattened me.

"Italian beef?" I asked, but didn't really need to. The heady, beer-salty smell was thick and unmistakable. "You made Italian beef." I drifted in and only then saw the handmade poster affixed to the chandelier hanging over the dining room table that read "Merry Christmas!" On the wooden table, two small packages and a third, the size of a breadbox, sparkled in shining wrapping paper.

"I hope you still like it," Mom was saying. "You loved it as a kid. I also have provolone cheese for sandwiches and potato salad." She pummeled my shame with a glorious smile and said, "Welcome home, Sawyer."

As far as I know, the Bible doesn't talk about what the prodigal son was thinking at the feast. Everyone just assumes it was a great time for everyone. You know, laughing, singing, and all. And I'm sure most of that is true. But I have to believe that while he was standing there, his father rejoicing, the servants celebrating, he felt a little like I did standing in the living room of my old house. Overwhelmed but ashamed. Stunned but not surprised by the generosity of his parent. Sad but unworthy of any tears. Grateful. In short, there must have been a storm raging in his heart, a magnificent torment that threatened to undo him.

"You shouldn't have gone out and bought me Christmas gifts, Mom. I—"

"I get you kids gifts every year, Sawyer," she cut me off. "I just didn't know where to send yours these last few years. So I just kept them in the closet for you. I knew someday you'd e-mail your new address or something." There wasn't a hint of scolding in her voice, but her honesty was brutal.

She handed me the big package first, and it was then that I realized she had written dates on each of them. "Christmas 2013, Christmas 2014, and Christmas 2015." It had been three years since Mom even knew where I was living.

"Of course, you are always so busy at the holidays." She opened the crockpot and gave the Italian beef a redolent stir. "The curse of the acting trade, right? Everyone gets the week off except for the performers."

I collapsed into one of the captain's chairs and folded my arms on top of the package in my lap. Hot tears flooded my eyes. I didn't care to stop them. They began to trickle Indian file down my cheeks. Normally, I would just blame them on my fatigue. I was tired, hungry, and not myself. But I was weary of the tricks and dishonesty. I wanted to say something honest like my mom, even if it was brutal. And so I did.

"It's all a lie, Mom."

She clinked the lid back on the crockpot and slid into a chair beside me. "What is, honey?"

The tears continued unchecked. "Christmas was. I am. The whole thing…" I was veering offtrack. I sniffed and rephrased my confession. "I haven't worked a Christmas in years, Mom. It was all an excuse. I didn't want to come home and face…everything…I don't know. And with Andrea being a successful dentist with a family and all, I just felt…I just didn't want to deal with it. I was ashamed to come back, and the theater gave me an excuse to lie. I hardly ever worked Christmas. Fact is, I haven't worked at all in over a year."

Mom was rubbing my back and shushing the tears away. "That's all in the past, Sawyer," she tried to reassure me. "It doesn't matter anymore. It's all part of yesterday. And today…" She brightened. "Today is Christmas!"

I tore into the presents and then into the Italian beef. Mom had bought me a new full-length wool coat for the 2013 East Coast winter, the Star Wars complete saga six-DVD set for 2014, and a Visa gift card for Christmas a few weeks ago. But the best gift she gave me was the Italian beef and the words "It doesn't matter anymore. Today is Christmas!" I wanted to believe her, and a small part of me thought that I could.

After plowing through two heaping provolone-drizzled sandwiches, a cereal bowl full of potato salad, and the lion's share of a pan of rice krispie treats, a delicious fatigue settled into my joints and limbs. I unsuccessfully boxed a prolonged yawn back into my throat. *How long had it been since I'd had a decent sleep anyway? Two days? Surely not.*

But it had been. *That lifetime ago with Rodriguez in my apartment was Friday. Saturday was swallowed by the bus ride. And Mom picked me up today…Sunday?* The discovery sent my head swimming and made me feel all the more exhausted.

"Honey, why don't you go lay down and get some sleep?" Mom was putting the plates into the dishwasher, and she gestured toward the hallway across from the kitchen. "The bed in your old room is all made up for you."

The offer was like a buffet to a fat guy, but I managed to hold out and say, "Let me help you clean up first."

"Oh, don't be silly, Sawyer. I'll take care of this. You go sleep." She paused, the slotted spoon still dangling in one hand. "I may try to go to evening church tonight since I missed it this morning. If I'm not here when you wake up, that's where I've gone. But it usually wraps up around seven or so, and I'll be home right after that."

"Sure, Mom."

Mom had been a rock of lightheartedness and optimism since she picked me up at the station. But in that strange moment by the dishwasher, I saw for a split-second behind her defenses. Her eyes pooled red and watery, and she wiped them quickly with the back of her hand. "Go get some sleep, Sawyer." She waved the spoon at me as if to shoo me away. "I'm fine here. Go take a nap."

I wasn't sure if the brief spell of tears was from joy or sadness. Regardless, she wanted to spend some time in church that day, and a little part of me was jealous of that. I couldn't ever imagine *wanting* to be in a church.

My old room was at the end of a short hall and on the left. I braced myself for the certain avalanche of nostalgia before pushing the door open.

I shouldn't have bothered.

If I still had lingering attachment to my old room, clearly Mom did not. The small room had been completely repainted from the macho blue that I had thrown on the walls as a teen to a sedate beige.

Lacy eggplant-purple curtains framed the two corner windows, and a dresser that looked like it once belonged to Mary Todd Lincoln stood in place of the chintzy one that used to shoulder my certificates, awards, and trophies. Even the bed was different. My narrow twin had been switched out for a queen that hogged most of the tight space. A thick downy comforter that matched the curtains stretched over the raft-sized mattress, and enough pillows for a sleeping hydra were piled at one end. A round end table with spindle legs and a digital clock stood nearby.

"Did you have anything to do with this?" I asked Noah, who had followed me into the room. He just stared at me. I think he was checking to make sure I wasn't going to make off with any of Mom's valuables.

I yanked back the heavy comforter, and a spill of pillows tumbled onto the floor. "Well, boy? If you're tired, feel free to join me." I arranged a rectangle of the fallen pillows on the floor and patted the center. "Believe me, I've slept with worse than the likes of you."

Noah never shifted his eyes from me, but he cautiously stepped over to the small bed I had made and eased onto the pillows.

I slid into the soft bed and sunk beneath the comforter. "Ooooh, memory foam mattress," I guessed. I had seen the commercials. "Have a nice nap, old boy," I called down. "Please don't kill me while I sleep."

Noah slumped to his side and stretched out his stubby legs. When I woke up, he was still there on the floor, snoring away like that old man in the children's rhyme.

FOUR

I thought I was hallucinating when I read the clock. *6:05?* I growled and shoved off the comforter. "Noah, you weren't supposed to let me sleep so long." I mashed my eyes and glanced out the window. Sure enough, day had ended. Mom's yard light was valiantly fending off the darkness. "Well, come on, boy. At least we didn't miss *The Simpson's*. Ever seen it? It's pretty funny."

I staggered out to the living room, but Mom had already left. Mom had the remote sitting neatly on the sofa table, and I clicked on the TV. Some local news hack was waxing eloquently about a food pantry that was collecting items for the survivors of a house fire. "*The Simpson's* must come on at 7:00 here," I informed Noah, but he was more interested in a white mashed chew stick under the table. I turned off the set and sprawled out on the couch. My back had tightened up since the morning, and I gave it a twist that crackled like gunfire up my spine.

My stomach rumbled.

I've read that stress can actually make some people gain weight. Luckily, I've never had that problem. Despite the calamity of my adult life, I was still only a few pounds heavier than I was in college. I certainly wasn't fit and healthy, but I looked relatively slim. If stress were ever going to make me gain weight, I'd look like Chris Farley's chubbier brother by now. But my stomach rumbled a second time, and I couldn't deny that I was inexplicably hungry again.

I wandered into the kitchen.

Bless Mom. She must have guessed that I'd want a snack. Her Bunn coffeemaker was topped off with a fresh pot, and a sleeve of bagels was lying next to it on the counter. She'd left a handwritten note that read, "Hope you had sweet dreams, sleepyhead. There's cream cheese and fruit in the fridge. I'll be home soon."

She left more surprises on the kitchen table. A Kohl's department store bag contained a folded pair of men's black dress pants, a snappy celery-green shirt, patterned tie, and black socks. On one of the chairs sat a stack of shoe boxes, each with the same style but different sizes. I didn't have the guts to total the price tags. Mom's generosity seemed to know no bounds. But I did intend to pay her back every cent.

Noah was watching me from near the sliding glass doors that led out onto the patio. When he saw me looking back, he turned a circle and pressed his nose against the glass.

"You need to go out, boy?" I was no dog expert, but I knew the look of nature's call. "Let me grab a cup of joe and put on some shoes first." I poured a steaming mug, threw on the new coat Mom had given me, and dragged open the sliding glass door.

The blast of air was startling, but I took in a bracing lungful and stepped outside. We crunched through the snow, and Noah seemed thankful for the company. He kept looking back to see if I was following as he made his way to his usual yellow-stained stops. It didn't take long for him to finish his business and escort me to the side door of the house.

He scrambled into the warm house and up the landing to the kitchen. But the dark stairway leading down to Mom's old beauty shop intrigued me. As a small kid, I'd spent a lot of time playing on those stairs. It was a perfect perch to eavesdrop on what Mom was doing and the ladies' conversations. It was also a quick jaunt to the refrigerator. The stairs were my playground and also my friend—that is, until they destroyed my favorite toy.

Perhaps the greatest toy ever imagined for a boy was the Evel Knievel wind-up stunt cycle, complete with poseable figurine, helmet, and swagger stick. A couple of knuckle-scraping turns of the dynamo could send Evel hurtling over all kinds of danger. Mom found one for me at a garage sale when I was eleven, and I thought it had to be the coolest creation this side of my Atari 2600.

I jumped Evel over pails of water, rows of Mom's curlers, and even once a plume of blue flame that my friend Ken created by spraying Mom's hairspray over a butane lighter. In retrospect, that last stunt was unadvisable, but as a kid, it was awesome. So I figured that if Evel could endure all that and the Snake River Canyon to boot, he could surely handle the basement stairs. As it turned out, the final score read, "Curlers/Fire/Snake River Canyon 0 – Basement Stairs 1."

When that cycle hit the tile floor below, the back axle exploded through the plastic gears of the rear wheel. The figurine skittered all the way across the floor under a dryer, and I never did find one of the handlebars. So much for my favorite toy. And so much for my cozy relationship with the stairs.

I drifted down the wooden stairs, reimagining Evel's fateful descent that day, only to discover that Mom's redecorating spirit had claimed the shop as well. Her old hydraulic chair and sink sat right where they had always been, but there was now only one dryer hunching in the corner where four had once stood. Clearly, Mom was still cutting hair from time to time because the sour tang of perm solution and dusty smell of hair spray still lingered in the air. But most of the room had been converted to an office of sorts.

It looked like Mom had been keeping busy. Near the modern-looking computer desk were two long utility tables strewn with papers, old scrapbooks, and stacks of plastic storage containers. A blocky Hewlit Packard printer squatted in the middle of it all, blinking happily. A pile of old theater programs lay beside it.

What have you been up to, Mom?

It didn't take me long to find out, and the realization unnerved me.

Mom had been scanning old pictures of me. Dozens of them. I found them half-tucked into a large manila envelope.

I put down my coffee cup and rifled through them. There were pictures of me as a small kid in my "bear" coat playing in the snow. There were pictures from birthday parties and Christmases. She had scanned twenty or so of me in high school. Most were from plays or musicals, but there were a few from prom and homecoming.

Sarah was in them.

I pulled those free from the rest. Sarah looked like a princess. Fresh. Beautiful. There were no cares in her eyes. The last time I saw her, there were plenty of lines around her eyes. I was responsible for most of them. But in these old pictures, she still looked young and innocent. Her smile flared like a klieg light.

I picked up the envelope and flipped it over. Mom had written her return address in one corner and pasted a mosaic of postage in the other. But there was no destination address in the center.

Mom's dog-eared address book was lying on the computer desk, and I began thumbing through it. I guess I thought that I'd just magically open to the address she was going to put on the envelope and I'd yell "aha" or something like that. That's how it worked in those Agatha Christie movies. But there were hundreds of old phone numbers and addresses scribbled in no discernable order throughout the yellowed pages. Many had been crossed, rewritten in pen, crossed out again with an arrow that pointed to some other obscure address.

I may have gotten my dad's shoulders, but I inherited my organizational skills from Mom.

Just then, the door at the top of the stairs rattled, and Mom breezed in, stomping snow from her boots.

"Sawyer? Are you down there?" She began clomping down the steps.

I tossed the address book back on the computer desk. "Yeah, Mom. Just down here taking a little trip down memory lane."

Her face pinched, and she bustled over to the tables and started pitching the pictures back into the plastic tubs. "Oh this? I meant to get this all picked up. I didn't expect—"

I stopped her. "Mom, who are you sending all these pictures to?"

She deposited the manila envelope in a tub and snapped the lid shut. "Look, Sawyer, I intended to have this all cleaned up. I didn't think that you'd..." She paused as though she was trying to make a decision. "It's for someone who still...just someone who wanted some pictures. It's really nothing. Don't worry about any of this." She turned off the printer. "So did you get something to eat? I figured you'd be hungry by now."

The question derailed my sleuthing. "Uh, just the coffee so far. I was going to, but the dog wanted out."

I followed Mom, who was already scurrying up the stairs. "Did you see the clothes I bought? I think I guessed right on the sizes for the shirt and pants, but with the shoes, I had no idea. So I just bought the same shoe in a nine, ten, and eleven. Was I close?"

"I wear a ten," I replied in monotone. Mom had shirked off her coat and tossed it onto a chair in the kitchen. Underneath, she was wearing an unflattering sweat suit and a pair of light-blue Nike shoes. "I thought you were going to church?"

"I did." She handed me the box of size 10 shoes. "Here, try these on."

"Evening services must be pretty casual these days." I nodded like I thought that was a good thing.

Mom worked a scrunchy off her ponytail, and her hair spilled around her neck. "I went to church *last* night, Sawyer. I just got back from doing my exercise therapy at the gym. You were still sleeping, and I didn't want to wake you."

The shoebox nearly fell from my hands.

Through the picture window in the front room, I could see the pale-pink head of a dawning sun just crowning over the woody horizon.

"This is a big morning for you. Meeting with Artie Chambers and all. I know you'll do great, sweetheart." She kissed me on the cheek, and hers was still cool. "And you'll look great too. You've always looked so handsome in green. Here, try on the shirt and tie too. When exactly is he expecting you? You said morning, right?"

I was only sent to the principal's office twice in my whole life. The first time wasn't my fault. The bus driver thought I had thrown the snowball at Kelly Jenkins at the bus stop when it was really someone else. The matter was cleared up quickly and to my satisfaction. The second time I was summoned, I was a little more culpable. Tony Guerrero and I had unearthed the entry on *reproduction* in the set World Book Encyclopedias from the back shelves in our classroom. The paragraph on *fertilization* contained a description that was far too mature for our twelve-year-old sensibilities. Twenty-five years later, I can still remember parts of it.

Anyway, Tony thought it would be hilarious to get some scissors and cut the description out to show to the basketball team later that night at practice. I didn't disagree. In fact, I volunteered to stand guard to make sure the teacher didn't see.

She saw.

We both got hauled down to the office, and I swear my heart was in my mouth. I wasn't so much worried about the destruction of school property as I was the *content* of the school property. Mom had been called. She met me at my classroom door and marched with me up the tile hallway to the principal's office where the whole sordid affair was exposed.

This trip to the principal, Mom stayed home but otherwise it felt the same. I drove by myself in silence, parked Mom's car, and walked the green mile to Artie Chambers's office. I didn't know what questions he would ask but I had my concerns. My biggest fear was that he'd ask if I had ever directed a show before.

I never had. But I still had debts, bad ones. I know I should have been thinking more about Mr. Bertollini and his legacy and all. But in that moment, all I could think was that I needed the money. I had borrowed rent, and it would be repaid. Even halfway across the country, my lender would find me. That was a certainty. I wanted to keep Mom out of it. So I figured I'd tell Artie Chambers whatever he wanted to hear as long as I got the check. I was an actor. That's what we did.

As it turns out, all that he wanted was my signature.

"So that's it?" I asked.

"All employees have to agree to a background check and get fingerprinted before they can work with the students. It's Illinois law, and it's a good one." He was sitting behind a large modular desk with papers tilting in untidy stacks across it. "You haven't been convicted of a sex offense, have you, Mr. Kent?"

"Well, not *convicted* of one," I replied. But one glance up to Chambers's tombstone eyes, and I could see that my attempt at humor had risen just slightly below the altitude of the Hindenburg. "No," I amended. "Never any trouble with that sort of thing."

"Good," he replied, but I wasn't sure he actually felt that way.

Physically, Artie Chambers was much as I had remembered him. He was lean, with an unassuming chin and retreating hair. He had a kind, uncomplicated face. His voice was not commanding. In theater parlance, he was an underling. He was not leading role material. And yet today, this underling had taken control of the stage. I was left to play a secondary role, and I was nervous with that. "Donna Thewlis will be down in a minute," Chambers continued. "She can bring you up to speed on what's happening with the production. She's quite talented and has a good way with the kids. I recommend you trust her." He paused. "By the way, you do have experience directing shows, don't you?"

"Absolutely," I lied. "You can count on me."

Artie propped his elbows and leaned over his desk. His fingers were steepled, and he leveled his gaze just over their bridge. "I'm not so sure I *can* count on you, Mr. Kent. Your history doesn't suggest that I can. You left quite a mess back here in Hanover, you know. You hurt a number of good people, very good people. You're only here now because of Ed Bertollini. I hope you don't let him down."

It was an awkward moment. Certainly not the time to discuss pay, but I needed to know. "I promise I'll be worth every last cent," I hinted and thought I was pretty clever, considering the circumstances.

"Yes," Chambers languished back into his high-backed chair. "I haven't had much time to discuss terms with the superintendent, let alone the school board. Because of his years of service, the school was paying Ed $4,700 for the Spring Musical. A director with no experience would receive $3,450. I imagine we can cut you a check for that upon completion of the show."

More awkward silence.

"That's terrific," I grunted into my fist. Chambers probably thought it was a cough. "If that's how things usually work, that's fine. I did have some expenses from dropping my, uh…previous work and getting back here to Illinois. In the theater world, you usually get a portion of a gig up front. For, you know, expenses and all."

Chambers stroked his small chin. "You make a decent point. I'll talk with the superintendent and see what we can do. But nothing can happen until we get clearance from your background check."

"How long will that take?"

"You'll need to stop by the courthouse and get fingerprinted. We don't do that here. They can probably give me a preliminary report by tomorrow. If everything checks out, you could start rehearsals Tuesday evening. I'll call you. You're at your mom's, right?"

"For now, anyway."

There was a timid knock at the door before a pleasant face peeked in. "Hey, Artie. Just checking in to see if you needed me?"

Chambers's face brightened. "Donna. Absolutely, please come in. Mr. Kent, this is Donna Thewlis, our vocal music director." He waved her into the office.

Donna had a quick, perky smile that I liked right away. Her brownish-red hair was pulled back, and she wore a hideous business suit and rectangular stylish glasses that so many of the twenty-some-things wear these days. But Donna didn't look twenty. She was more my age; her wide, chunky hips betrayed her. But she was still attractive even in an ugly business suit. She had the kind of "pretty" that young men miss but old men see. "You two may know each other. Donna is a Hanover grad. Let's see, you graduated in…"

"'98," she admitted sheepishly.

"So you were a sophomore when Mr. Kent graduated. She was Donna Myers back in those days."

"Hi, Donna." I shook her hand. "I knew you looked familiar."

"Well, you two will be spending a lot of time together over these next two months." Chambers was already back in his desk, moving stacks of paper around. I got the sense that he did a lot of stack moving to fill up his days. "Donna? Why don't you take Mr. Kent down to the auditorium and show him around?"

It was obviously a dodge. Chambers was done with me, and now, he was passing the albatross. Donna accepted graciously.

Hanover Township High School had changed measurably since I had left. In the mid-1990s, the school had received a building grant that allowed it to tear down several decrepit wings and add a veritable labyrinth of hallways, classrooms, a gymnasium, and an auditorium on the northern flank of the school.

Donna led me down one of the shiny new hallways. On both sides of the hall were old pictures of graduating classes, the earliest dating to 1907. I had seen them before. They used to be hung in the hallway leading to the lunchroom. It gave us kids something to look at while waiting in line to have our lunch tickets punched. Back then, the faces were old and arcane, a mystery to be solved. But today, the black-and-white faces seemed to recognize me. They stared at me with accusing eyes. *What are you doing here? Another chance at failure, Kent?* I was sure they were heckling. *Screw this up and you'll outdo your old man. What a failure!*

"So Chambers said your maiden name was Myers?" I asked Donna as we clicked along the hallway. "Were you in any of the theater productions back then?"

"All four years, including Camelot and West Side Story with you." She unlocked a pair of steel doors and pushed them open. "And let's cut the crap right now. If we're going to work together, I don't want to start off with lies. You don't remember me at all, do you?"

"Not exactly."

"See? That wasn't so hard. And it's okay. Back then, all of us girls knew who you were. None of us expected you to know our names. Sarah had your attention."

We strolled through the doors onto the wings of a splendid auditorium. "This is our new space. Ed is pretty proud of it, as you might imagine."

Mr. Bertollini had every reason to be proud. The stage was enormous and complete with a fly system and balconied house. "How many does it hold?"

"About 1,200. Enough for the entire student body and staff to sit in here for assemblies. A far cry from the old gym, where we used to stage our shows, huh?" Donna was staring up into the darkness of the high ceiling. She seemed as proud of the place as I was impressed.

"I think the most we could jam into the old gym was about 400, not that we sold out many of those shows."

"How about here?" I teased. "Any sellouts since you moved to the auditorium?"

"Hardly. But that was Ed's goal for this show. Three nights, 1,200 butts a night. A pretty tall order."

"Eww, here's something I don't like." I had wandered to center stage. "Look how wide this proscenium mouth is. We'll have to cut that down with curtains to protect our sight lines. But worse is the depth of this apron." I stepped off the distance from the main curtain to the front of the stage lip. "What is this, eighteen to twenty feet? That puts stage pieces a long way from the front row of seats."

Donna seemed surprised but in a good way. "That's exactly what Ed said the first time he came in here. 'Who designed this stage front? Barnum and Bailey?' But he managed to find some tricks to make it all work. It's not as intimate as the old gym, but you know Bert, he could make magic in a shoe box."

Donna's eyes suddenly seemed less bright. She pushed her glasses back up the bridge of her nose. "Have you been up to see him?"

"Actually, I just got into town." It was a genuine excuse, but it didn't seem very satisfying. "I was going to try to slip up there soon. Maybe this afternoon after we're done here. Have you been up?"

Donna nodded. "Just for a minute. I have my daughter this weekend, and I'm pretty protective of our time. But I figured I owed it to Ed to at least pop in."

"How'd he look?"

"Small. Weak. Terrible. You know, Bert always seemed so...big. He'd walk into a room, and everyone noticed. It's bad seeing him this way. Unconscious. Pale. Tubes running everywhere." I think she actually shook her head to chase away the thought. "Look, here's Ed's binder. I found it with his stuff in his classroom. He's probably got notes on the first few scenes at least. You know how organized he always was. He liked to have most things nailed down before rehearsals began. I can e-mail you the rehearsal schedule and cast list. You've got e-mail, right?"

"Yeah." I could have said, "That's assuming Mom's computer is hooked up to the Internet. I live with her. I have no car, no money, and only a single change of clothes." But I didn't.

"If Artie gives us the green light tomorrow, you can start blocking Act 1. I've already begun morning vocal rehearsals with the company." She clunked into my hands a phone-book thick three-ring binder. It had a multicolor *G* printed on its white cover, and the title of the show flourished beneath it.

"So we're doing 'Godspell,' I see." I didn't mean anything by it, but Donna nearly came unglued.

"You didn't even know the name of the show we're doing?"

"There's a lot of things I don't know," I tried to joke.

Her white teeth flared. Even angry, I had to admit, she was kind of pretty. "Look, Mr. Kent—"

"Call me Sawyer."

"Look, *Mr. Kent*, if you came here to make this return somehow about you, then you need to walk right out of here and take the first plane back to wherever you came from. I don't know how it works in the big city, but at Hanover, these shows are first about the kids. After that comes the parents and friends and way down the totem pole can come your ego." She took a breath before firing one last salvo, "And somewhere else in the mix—way ahead of your ego, mind you—should come the reputation of Ed Bertollini. This was going to be his last show that you, by some quirk of delirium, managed the good fortune to inherit. So you need to consider all of that before you agree to have your name printed as *director* on the program." She flattened the front of her pantsuit with her hands.

"Are you done?"

"For now, I think."

I was never much good at confessions, but this one poured out like easy liquid. "Look, Donna, I don't know much about what I'm getting myself into. That's painfully true. I didn't even realize that this was to be Mr. B's last show. But I can tell you for certain that this isn't about me. Hanover is the last place I ever thought I'd see again.

And if I had even a shred of dignity left, I never would have come back. But I don't, and so I'm here. And if you'll help me, I'll do my best to make this a great show for Mr. B."

My unvarnished honesty was apparently enough to cool her. "All right. I just felt like I needed to get that out in the open."

"At least I'll never have to question where I stand with you. Who'd you learn your diplomacy skills from, Artie Chambers?"

"Are you kidding me?" She took a step back. "Artie's the biggest teddy bear I know."

"That hasn't been my experience with him. 'Bear,' yes. 'Teddy,' no."

"All you need to know about Artie is one thing. He leads with his heart. He's never been the most dynamic person, but he's made his way up to principal because he is loyal and kind. Two qualities that will take you a long way in Hanover. To Artie, this school is his family. Hurt his family and you'll see his claws. He's just worried that you'll do that. You did it before. You know, he was close to Mrs. Gibson. They even dated for a while."

"Artie Chambers dated Sarah's mom?" I was incredulous.

"A year or two after her husband died. Ed actually set them up, but Johanna said she didn't want to divide her time away from Sarah. Artie was heartbroken. I think he really loved her. They stayed close all those years, not as close as Artie would have liked, but he was a gentleman. I think he cried as much as Sarah when the cancer took Mrs. Gibson."

"How do you know all that?"

"Ed told me. He enjoyed playing the role of cupid, for better or worse." The knowing look she gave me was half irony, half stiletto. Obviously, she knew that Mr. B was the instigator between Sarah and me.

We waited in the auditorium for a few minutes for the passing bell to sound. I admired the gallery of musical posters that lined the wall outside the green room while the herd of high-schoolers stampeded outside. When the coast was clear, Donna walked me to the door. On our way, we passed the old gym, and I insisted on a look.

The old gym was a wooden palace built right out of the post-modern blueprints of the 1920s. On one side, it had a bank of permanent wooden bleachers with crafted stairs that stretched from the floor to the bottom edge of an oak-planked Quonset hut roof. On the opposite side was a shallow, black-box stage framed by a red brocade curtain and valence. The whole room reeked of wood, sweat, and municipal wax—the most wonderful elixir of my teenage years. The first sniff sent me hurtling backwards to my youth, Mr. B, and Sarah.

I've read that scent is the sense most closely tied to memory. It's gotta be true. The walls of Camelot suddenly rose up to my left and right. The stairway where I held a dying Maria and the Brigadoon town square materialized over the jump circle. And just as suddenly, thunderous applause sounded in my innocent ears.

The virgin thrill of hearing a crowd roar for you is more intoxicating than liquor and twice as addictive. But it's never quite as exquisite again after that first time you hear it. I stood at the lip of the old stage, closed my eyes, and imagined guzzling it down all over again.

"Do you two want to be alone?" Donna said from the doorway. "I can give you and the gym another few minutes if you like."

Normally, I would have appreciated the clever jibe, but the nostalgia had colored me serious. "You know what's tragic about these shows?" I was still standing there on the stage like some great sage engaging his pupils. I know it must have seemed overdramatic, but I was caught up in the truth of it and didn't care. "These shows end. The crowd applauds. Then afterward, family and friends rush forward and tell the kids how wonderful and talented they are and how they should study acting in school or audition for Broadway."

"What's so tragic about that?" Donna waltzed right into my melancholy trap.

"Sometimes, the kids believe them."

FIVE

I needed a drink.

Okay, I didn't really *need* a drink, but I sure felt like I did. My tolerance for tension had gotten pretty low over the last several months, and whiskey was what I turned to for fortitude. Trouble was, there would be no whiskey at Mom's place. So I made an ill-advised decision to swing past a gas station after my stop at the courthouse and grab a jug of something cheap. I only had $38.09 left from the money Mom gave me to get home, so I dropped $7.99 on something called Tucker's Finest. Clearly, Tucker was an underachiever.

I have to admit that I felt guilty smuggling the bottle into Mom's house. Noah stared me down the whole way like a Russian custom's officer. I sneaked a few mouthfuls, chased them with mints, and hid the bottle behind some old boxes in the closet of my bedroom. Noah sauntered away disgusted.

There wasn't much shame in my last life when it came to booze. But in this world, things would be different. You don't drag along an ex-wife on a date. That's a little what toting the bottle into the house felt like. But the thought of going on and living a new life without my old companion made me feel…To be honest, it made me feel a little afraid.

I found Mom down in the basement. The boxes of pictures and envelopes were nowhere to be seen. She was tidying up her computer desk and dusting with a fake yellow feather duster. She lit up when she saw me. "So how did it go at the school?"

"It was touch-and-go at first. But once Chambers got a good look at this snappy tie you bought me, well, how could he not give me the job?"

"I'm sure he was very impressed," she teased back. "Had I bought that vest I was looking at, he might have made you dean. So when do rehearsals start?"

"They already did. The music rehearsals anyway. I have to wait until my background check goes through. Don't give me that look, Mom. I'll pass it. Anyway, I'll probably start tomorrow night. The music director is sending me the schedule and cast list. Is your computer hooked up to the Internet?"

"Of course." She acted insulted and pressed the blue button that fired up her HP Pavillion 110 desktop. "So you met Donna then?"

"Do you know everyone in Hanover, Mom?"

"Most of the good ones."

Well, to answer your question, yes. We met, and she told me exactly what she thought of just about everything, including me."

Mom percolated a little laugh. "That's part of Donna's charm."

"Only if you find a sledgehammer charming."

"You know, she's not married."

"Dear lord, Mom. Are you kidding me? I'm home for one day, and you're already pairing me up with the music director? I think you've been watching too much cable television."

"I'm just saying that she's a great gal and that maybe you two would enjoy each other's company."

"Well, that great gal hasn't sent me the schedule yet." I clicked off the computer. "And it looks like we'll have plenty of company with each other, whether we want to or not."

Mom fussed a little longer with the duster, and I followed her upstairs. "I've got the room number for Ed if you want to go visit." She peeled a Post-it note off the wall by the telephone. "I'm only saying because tomorrow, I have a pretty full day and will need the car. So if you wanted to go, today might be—"

"I heard he didn't look good, Mom. I'm not sure I'm ready to face that. Not this soon anyway. He's unconscious anyway. He'll never know whether I came or not."

My mom always had a way of pulling the salient string out of a knot. She did it again when she said, "I don't think you should go for Ed's sake. I think you should go for yours."

I chewed on that thought for a while and imagined how much better it would taste with a swallow of whiskey, even Tucker's Finest.

"Sometimes, there are hurdles in life that we need to take in turn," she explained. "Don't you think it would be better to have seen Mr. Bertollini before you see all of his kids tomorrow night?"

I probably should explain that I hate hospitals. I'll go to any length to avoid visiting them. When I was little, my grandma was shuttled in and out of one for months before she died. She had triple bypass heart surgery (pretty rare in those days), and Mom dragged me daily through those antiseptic halls. In my mind, the place was a haunted house with desperate voices moaning behind the half-closed doors, blood-flecked tile floors, somber doctors whispering over charts, and the ever-present wreak of disinfectant—Death's aftershave, I was sure.

Mom says I'm crazy. She told me that I loved visiting Nana in the hospital, even begging to go see her. Mom claims my abhorrence for those places developed later. Maybe she's right. I think the last time I willingly entered a hospital was after Sarah and I were married. It was a bad day. It was the day the baby died.

The intensive care ward was located on the fourteenth floor of St. Sebastian hospital. I punched the number 14 button and rode the elevator in silence with a frocked orderly, a nun, and a young Japanese guy with an iPod who hummed *You Can't Always Get What You Want* all the way up.

Like I said, it had been a while since I'd been in a hospital, and I made a mistake right away. I tried to find Mr. B's room by myself, and a nurse stopped me directly. "Can I help you, sir?" She sounded like she wanted to berate me more than help me.

"I'm just trying to find room 1431. I was guessing that it should be down this hall."

"It is. But you need to check in with the nurse's station first. The ICU doesn't work like the other wards. Not all patients can receive visitors, and even then, it might be for only limited amounts of time." She led me to a round half wall behind, which lay some kind of mission control center. Three nurses in brightly patterned smocks were zipping back and forth behind the counter. "Now, who are you here to see?"

"Edward Bertollini. I was told he was in room 1431."

"And are you family?"

"Yes," I lied.

"Let's see," she punched a few keys on a computer and looked over the rim of her glasses. "Yes, Mr. Bertollini is in room 1431. You are aware that he is currently unresponsive."

I cleared my throat. "I knew that, yes."

"And your name?"

"Sawyer Kent."

I've been to a few funeral visitations before. Every time, I get a fluttering dread as I make my way through the line and nearer the casket. I think it's the apprehension of what the body will look like, I don't know. But room 1431 felt more like a visitation than it did a visit.

I shuffled past a plastic privacy curtain to the bed.

And there he was.

It was a cruel sight. He looked so small, frail, lying there in that bed with tubes running everywhere. His wispy hair was matted down, and his proud bushy moustache lay flat and dull-gray over his chalky lips. He was wearing one of those dehumanizing gowns and his thin hairless legs poked out the bottom. A lemon-sized bruise on his temple added a further indignity.

It wasn't Mr. B. At least the unconscious body lying there bore little resemblance to the man I once knew. In some ways, it made it easier.

Donna was right when she said that Mr. Bertollini always seemed big. He wasn't a big man physically, but he was a prodigious presence. The first time I ever saw him was my freshman year, when all the English I classes were pooled together to watch the movie *Romeo and Juliet* on a projection TV in the library. Most of us had old Mrs. Thackery, whose wrinkled face looked like she'd been sucking persimmons for the last decade. None of us knew how old she was, but we used to joke that when Mrs. Thackery said she taught Shakespeare, it meant that she really taught William Shakespeare.

So we were all huddled together like galley slaves, scared to move a muscle for fear she'd break our necks with more grammar homework when in walked Mr.B. And when I say he walked in, it was more like he *paraded* into the library with entourage in tow. His students were laughing and smiling. A few lucky ones were near the front of the queue by Mr. B as he pointed out where to sit and gave them directions. They dutifully obeyed.

During the movie, he made pithy remarks about lovesick Romeo, Benvolio's costume, and the gorilla-faced nurse. But among the laughter, he sprinkled in thoughtful questions about the nature of love and hate and its powerful communicator—theater. Old Mrs. Thackery just sat there in the dark marking papers like the Charon pouring over his to-do list at the River Styx.

And it seemed to always go that way with Ed Bertollini. He overshadowed everyone else. Heck, even when Juliet scampered out of the bed half-naked, my first response was to not to stare a hole through the screen but to see what kind of reaction it stirred in Mr. Bertollini. He stood there serenely, taking in Juliet's sudden nakedness with a dignified calm that suited a man of the arts. I casually turned back to the movie and mimicked him.

He drew a crowd, and one that wanted to follow him. Kids wanted to get close. They were desperate to seep into the inner circle. They were jealous of the charmed few who did. I was one of those few.

Yet as public of a life as Mr. B led, he was fiercely private. He rarely let anyone penetrate the safe boundaries of his wit and creativity. He kept people farther than arm's length. He would work with them, laugh with them, even travel with them. But few knew what was happening inside of him. Never would you hear him talk about subjects that ventured close to his heart. Any dangerously tender moment would be cleverly deflected with humor. Most people found that aggravating, but it didn't stop them from trying.

I don't really know why he was so private, but I have a guess. I think at the core of this considerable man was a nagging fear that he couldn't live up to everyone's expectations. He was afraid that if he allowed them to pull back the curtain, they'd only see a tiny, unimpressive Oz pumping furiously on pedals and tugging at levers. His magic remained protected behind his mystery.

He shouldn't have worried. He let me see behind the curtain flap, albeit sparingly. And certainly, I saw that he had a few warts. Mr. B played favorites, and he doted on them. He also had a temper that vented itself in creatively disturbing bursts of profanity. And he could hold a grudge. Not a little grudge. I'm talking a full-blown, Italian blood-stoked grudge that had a better memory than ENIAC.

But stronger than all of that was a heart that could love so big it seemed impossible that it fit in that barrel chest of his. He gave without regard to himself. His priorities were always outwardly focused. He would paint another man's house while his own peeled down to the planks. Mr. B was genial, charismatic, talented, and just plain big. That's why the scrawny, bare-legged man breathing through a machine in the bed next to me just couldn't be him.

A plump nurse with short mousy hair swished into the room without knocking. She began changing out one of the plastic bags dripping who-knows-what into one of Mr. B's veins. She didn't say a word, and I felt like I should fill the awkwardness with a question or comment, but I couldn't think of anything to say. Fortunately, the door opened again, and she broke the silence by greeting the newcomer. "Oh, hello, Dr. Stratton."

"And how is Ed doing this afternoon?" I was surprised by his casual tone and familiar use of Mr. B's first name. But most everything about this doctor exuded informality. I have to say, I kind of liked it.

He was clean-shaven and tanned with sandy hair that seemed like it belonged more on a surfer than a doctor. And he was younger than me by maybe only a year or two, but his green eyes and quick smile made him seem younger still. He wasn't wearing a lab coat or scrubs. Come to think of it, he didn't even have a stethoscope. Instead, he was casually attired in a white polo shirt and a pair of tan Dockers. I had to wonder if he realized it was still January outside.

Dr. Stratton took Mr. B's pulse and checked his vitals on the computer monitor. "Has the surgeon been in for an evaluation?" he asked the nurse.

"Not yet. But I would expect her back on the floor by four thirty or so. Will you be here that long?"

"It looks like I will be now," he said without a hint of sarcasm. "I really want to see what Dr. Schaeffer wants to do about these ICP numbers before I leave."

The nurse nodded and left, and Dr. Stratton turned to me. "And you must be Sawyer Kent," he said graciously.

"I'm sorry," I think I stuttered. "Have we met before, Dr. Stratton?"

"No," he grinned. "The nurse at the station told me that a Sawyer Kent was here when I checked in." He extended his hand.

You can tell a lot about a man in the way he shakes your hand. A limp hand means he doesn't care or wasn't raised well. But a firm handshake can tell you even more. See, lots of men think it's an opportunity to impress you with their strength. If they give you a vice grip and stare you down, it speaks of arrogance or that they are hiding something. My guess is that Napoleon gave everyone knuckle-cracking handshakes. But Dr. Stratton just gave me a warm firm handshake, looked me in the eyes, and said, "Please, call me Jim." He pulled up a chair and sat in it backwards.

"So how is he doing, Jim?" I tested out his name, and it didn't seem as odd as I thought it might. "You said something to the nurse about a surgeon and ICU numbers or something?"

"ICP," he corrected me but not in a superior way. I have to say, I really liked this guy, even if he did work in a hospital. "ICP stands for intracranial pressure," he continued. "And unfortunately, it appears that there still might be some small hemorrhaging inside Ed's skull. I was hoping the surgeon could give me an indication of what she thought and if she believes Ed needs more surgery."

"And if he does?"

Jim folded his arms over the back of the chair. "It's really hard to say at this point. There's always a risk with surgery. But he's also at risk in his current condition. For now, we need to hope that, if there is bleeding, it stops and the pressure on his brain subsides. But even after that, Ed would have a long road to recovery."

His estimation wasn't unexpected, but it was still hard to hear, especially with Mr. B lying three feet away. "Well, it sounds like Mr. B is in good hands anyway."

"We'll do our best. So how about you? How is the play going?"

The unexpected question was like a mortar shell to my gut. "The play? How did you know…" I'm sure my face must have screwed up like Luke Skywalker's when Darth Vader told him he was his dad.

Jim reloaded with a disarming smile. He waved off my stammering. "I need to apologize. I haven't been completely fair with you. When the nurse at the desk told me that a Sawyer Kent was in the room, I already knew a little bit about you. Sarah told me that you might stop by at some point."

Forget the mortar shell. His last revelation was more like a warhead detonating. My brain scrambled with implications. *Sarah? Here? Expecting me?* I tried to spew them out all at once. But the questions were swirling like gumballs in a machine. I could only slowly roll one out at a time. "Is Sarah here now?"

"No, she's left for the day. I told her I'd try to stay around long enough to find out what the surgeon had to say. She may be back tomorrow, I don't know. I think she's still trying to get settled in at her friend's house."

If I was thinking more clearly, I would have wondered why Dr. Stratton knew such details and why he'd share them with me. But I was flummoxed, and I was consumed with getting those gumballs out of my head. "How long has she been here? And when she said that she knew I might visit, was that a bad thing? I mean, was she unhappy with that idea? And who's the friend she's staying with? Is it here in Peoria?"

Jim kept his responses to these questions a little more close to his vest. Either that or he didn't know much more. He told me that Sarah had flown in Friday, but given Mr. B's uncertain condition, she immediately began searching for a longer-term solution for housing. The hotel she was staying in would get pricey. And on top of that, well, it was a hotel. He went on to say that one of her old classmates was now a veterinarian and had a large house on a lake. When she heard about the circumstances, she invited Sarah to stay with her. Jim said the classmate lived in Sarah's old hometown, at least he thought so.

The small spurts of information burst against my head like the torrent from a fireman's hose. I had no idea who the classmate was, but I knew the lake. Hanover only had one lake. And the neighborhood that circled it was only a five-minute bicycle ride from Mom's place.

I was trembling, I'm sure, as I excused myself from the room and shambled back to the car in the parking deck. I wasn't used to handling so many calamities all at once. For the last year and a half, my biggest problem was convincing Rodriguez that he couldn't crash at my place for the night. But now I had Mr. B dying, a play to figure out how to direct, no money and no immediate prospects, and now Sarah back—back in Hanover, a town too small in which to decently hide.

I fired the car to life and burned a trail home. My new friend Tucker was waiting. And I can tell you for certain, Tucker never had a finer hour.

Given my condition, I should never have cracked open Mr. B's production binder. Like I said, alcohol coaxed out the despondent philosopher in me. One look at his familiar printer-perfect handwriting sent me on a maudlin downward spiral that Diogenes would have been proud of. The binder was stuffed with exacting staging notes, set drawings, and rehearsal checklists. I found the cast list with contact information tucked into the inner pocket. The entire libretto had been photocopied (one-sided) and placed on the rings so that the text appeared on the right and the back of the previous page lay open on the left so that he could make blocking notes. I even found a drawing of the production T-shirt and phone number of the silkscreen company that was producing them. In short, there was nearly everything I needed to direct the show laid out for me in Mr. B's meticulous script. It should have elicited a celebratory relief. Instead, it broke my heart.

This was going to have been Edward Bertollini's curtain call. And it was clear that he wanted to go out with a statement. It made no sense to me that he would choose me to be his voice.

"Godspell" was originally written to be staged on a playground. Jesus would show up and start painting faces and telling stories that would draw the other players together. I had seen it before. A buddy of mine I met in *Ragtime* had landed the role of Judas Iscariot in a production that was playing on the West Side. I remember thinking that Jesus was sort of a charismatic, hippy magician that made people happy. The cast sang great songs, and in the end, for no good reason, they crucify the magician. Great music. Weird show.

Mr. B was planning on telling a very different kind of story. He had drawn set designs that imagined a filthy inner-city slum. He had originally gone to college to be an artist, and his skill still showed itself in his detailed sketches of the set.

Stage left held a series of derelict row houses with crumbling stairs and barred windows. Upstage center was the corner of a fleabag hotel. A rusty fire escape provided a balcony on the second floor. Barely visible in the distance was the courthouse, a white plastered building. Mr. B had drawn it with a grilled door and large windows that gave it the appearance of a skull looming in the background. Stage right was littered with other rundown buildings: a pawn shop, a tattoo parlor, and a shuttered garage. And speaking of litter, he planned to have it everywhere, garnishing the set like tinsel on a dilapidated Christmas tree.

Mr. B had also cut the show's opening number, an ensemble called *Tower of Babel* that had philosophers from throughout the ages blathering at each other in sort of a musical mess. Instead, he had written this beginning, "Curtain pulls to reveal dark stage. Only vague shapes of the buildings can be discerned. A soft, low tone is heard, followed by the sound of an argument. Tableau 1 is lit downstage right. A man and woman fighting. He has her by the throat. Other voices gather in the sound, and the tone begins to crescendo. Tableau 2 is lit stage left. A pair of gangbangers shooting craps by the broken stairs. More city sounds add to the cacophony. Shouts and cries and the murmur of a police radio. Tableau 3 is lit upstage right. A young girl, pregnant and forlorn, is seen carrying a plastic grocery sack. The sound swells to its zenith. A mad rush of sounds and then a gun shot. Stage goes completely black and silent. And then out of that darkness comes the voice of John the Baptist (dressed as a newsboy) singing the opening song 'Prepare Ye the Way of the Lord.'"

To the side of these stage directions, he had written, "This is the world Jesus entered. Desperate and broken. It's the same kind of world he reaches out to today."

I had never known Mr. B to be very religious. I knew he had gone to Catholic grade school and attended Mass on holidays, but I had always seen his Catholicism as more cultural than spiritual. Obviously, I was wrong.

I took a last swig of the whiskey and flipped through the rest of the binder. The stage directions thinned out in the second act, and he had nothing written for the final two numbers. But it was enough. Enough to get started and enough to feel unworthy of the task ahead. This show was to be his holy grail, and I was certainly no Galahad.

I closed my eyes and fell back on the plush bed. I was tired, probably more from the whiskey than anything else. Sleep came quickly. And as I slept, I had a repeating dream. It was of me and Rodriguez shooting a never-ending game of craps beside a crumbling staircase on the set of Edward Bertollini's magnificent stage.

SIX

Two surprises were waiting for me when I woke up. The first was Noah sleeping soundly on the bed near my feet. It wasn't so much that he was near me. I was pleasantly aware of the incremental détente between us. But what baffled me was *how* he managed to get there. This was a dog designed to sit, sleep, and occasionally glare. How those stubby legs had propelled his squat body onto the bed was a trick to confound Chris Angel. Noah was curled up like a black velvety doughnut and snoring lightly. When he heard me stir, he wriggled closer and shoved his wet nose under my hand. I gave him a little pet on his head. I had to admit, this stocky little guy was starting to grow on me.

The second surprise lay on the dresser. Stacked in a neat pile were several pairs of jeans and a whole tower of shirts. They weren't new, at least they bore no tags, but they didn't look terribly worn either. I shook out a pair of the jeans and tried them on. They were a little long, but otherwise, they fit pretty well. "Did you have anything to do with this?" I asked Noah, who replied with a prolonged yawn and stretch of his front paws. "Mom didn't tell me you could high jump. Guess you can sew too, huh?"

I tossed on a soft flannel shirt and strolled into the kitchen. Mom was there clutching a mug of coffee and sipping it gingerly. "Oh, they look like they fit perfectly. I thought you two were about the same size." She stood up and admired my new ensemble.

"Almost perfect. The jeans are a little long, but I can roll them. But you shouldn't be spending so much money on me, Mom. I'm already into you for several hundred, at least."

"Relax, Sawyer." She waved me off. It was one of those mom gestures that would tolerate no rebuttal. "And don't worry. I didn't spend a thing. They were a gift from an old friend of yours. You remember Timothy, surely?"

"Timothy?"

"Timothy Kavenaugh? I saw him at church Sunday night and thought you two were about the same size. Remember, my first job I had was at Sears in the men's department. That's where I met your father. I've got an eye for sizes."

"Too bad you didn't have a better eye for men," I smirked and felt bad right away for it. This wasn't a time to bring up those sour memories. "So what's old Tim up to these days?" I deftly steered the subject. "Aside from playing Santa Claus, that is"

"Oh, he's the chiropractor here in town. He's got a beautiful office with a connecting health club. And he's really good. In fact, he's the one who got me up and kicking again after I fell on the ice back in November. Wait till you see him, Sawyer. He's all grown up and dignified now. And you'll just love his wife, Kate. She gives the best hugs in the tricounty area."

"I can't wait," I mumbled as I poured my coffee. "Can't wait."

I knew Tim, knew him well. He was one of the few friends who stuck with me through my awkward transition from sports to theater. We played little league and JFL together through junior high school, but he stuck with sports, especially football, when we entered high school. As it turns out, he became one of our better players on an absolutely dismal varsity football team. I think he was just dumb enough to keep sticking his head into the pile no matter the score. Our team, the Falcons, was often referred to as the "Fail-cons," and that was by our most ardent supporters. I won't tell you what we were called by the people who hated us. But it all added up the same, we were free meat most every Friday night. Tim Kavenaugh was just ornery enough to bite back.

But he was loyal, I'll tell you that. When all the other guys jettisoned me when I quit playing sports, Tim stuck by me. I think he saw every single one of my shows. He'd stand up at curtain call, jam his two forefingers into his mouth, and let loose with a whistle that could shame a steam engine. He was unabashedly proud of me, even if he didn't really understand what it was all about. He was a good guy. And on top of that, we shared another bond. See, it was Tim who taught me to drink.

Yep, that's where it all started, down in Tim's basement. I suppose I could blame him for some of my troubles, but the favor was returned. As he liked to joke, especially after a few cold ones, he may have taught me to drink, but I helped him raise it to an art form.

It was never anything close to art. But the line made us laugh all the same.

Really, all I did was show Tim how we could capitalize on circumstances. Tim had an older brother named Jerry, who worked at the local grocery store. Jerry was not a particularly promising young man. Heck, I could tell that, and I was only fifteen. So we convinced Jerry to leave a case or two of beer in the alley behind the stockroom on nights when he worked late. In return, I gave him the phone number of my sister Andrea and the numbers of all her friends. Apparently, Jerry had never heard of the phone book. Either that or he somehow thought my approval would carry weight with the ladies. Regardless, he would routinely stash the loot in the alley behind some milk crates, and then Tim and I would stroll by and tote it home.

And when I say "home," I mean Tim's house. Alcohol in my house would have stood out like Chewbacca in a chorus line. But Tim's dad loved his beer. He loved it so much that he had two extra refrigerators—one in the garage, one in the basement—to keep his brown-bottled beauties handy. All we had to do was replenish what we drank. Tim's dad was never the wiser. Either that or he just didn't care. In retrospect, that was a distinct possibility. I mentioned the refrigerator in the basement. I hate to tell you what we did to it after knocking back a few of Jerry's ill-gotten gain, and yet Mr. Kavenaugh never made a peep about it. I tell you, we'd whack on that old fridge like it was our own personal punching bag. We'd use it like a tackling dummy. We'd karate kick it, shoot it with Tim's bb gun.

Once after far too many beers, I decided to see if an axe could penetrate its 1960s cold-war armor. I swung and missed and bashed a hole through the cheap paneling on the wall. Tim and I just moved the refrigerator over to cover the indiscretion.

In many ways, that incident was a lot like my adult life. I made mistakes, did stupid things, caused damage, then rather than own up to them or repair them, I'd just move around the furniture to hide it all. And I guess that's why I wasn't too keen on seeing Tim and his wife.

Tim and I graduated high school with vastly different prospects. My future looked golden; his, more like tin. But apparently, he had made something special of himself. And here I was, so pathetic that I had to borrow his old clothes.

"You didn't tell me you hurt your back," I said as I stuffed a bagel into the toaster oven. "Back pain is terrible. It affects everything."

"Oh, it was a silly accident. I was taking Noah out for his morning walk and just slipped. I felt more stupid than hurt, at first. But I'm much better now. Timothy has done wonders. But I have decided no more morning walks until the snow thaws. Got a membership to the gym instead."

"Well, good for you, and good for old Tim. Glad to hear he's doing well."

"I was hoping you could tell him yourself. I have an appointment later this morning. I know he'll be delighted to see you."

"I don't know, Mom," I hedged. "I really need to go over some rehearsal stuff. I haven't even met the cast yet and—"

"Rehearsal isn't until seven tonight."

"Even so, I…Wait a minute. How do you know that? I haven't heard from the school yet about—"

"Donna sent a short e-mail this morning," Mom cut me off again. It seemed that my preferential treatment as a guest had already worn off. She was treating me like her son again. "She said, and I quote, 'Rehearsal at seven. Pick up auditorium keys in the office before it closes at five.'"

"Curt and to the point." I shook my head. "Sounds just like her. Any other directives from Ms. Thewlis?"

"She also said don't be late." Mom smiled. "She wrote that last part in all caps. So you see, you have plenty of time to see Tim and still get back to work on rehearsal before it starts tonight. And regardless"—she plunked her coffee mug into the sink—"You need to go and thank him, Sawyer. I didn't raise you to be ungrateful. His wife drove over here early this morning so you'd have something to wear. The least you can do is say thanks."

"Why do I have this strange feeling that since I've been home, you've been carefully orchestrating where I go and who I run into?"

"Because I'm your mom. And probably because a little of it's true."

"Anyone else that I'm scheduled to meet in the near future?"

"Like who?" She batted her eyes and feigned demur.

I know what I wanted to say. I wanted to blurt out Sarah's name, wanted to ask if she had seen her. Did she look well? Was she happy? But I kept the impulse trapped behind my teeth. Sure, I wanted to say it, but a bigger part of me was too much of a coward to hear the reply. Instead, I remained cryptic. "Oh, I don't know. The mayor of Hanover, a few important merchants, maybe the local veterinarian."

If Mom knew that Sarah was staying with a vet/classmate, she didn't let on. "I think we'll just stick with Timothy for now," she returned. "A woman has to be allowed a few secrets, doesn't she?"

Tim's clinic was pretty impressive. It was located in the old hardware store off the square, but a stranger would never have been able to tell. The whole building had been gutted and reappointed with crisp, state-of-the-art furnishings. Even the old indoor lumber stockade had been converted into a two-story fitness center. Outside stood an electric marquee that blazed against the January sky with the words "Kavenaugh Wellness Center." The last A in Kavenaugh had been replaced with a stylized stick figure of a man bursting forward in newly acquired vitality. I thought that touch may have been a little over the top, especially for a guy who was once best known for having defecated in the McDonald's urinal. But still, like I said, it was impressive. I was glad for Tim. But it also made me feel pretty small.

I ducked into the waiting room with Mom and hid behind an old copy of Field and Stream. I don't know the first thing about hunting or fishing, but I was determined to read every page if necessary to keep from making eye contact with anyone else in the room. Occasionally, I heard the nurse call out names, and slowly, the waiting room thinned out. I was deeply engaged in a narrative about Wyoming's trout habitat when I heard Mom's name called and felt her move out of the chair beside me.

The waiting room grew silent, and I dared a peek over the top of my magazine. I was the only one left in the place. Even the young lady behind the check-in counter was gone. I could hear Mom's voice and laughter trickling back from the warren of rooms when I realized the time. It was noon, and evidently, the staff had all vanished for lunch. I have to say that it made me finally relax a little, but then Tim came bouncing around the corner. He had a grin so big it made his eyes squint, and he threw out his hands and yelled, "Finny!"

I should probably explain that I have collected a few nicknames over the years. Rodriguez called me Shakespeare. Sarah had a few that I won't mention here. But Tim always referred to me as Finny. It was the name Sawyer that did it. Somehow, Tim thought that Huck Finn's first name was Sawyer or that Tom Sawyer wrote Huckleberry Finn or something. I tried to sort it out for him once, but he said he didn't care. He liked the name Finny and seemed almost hurt that I didn't force myself above such distinctions, so Finny it was.

I hadn't heard the name spoken in years, and the way it poured so joyously out of Tim's throat made his clothes I was wearing not seem so ungainly. He gave me a big gangly bear hug and said, "How've you been?" Then he stood back and assessed, "Geez, you look kinda terrible."

He wasn't trying to be funny. Tim had a cleaving honesty. I wanted to return the insult, but the truth was he looked great. Tim was always a handsome guy. Tall, well-built, with wavy black hair. He sort of looked like a dark-haired Ben Affleck, but without the ego. See, Tim never had any clue how handsome he was. That was one of our differences. As an actor, I always knew how handsome I was. It was impossible not to. Casting directors don't hold back on their appraisals of physical assets and liabilities. Like all actors, I learned to exploit my looks. Apparently, that practice never rubbed off on the chiropractic world.

"Thanks," I smirked. "I know I look terrible. But I'm guessing it's mostly these ugly clothes."

Tim let out a laugh that sounded like a bark, and that golden smile split his face again. "Finny! Clever as ever."

"But seriously, Tim. Thanks for the clothes. I left town on pretty short notice. And at the rate old Artie Chambers pays, it may have been a while before I could do much shopping."

"Think nothing of it. It worked out well for me too." Tim gave me a slap on the shoulder and leaned in conspiratorially close. "My wife loves to shop. And I'm too cheap to buy bigger closets." He laughed again with one of those eye-squinting smiles.

"Well, thanks. And thanks also for patching Mom up. She says you worked miracles."

Tim shook off the compliment. "Ah, just happy to be helpful. We all go way back, ya know. Hey, by the way, your mom tells me that you're a little gimpy yourself. What was it? Fell off a platform or something? You should've chosen a less dangerous career."

"You have no idea."

"Did you get any therapy for it?"

"Well, it depends on how you define the word *therapy*."

"Finny," Tim said it like he was scolding me, "that's no good. Did you at least go in for a diagnosis? Get an x-ray or something?"

"Well, the theater company ordered an MRI for me, but I never went. Figured they'd just tell me that I had a bad back."

"So still clever but still stubborn I see." He shook his head. "And let me guess, your back got a little better after a while, but now since the weather has turned cold, it's gotten worse, especially in the mornings."

"Uh, yeah," I mumbled. I honestly was a little surprised. Back in the day, insight wasn't one of Tim's stronger suits. "So when did you get so smart?"

"I just know a little about backs. Perks of the job." Then he said something I was hoping he wouldn't. "Tell you what, Mrs. K," he said to my mom. "If you can spare a few minutes, how about I take Finny back and take a look at that back?"

"No. Really, it's okay." I put my hands up in protest. "Look, Tim. I appreciate the clothes and all, but you don't need to make me your personal charity case."

The words were too strong, and I could tell they wounded him. "It's not charity," Tim's voice was flat. "I just like to help people get rid of pain. You can do whatever you want."

I could feel Mom's ire burning a hole into my back, and she was right. She started to say something, but I cut her off. "What I mean is…" What did I mean? Actually, I think I meant exactly what I said, but I softened it by saying, "I'm finding myself falling further and further in debt. I don't know when I'll be able to pay you back. I don't have any insurance or anything."

My confession didn't move him. He gave a dismissive wag of his big calloused hand. "You know anyone with Medicaid? Heck, they might as well not have any insurance either, at least from my end of things. The state pays so little I don't even bother turning it in. Like I said, I like to help people get rid of pain. I'm pretty good at it. But only if *you* want to. I learned a long time ago that I couldn't force unwilling people to get treatment."

Mom's stare had long since melted a hole through the buttons on my flannel shirt, at least it felt that way.

The truth was, my back had been getting progressively worse. And the prospect of medicating it with cheap hooch was growing more and more complicated. So I relented. "Well, if you're up for it, I can probably squeeze an appointment in to my packed schedule today. It may cost me my afternoon nap though. I want you to know that." I returned a friendly slap on Tim's shoulder, and he brightened. "Someday, I'm gonna pay you back though. Okay?"

Then Tim said something very strange that I should have asked about, but I didn't want to spoil the rehabilitated mood. "Oh, you'll pay, Finny," he crooned, and I couldn't figure if it was a joke or not. "You'll pay."

Tim led me back to the x-ray room first and took some shots of my spine. He poured coffee while we waited for the images to process, and he showed me the rest of the clinic, right down to the utility closet where he kept the mop and spare toilet paper. He was vigorously proud of the whole place, and he should have been. But when he threw my x-ray up on the rectangular illuminated screen, he grew somber. "Mmm-hmmm. Yep. Mmmm-hmmm. Yep." There may have been a cluck of his tongue or a tsk in there as well, but I'm not sure.

"What is it?" I put down my coffee and slid to the front of my chair.

"You have an advancing case of degenerative disc disease with an L5 herniation."

"So what's that mean?"

"It means that you've got a bad back," Tim replied drolly. "It also means that if you don't do something about it, it'll get worse."

"I suppose you have something in mind?"

"Why don't you step into that room over there."

Tim slipped effortlessly into doctor mode. He had me try some impossibly painful stretches and rotations of my back before twisting me like a pipe cleaner and trying to crack my back. "Oh man, Finny," he lamented. "You are as tight as a brick back there. Here, lay on this table."

We moved on to a motorized, undulating gizmo that he called the Leander Table, and he systematically moved up my spine, adjusting every vertebrae it seemed with a firm shove of his hand. He finished by popping my neck and having me sit in a chair while electrical stimulation worked the sore muscles of my lower back. After we finished, he had me try some of the stretches and rotations I had tried earlier.

"You've got to be kidding me." I don't know if I was more surprised or pleased. I had several more degrees of flexibility than before we started. The best part was, the pain was minimal. "Did you slip me some vicodin or something while I wasn't looking?"

"You'll need more than vicodin if we don't keep up these treatments. This was just a start." He handed me a trifold brochure that had drawings of a guy stretching his back like a cat and other odd contortions. "And I want you to do these at home in between sessions. You'll be surprised how much they'll help. And one more thing…"

"Only one?"

"Well, one for now. How much exercise do you get these days?"

It was a deflating question. I considered any activities that involved pain, sweat, and self-discipline to be absolute anathema. Rodriguez and I had sworn them off years ago. "Besides the twelve-ounce curls"—I mimicked the raising of a beer can to my mouth—"not much. I figured I'd save myself until I got really fat."

"Well, that's part of your problem." Tim started to say something about blood flow and disc herniation or some such thing, but I got distracted by a poster on his wall of a skinless man that showed all his muscles and nerve endings. Nearby was a plastic spinal column that looked like it had been used regularly for demonstrations and a whole blinking wall of electronic equipment. Tim was really a doctor. I couldn't get over it. I know that sounds stupid, especially after he had just treated my back. But if you knew him in high school, you'd have a tough time swallowing that fact too. It made me start chuckling.

"What? What's so funny?"

"You. You are." I shook my head incredulously. "This place and all this stuff. I don't mean to sound insulting, but I'm just amazed. You've really done well for yourself, Tim."

The compliment was a little too much for his ego. "Nah," he gave another one of those dismissive wags of his hand. "I just grew up and started to work hard. Anybody could have done the same. It's nothing like what you've done." His face lit up. "I mean *Broadway*, Finny? Big cities? Actors and celebrities? I can't wait to hear all about it. Kate and I were hoping maybe you could come over for dinner some night. You know, you're somewhat of a celebrity in these parts."

"Yeah, like Bin Laden in New York City."

Tim's excitement cooled. He knew some of what I meant. "Well, there are still people here who care about you. And most of us would love to hear all the stories."

"Maybe after ten or twelve shots of whiskey," I joked but quickly wished I'd hadn't. Standing there in his Kavenaugh Wellness Center polo shirt and khaki's, Tim suddenly seemed awfully respectable. "But I suppose you don't do that kind of thing anymore."

He let out a long sigh that sort of whistled. "Yeah, I can't say the whiskey agrees with me much anymore. But I still enjoy a glass of red wine now and then. Lots of antioxidants and good for digestion," he smiled, but I think he was stone serious.

I couldn't stop the chuckle tumbling out again. "Look at you. Don't get me wrong, it's wonderful. But you're just so grown up and dignified. I bet you're even on the school board and everything."

"I'm not on the school board," he remonstrated, but then a sly grin slipped out. "I'm on the Chamber of Commerce."

"See!" I smacked him on the leg, and we both howled. It was a small gesture, but I think we both felt the last of the mild awkwardness slough away. It was genuine laughter we shared, and the chairs we sat in suddenly seemed as familiar as the dumpy couch in his old basement. "I'm proud of you, pal. You've really done great. Still a little surprised you found someone to marry you though. What is she? Nearsighted or is she completely blind?"

Tim barked again at that. "Let's just say that she's opted to look past several of my more obvious faults."

"And you've probably got kids by now too, I'm guessing."

Tim held up his hand and splayed out his fingers."

"Five?" I may have even gasped. "Holy smokes! You have been busy."

"Well, once the world got past the Y2K scare, Kate and I just figured we make up for lost time. The turn of the century has been a pretty productive time for us."

"And exhausting too, I bet." I gave Tim a knowing wink. "Good for you, pal. I really am happy for you. It seems like you've really got things on track. I just wish I knew your secret."

Tim's expression changed when I said that. It wasn't a bad look or anything. It was more like he'd intercepted covert information, like when a baseball player gets the "steal" sign. "It's really no secret. I got out of high school and floundered for a while. I took a few classes at the community college, but that felt too much like high school. I knew that my football glory days were gone, and so I started looking for something new. Medicine seemed like a good fit, and that gave me some direction. But things really changed when I went off to Eastern Illinois University and I met someone."

"So how long after you met Kate did you two get married?" I wanted him to know that I had been following along. I used to have a well-earned reputation for daydreaming.

"Actually, I met Kate in graduate school, but I'll let her tell you that story. She tells it better than I do." I thought Tim was going to say something else, something about what happened to him at EIU, but changed his mind. I guess he decided not to steal second base after all. "So I'd like to see you back here in a week." He marked something on a complicated form he held on a clipboard. "Same time as today? Maybe we can grab a bite for lunch afterwards. There's a great café that just opened up on the corner."

I hesitated. "You've really done too much already. Thanks, but—"

"Does your back feel a little better?"

"Well, yeah, but—"

"Do you want it to keep getting better?"

"Sure, but like I said—"

"Then you'll come back next Tuesday at lunchtime for another adjustment and electric stim."

"And you get stuck with another patient that can't pay."

Tim gave another one of those sly grins. "Oh, I have an idea about payment. You'll be able to pay. What are you doing on Thursday mornings?"

"Sweeping up around here, I'm guessing."

Tim seemed surprised by my answer. "Nah, none of that, Finny. Besides, I already have someone who takes care of that." He paused for a second, a hem or haw tripping him before he plowed ahead. "We've got a men's Bible study we've just started on Thursday mornings. Great guys, and really good stuff, Finny. Thought provoking, but unbelievably practical. It's a neat deal. How about you come with me? I'd love the company. And I'll keep treating your back on Tuesdays."

More than a hem and haw sat poised behind my lips, but Tim was already sweetening the deal. I could tell he was nervous. "Tell you what"—he put down the clipboard and stood—"just go with me twice. Just two times. And after that, if you don't think it's worth your time, I won't ask you to come anymore."

I was never good at economics, but this was obviously a pretty good bargain. The best part was that I wouldn't be freeloading. It was quid pro quo. I wouldn't have to feel guilty for the services. Still, I couldn't let Tim off the hook too easily. "I don't know, Tim." I rose to my feet to meet him eye to eye. "I go to this Bible study thing with you, or you don't treat my back? There are some courts in this land that would call that extortion."

Tim's ear-tickling smile was back in full glory. "I suppose there's a fine line between ministry and extortion, Finny. But I'll let God sort it out." He gave me another fraternal slap on the shoulder. "I'll pick you up at 5:15."

"5:15 *a.m.?*"

"Well, it's twenty-five minutes to the church," he said unapologetically. "And we want to get there before all the good donuts are gone."

I spent a couple of hours poring over Mr. B's binder before heading up to the school. I collected my keys from the office and borrowed a roll of masking tape from the supply cabinet. The tape was to mark out stage walls and set pieces and exit/entrances on the floor so that the kids could get a sense of their location and the distances between them. Mr. B used to do it for us, and I remember that it made the transition from a blank stage to one with real walls go much more smoothly. But when I arrived at the stage, I discovered that my work already had been done for me.

Mr. B had done it. Probably no more than a few days ago. I could tell because the tape was still clean, no shoeprints or rub-outs. And I knew it was Mr. B who had put it there because each strip was labeled with magic marker in his handwriting.

I crouched down and ran my fingers over the papery strip of tape just as he must have done. I tapped it with my index and forefinger and then smoothed my thumb along its length to make sure it was adhered. The line wasn't quite straight near its end, and I frowned as I traced the small arc. I'm sure the small imperfection annoyed Mr. B too, but he was too busy to bother with its correction. Mr. B liked things clean and in line, when he had time for it. I started to make a repair but stopped. How could I? This was his world. His stage. God help me, it was his strip of tape. And he had stared at this simple line just like me and let it pass.

I know it sounds crazy, but in that moment, I suddenly felt close to him. Much closer than I did when I stood by his naked feet at the hospital. Mr. B's presence was here—here on this stage. I felt connected to it. It seemed certain that he would know what happened here. And for the first time, my self-interests were replaced by an overwhelming desire to make him proud.

"You ready to go tonight?" It was Donna. She had entered the auditorium and was lugging a bulky music score over to the upright piano. "The kids have the opener, 'Prepare Ye,' down, and 'God Save the People' was pretty tight in this morning's music rehearsal. I should have asked if you planned to block the show in order of scenes. That's how we're learning the music."

"That was my plan, yeah," I said flatly. I had eaten dinner, but my stomach rumbled. "I think it will improve the execution."

"First night and you're already contemplating your execution?" she replied dryly. "A bad sign, Mr. Kent. A bad sign."

The comment made me laugh, and I needed it. "Just promise to not let me dangle on the gallows for too long. That's never pretty."

The kids began to enter in drips and drabs. I think some came early out of curiosity. But they were all seated, librettos poised on their laps at exactly seven. It was heartening to see that Mr. B's insistence on punctuality had not been lost over the years.

I called out their names from the cast list, and Donna glued them with makeshift nametags made from the masking tape.

"Godspell" was written for only ten players, but Mr. B had cast sixty-two. No doubt it would take a while to connect names with faces, so I concentrated on the main characters. Drew Boulton was my Jesus and an obvious choice. He was tall, good-looking, and most certainly the man among the boys. He had a full beard and mustache that even I envied and looked every bit the part of the leading man. Judas was square-jawed and a little acne-pocked but otherwise a convincing villain. John the Baptist, on the other hand, looked like an infant. For a minute, I thought someone had brought his kid brother to rehearsal. But when I called the name Eddie Parker, the little guy thrust up his skinny arm, beamed cherubically, and piped, "In the house, milord."

Though tiny, Eddie Parker was stuffed with personality. "So who cast the Keebler elf?" I whispered to Donna.

"Just wait till you hear him sing," she nodded confidently. She hammered a chord on the old piano, and the kids all stood. For the next few minutes, she took them through a series of vocal warm-ups that sounded much fuller and grand than I expected. They finished with some shoulder shrugs and neck stretches that I thought were a little over the top, but I didn't say anything. They sat back down in the seats and stared at me like a jury studying the accused.

"Sounds good," I said because I couldn't think of anything else. The image of Donna's noose and scaffold flitted through my mind. Fortunately, the Keebler elf raised his hand, and the sea of eyes turned to him.

"Yes, uh...Eddie" I squinted at the masking tape tag he had reaffixed vertically down his shirt. "You have a question?"

"Who are you?" he chirped innocently.

"Well, uh, I'm your director, at least for now. I'll be filling in for Mr. Bertollini for a while."

"For how long?"

"Well, Eddie, umm, I don't really know for sure. Hopefully not too long." A few kids grimaced at the perceived insult, and flop sweat budded on my forehead. "What I mean is, let's all hope that Mr. B gets back on his feet again soon. I'm sure he's missing you."

"You graduated from here and went on to Broadway, right?" This time it was Drew, the man-child, who spoke. His voice was smooth and confident. "My mom said that you and Mr. Bertollini were really close."

"Didn't you marry his daughter?" The question was thrown from the back. But before, I could respond, I could see a flock of hands fly to mouths, and whispers exchanged.

"Not his daughter, no. I was married to his niece for a while though."

"Do you know any famous actors?" Another faceless voice asked.

"Well, I guess I'd say yes. I managed to work with some really talented people over the years. I'm not so sure you'd recognize their names though. But all that really isn't important. What is important is you, and this show that we're—"

"So were you, like, Mr. Bertollini's greatest actor ever or what?" Eddie was clearly stuck on the earlier conversation thread. I couldn't blame him. Precocious personalities and short attention spans tend to travel in pairs.

"I wouldn't go that far, Eddie. But he was a great mentor to me, yes. I owe him a lot. He taught me things…Well, he taught me a lot." There was more I could have said, but I didn't trust my quavering chin. "Mr. Bertollini's a special man. You know how it is. Once you meet him, he makes an impression."

"So what do you want us to call you?" It was Eddie again. "Director? Mr. Director? Director Man?"

"You can just call me Sawy—"

"Mr. Kent." Donna interrupted from the piano bench. "You'll refer to him as Mr. Kent."

A tense quiet settled in, as is typical after an edict has been proclaimed. I think the kids could sense my unease, and they took some sympathy when I admitted. "Look, guys, this is uncharted waters for all of us. You don't know me, and I don't know you. But one thing we do have in common is that we all know Mr. B. So if you want to call me Mr. Kent, Mr. Director, or even 'Hey, you,' I'm good with that. All I ask is that whatever you do, please don't slip and call me Mr. Bertollini, because all of us will probably break into tears if you do." And then an idea burst in my head. "Come over here and let me show you something."

I led them back into the stage-left wings, where a gallery of past musical posters hung on the black wall. "Mr. Bertollini started the musical program here in 1975. See? Oklahoma up there in the corner. And since then, Hanover has been known for staging fantastic musicals. People walk out and can't believe that the show they've just seen was performed by high school kids. Some of you came and saw those shows as kids and felt the same way, right?" Their eyes were all pasted on the various posters, and several nodded their heads. "Now, just look up there. If you look hard enough, you can see people you know. Maybe your mom or dad. Maybe an older brother or cousin, or even someone who used to babysit you. You can even see me up there in Brigadoon, Camelot, and West Side Story. We're all up there, embedded in those posters, those shows. And in just a couple of months, you'll be up there too.

"See, now it's your chance to carry the flag. Now it's your chance to make a mark. And all those other actors from all those other shows, they're counting on you. They're counting on all of us. So how about we get started on Act I scene I?"

The rehearsal went better than I expected. We blocked the opening montage with the tableaus fairly quickly and moved on to the opener, "Prepare Ye." That one was still pretty rough by the time the clock struck eight thirty, but at least the basics of the choreography had been installed. What was even more heartening was tiny Eddie's voice. Donna hadn't exaggerated. That little elf had some pipes.

"Everyone has a ride home, right?" Donna called to the kids as they gathered their librettos, tugged on coats, and snapped open cell phones. "Don't forget we don't have vocal rehearsal tomorrow morning, but we do go over music Friday. Be ready for 'Prepare Ye' and to move on to 'God Save the People' and 'Day by Day.'" Most of the mob shuffled out, but Eddie was still sitting in the front row, pounding out an extended text message.

"You've got someone on the way, right?" Donna asked him.

His eyes didn't leave the miniature keyboard. "Yep. Mom will be here any minute. Just texting my woman to tell her I'm on the way over to study for tomorrow's science test."

"Hey, nice job tonight, Eddie," I threw in as he snapped his phone shut and gathered his stuff. "Terrific voice. You're not related to Rick Astley, are you? Maybe his long lost son or something?" I don't know why I ever thought he'd catch the reference.

"Who's Rick Ghastley?"

"Rick *Astley* was a singer in the late '80s. Kind of a small guy but a big voice. It was just a joke."

Eddie didn't seem to take it that way. He thoughtfully chewed over the notion before saying, "Could be. I *am* adopted. Was he as handsome as me?"

"Good night, Eddie," Donna moaned, and Eddie was out the door.

"Let me guess, he's really thirty-five, but the school lost his birth certificate."

"No, he's only a freshman. But don't let him fool you. He's going through a lot right now. I was concerned about him tonight."

"What? That he'd bring his agent?"

"No," Donna remonstrated, but she grinned before getting serious again. "Eddie is the one that found Ed collapsed at his home. Apparently, he had stopped by to drop off his T-shirt order, and when no one came to the door, he peeped through the window. Fortunately, the house was unlocked. Eddie managed to call for help right away, but I guess he was a mess afterward."

"Geez. I would never have known by the way he acted."

"Yeah, his folks were pretty worried about how he'd react tonight. The Parkers and Ed are tight. Ed used to say that Eddie was his namesake, and I'm not so sure that he was joking. And as you can imagine, Eddie idolized old Bert. I don't know if you knew this, but last year, Bert was hospitalized for a week or so. Apparently, Eddie fell ill about the same time. It was a pretty big deal. Little Eddie nearly died."

"What happened?"

"I don't know. His parents were pretty vague about everything. One of the counselors said something about him having kidney problems, but they don't tell us much. Confidentiality and all."

"You're kidding me."

Donna took my shock in stride. "One of the things you'll learn pretty fast when you work with high-schoolers is that you just never know the whole story about them. Some of these kids come from unbelievable backgrounds. Homeless. Crack-head parents. Abusive boyfriends. But they walk in here and pull on a brave face. You just never know."

"I'll try harder to watch what I say around 'em, especially Eddie."

Donna softened at that. The padded shoulders of her tweed jacket visibly relaxed. It seemed that the steel-plated armor of General Thewlis was lowering for a brief salute. "You did really well with the kids tonight," she allowed. "I have to admit, I expected utter failure. But you have a real natural way with them. I think you might do okay."

"Well, that's a shame, now, isn't it?" I chided. "I was hoping to make a disaster of things, just to keep my Hanover karma consistent."

"I didn't say you *would* do okay. I said *might*."

"Well, regardless, thanks, Ms. Thewlis."

"You're welcome, Mr. Director Man."

SEVEN

Karma turned ugly Wednesday night. Several kids were missing for a basketball game, including Jesus. The rest of the cast had trouble recalling the opener dance steps, and I had to spend nearly half an hour reteaching it, all the while reminding them to leave space for those who were missing. Voices were flat, faces flatter. It felt like herding zombies. And on top of that, I was informed I would have to administrate the selling and distribution of the show T-shirts.

"What am I supposed to do with this?" I asked Donna when she handed me the large manila envelope.

"Collect the twelve dollars from each kid who ordered a shirt. Oh, and make sure if they pay by check, it's made out to Hanover Township High School, not to you. They make that mistake all the time. Then keep track of all the sizes and who's paid and turn everything into the office, but *before* you pass out the shirts."

"When do the shirts come in?"

"They don't. You go get them when they're ready. Probably in a couple of weeks. The school has already paid the silkscreen company. You just turn in what you get along with any ticket money they give you. Did I mention that the kids will also be giving you ticket money?"

"Don't we have someone to take care of all this stuff?"

"Yeah. It's the director." Donna smirked from behind her rectangular glasses. "That's why they pay you the big bucks."

"I suppose I'm in charge of costuming too."

"Oh, no. We have a costumer, and wait until you meet her. She'll make your head spin."

So I guess what I'm saying is that after Wednesday night's rehearsal, I had plenty to pray about Thursday morning, when Tim's headlights came lasering into the driveway.

I was in no mood to pray.

"Ready to go, Finny?"

"The last time I was up at 5:00 a.m. was because I hadn't gone to bed yet."

"Oh, come on," Tim said valiantly. "It's a beautiful morning here in Central Illinois."

"How do you know? We can't even see it. Two times," I muttered. "You promised I only had to do this twice."

We drove most of the way in silence. Tim played some talk radio from a station out of Chicago. We crossed the river and drove through the sparse dark streets of Peoria. The sun was still a long way from making its appearance when we pulled into the church parking lot.

"This place is huge," I squeegeed a portal into my fogged window. "Gotta tell you, in the dark with the overhead lights and all, it looks a little like a prison. How many people go here?"

"On a typical weekend, we run about two thousand inmates," Tim smiled and threw the car into park. "Come on. I'll show you around."

Poplar Creek Community Church had started in the basement of a lawyer's office, expanded to a warehouse loading dock before finally burgeoning into the complex of buildings at its current site. Tim and his wife had been there through most of the transitions, and he was dutifully proud as he escorted me through the narthex and into a spacious vaulted atrium that overlooked the church lake. Four flat-screen TVs blared the ESPN morning show, and a coffee bar pumped delicious smells into the air. "We meet in here, not the sanctuary," Tim informed me before darting off to the snack table. I have to say, it didn't feel much like a church.

Nearly a hundred men of all sorts hobnobbed around the circular tables, munching on donuts and sipping coffee from Styrofoam cups. Some were old, some my age, and a few looked like college kids. And they ran the socioeconomic gamut too. I saw men wearing everything from business suits to polo shirts to overalls to seed caps. The guys all wore nametags written in magic marker. I saw a Mario, a DeShaunta, a Lun, and even an Ichabod. It was like a mini United Nations. And Tim seemed to know most of them.

A tall weather-faced man in a Bass Pro Shops sweatshirt finally got everyone's attention, and we settled into tables.

"What happens now?" I whispered to Tim.

"We slay a goat and dance in its blood," he smirked.

"Gentlemen," the Bass Pro Shops guy said, "I want everyone to know that this is a safe place."

"What's he expecting? An Al Qaida attack?"

"Shhhh," Tim scolded me.

"What is spoken in confidence here, stays here," the guy continued. "We're here to be better men. We're here to be the men that God has created us to be. But to do that, we need to be able to say what's on our hearts."

He finished with a few other words and introduced the speaker, Dale Patterson, a late fifty-something man with a slight southern drawl and engaging smile.

I checked my watch. This could be a long hour and a half. I should have gotten more coffee.

But then old Dale said something I wasn't expecting. "Men, how did you know when you became a man?"

It was a pretty good question. The day I threw away the baseball glove came to mind. But there were other answers that crowded in. They were shameful moments that came later in my life. And they weren't the kinds of things you couldn't mention in church. But then surprisingly, Dale spoke them for me.

"The first time you had sex with a woman?" he asked with a knowing smile, and a rustle of uncomfortable laughter scurried through the tables. "The first time you won a fist fight? First time you got drunk? Maybe it was the first time you went to a strip club or bought some porn. What is the definition of manhood?"

I'm glad I was out of coffee because I might have spit it on the floor. I didn't know you could say real things like that in church.

"See, guys," Dale continued. "For most of us, the world has blurred the lines of what it is to be an authentic man. And so we wander, just trying to figure it out for ourselves. The good news is that the Bible gives us the perfect definition of a real man through the example of Jesus Christ. And the starting point of becoming a real man is encountering him."

It sounded like it was going to start getting preachy, so I checked my watch again and began doodling on my coffee napkin. It was kind of a shame. Dale had gotten off to a good start. And I had to admit, these guys here seemed like a pretty decent bunch. But I'd heard before all about what I haven't done. Another sermon wouldn't change anything.

But then Dale said something else that was so true that it stole back my attention. "The problem is, though, most of us men are dragging along baggage from our pasts that make it hard to move forward. And though we don't like to admit it, most of us bear wounds that haven't healed. Some of us have a 'loner wound.' Some carry an 'overbonded with mother wound.' And all of us have what I call a 'heart wound' that only Christ's blood can heal." Then he took a deep breath, and I swear he was looking right at my table. "But today, I want to start with a very common wound. It's called 'the absent father wound.'"

I won't try and recite the entire talk, but he basically said that many boys grow up without a father to give them any sort of direction for being a man. He told us that nearly 40 percent of boys today didn't have a father of any kind in their home. And that didn't count the homes where Dad lived there physically but not emotionally.

These absent fathers, whether absent physically or emotionally, generally don't tell their sons the three things every boy needs to hear from his dad: "I love you. I'm proud of you. And here is what you're good at." Dale went on to explain that God basically did this for Jesus when he was baptized and at the Transfiguration. God said from heaven, "This is my son with whom I am well pleased. Listen to him."

Anyway, Dale said without that affirmation from a father, many boys fall into patterns of anger, pain, addictions, sexual promiscuity, and the sense of being lost. Worse yet, most of these boys have an impossible time of understanding a loving yet rebuking Heavenly Father. They have no fatherly reference point.

That was me.

I had never thought of it that way before. But that was me.

Old Dale finished by saying that all of us are affected by our past, but that doesn't mean we have to be prisoners to it. He promised that over the next several weeks, we'd be unpacking some of those issues that stand in the way of becoming authentic men for God.

For the last twenty-five minutes or so, we had some discussion questions to banter at our individual tables. They passed out workbooks that summarized the message for the day and left blanks for us to write down individual thoughts. I didn't say a word, and neither did Tim. We didn't write anything either. When the clock struck seven, we hustled out into the frosty parking lot. The sun had come up, and it was glowing like a bonfire in the east, but it was still too distant to warm me. Tim fired the car to life, and we started home.

It was quiet. Tim forgot to turn on the radio.

He was just glaring at the road. The car was uncomfortably silent, except for the steady rumble of the engine. It was the kind of silence that stifles men. Something probably needed to be said, but I wasn't sure what. Finally, I got up the courage to lead with, "So do you talk to your dad much these days?"

It was the best and worst question I could have asked.

"Not since he passed away three years ago." Tim never took his eyes off the road.

More stifling silence. I thought about turning on the radio.

"You know, he never once told me he was proud of me," Tim suddenly blurted. "Not after all those football games. Not when I got married. Not even when I graduated from chiropractic school and got my license. Not once."

"Yeah, but you know he was," I offered. "He just didn't know how to say it. You heard. Dale even said that we can't just blame our dads. They came from a different generation. You have to move on."

Tim didn't appreciate my faux counseling. "Shut up, Finny," he snapped. "You had a father that you wanted to murder and a wife who tried to kill herself. So maybe you should just think twice before instructing me how I should feel about my dad."

He was right, but I could tell that he regretted the way he delivered the truth. "Look." He shook his head. "I shouldn't have said that. I'm sorry, man. I asked you to come today and be my guest. Here I am snapping at you. Sorry, Finny."

But I had travelled past Tim's confession. What he said was true, and it stirred old, decayed feelings about my father. They swirled, tossing up with them resurrected motes of anger, resentment, and shame. "I hated him," I admitted. "I still hate him. And Sarah paid the price for most of it. He didn't deserve to live. We should have dug that pit outside his front door. Remember? We were going to fill it with spikes and broken beer bottles."

We must have traveled another four or five miles without anything else spoken. After a while, Tim switched on the radio. We sat there, watching the morning sun claim the sky and listening to the squawking voices like we cared about the traffic on the interstates outside Chicago.

But all the while, I knew that something genuine had been exchanged in the car and in the church before that. It was the first real dialogue about something that mattered that I had, had in a long while. And even though painful, it set my heart pumping. I looked over at Tim and could see the thin wet line where a tear had escaped his eye.

It was then that I knew I would come back to this place. Tim made me promise to come only twice. But that wouldn't be a problem. I wanted to hear it all.

EIGHT

"**C**ut!" I hollered. "Cut, cut, cut. Come on, guys. We've been over this for days now. On the last stanza of 'Prepare Ye,' you need to return to positions and strike any props with you. We've got to make room for the dumpster. Eddie? Didn't I tell you to travel upstage right and take yourself out of the scene?"

"Yeah."

"Then why were you still standing stage center?"

"Because I don't know where upstage right is," he replied matter-of-factly.

That stopped me in my tracks. "Okay, guys." I rubbed my hands together. "How many of you are confused when I give out stage directions and don't really know where I want you to go?"

The forest of hands that went up shouldn't have surprised me. I didn't know stage directions either until Mr. Bertollini taught me.

"Okay, everybody, just take a seat where you are. Just sit down, and I'll explain. It's actually pretty easy because all directions are in reference to you as an actor. So when I tell you to go stage right you go this way." I pointed to my right. "And so stage left is which side? Julia?"

"Over there, right?"

"Exactly. Now, does anyone know where upstage is?"

"Opposite of downstage?" Eddie volunteered.

"Thanks, Eddie. Downstage is toward the audience and upstage, as Eddie has so insightfully informed us, is back there." I could vividly remember Mr. B having the same discussion with us as he pointed and marched all over the stage. And then I remembered something else he taught us. "Does anyone know why it's called upstage and downstage?" There were no responses, but the faces were intrigued. "In the old days, all the stages were raked. That means they were slanted down toward the audience. They built them that way so that the actors could still be seen when they walked away from the audience. So for the actors, they were literally walking slightly up the stage. But today, we just rake the audiences' seats out in the house, and it has the same effect."

"What does 'strike' mean?" It was Eddie again.

"Strike?"

"Yeah. You said something about 'striking' something."

"Oh, I said to strike the props. That just means to remove them. See, we have to clear center stage for Jesus's entrance. And with him rolling in on a dumpster, we need plenty of room. So those old tires, the turned-over bench, and any other loose stuff we have cluttering the middle has to be struck. We need it clear for Jesus to take center stage. Got it?"

We ploughed on through the next scene, but it was pedestrian work. I could see the kids thinking before moving, unsure if they were right and wondering how I'd react if they were wrong. They were moving mechanically, by assignment, not with natural purpose.

We had a long way to go.

Two parents showed up for the last half hour of rehearsal and hovered in the back of the auditorium. It irritated me. I couldn't stop peering back to where they were standing, hoping they had left. Rehearsals are usually closed to the public, and for good reason. You don't eat an apple while it's still a seed. It's meant to be consumed only when fully ripened. The same is true about a show.

The witching hour finally struck, and the kids shambled out. I wandered over to Donna at the piano. "So who are the helicopter parents back there?"

She peeked above the upright. "Oh, those are the Parkers. Eddie's folks."

"Well, what do you think they want?"

"Who knows? They're taxpayers. Maybe they want to see if the district is getting its money's worth with its new director."

"They keep looking over this way," I whispered. "Do you think I should go over and say something?"

"No." Donna squared up some loose sheet music and put it in a folder. "I think you should stay right here and keep asking me questions that you already know the answers to."

"Thanks for support."

"Anytime."

I skipped down stage stairs and met Mr. Parker in the aisle. His wife stood back a pace, like a timid child waiting for someone else to test the pool water first.

"Mr. Kent," he said jovially. "I'm David Parker, Eddie's dad. It's nice to finally meet you." He pumped my hand like we were long lost relatives.

"Well, I've only been here a week, so…"

"Uh, well, I meant, um, that the way Eddie has talked about you, it seems like I've known you for longer." Another bright smile.

It was a very odd beginning. He kept smiling, but all the while, he was looking me up and down like a nervous suitor. I got the sense that he wanted to find something in me to like regardless of what he had heard. He seemed nice enough though. Just a little anxious. "Oh," he said as though he'd forgotten. "And this is my wife, uh, Cindy."

Cindy was as apprehensive as David was forward. Cautiously, she extended her arm and shook my hand limply. She was looking me up and down too. But she had the look of a hostage. Had David not been so friendly and physically unimposing, I would have wondered if there was something really dysfunctional about them.

"So I hear that you and Mr. Bertollini are friends?" I broke the awkward silence. "How long have you known him?"

"Since right before Eddie was born, of course," David replied, but Cindy needled him with nervous eyes. "Well, what I mean is…" He cleared his throat. "We moved here just about then. Fourteen years ago. Ed went to St. Mark's, where we started attending. We met through the priest there." Cindy remained a step behind his elbow, listening carefully to every word as though she was parsing for grammar.

It was all just a little weird. Then again, Eddie was kind of weird. At least I knew where he got it.

"So anyway"—David and Cindy began to back-peddle up the aisle—"we just wanted to come by and say hello. Eddie is really enjoying you and the show. It's so nice to finally meet you." Cindy gave David another sharp glare, and they left.

"So are they always that strange?" I asked Donna as she pulled on her coat.

"No, they're usually pretty normal and nice. My guess is it's just you."

I propped my elbows on the top of the upright piano. The auditorium was empty and hollow, except for us. "Can I ask you a question, Donna?"

"If you must."

"How do *you* think it's going? The show, so far. I mean, I haven't been around teenagers since...well, since I was a teenager. And I know that we've only had a few rehearsals. But everything seems so clunky and mechanical. And it's not the music. I meant to tell you that. All joking aside, I'm really impressed how well the kids sing. But as far as the rest of the rehearsals go...I don't know. What do you think? Is this typical?"

"All joking aside?" She drummed her fingers on the top of her leather satchel. "Yes, the kids are a little stiff. But it's not what you're doing. They just have to get used to you. They need to get used to each other. It only takes a few hours to cast a show, but it sometimes takes weeks for that cast to become a company."

"And I've got...how many weeks?"

"Seven. We open seven weeks from yesterday."

"Thanks for the pep talk."

"Pep talk?" She turned to leave. "I was hoping to depress you."

"Mission accomplished."

"Amazing. We communicate better than I thought." She flashed a fabulous smile that actually made me brighten a little, and she left.

I stood there in the silence that followed. It was an overwhelming silence constructed from my own inadequacies. "Seven weeks, Mr. B," I called out to the empty catwalks. "I need you to get better soon. I don't think we can make it without you." It was a stupid thing to do, I know. But it made me feel a little better, and no one was there to hear it anyway.

At least at the time, I didn't think anyone did.

I had trouble sleeping that night. And it wasn't because I wasn't tired; I was tired to the bone. But I couldn't get my brain to shut off. It was trapped in an anxious cycle that started with thinking about the lousy rehearsal and how little time we had until opening night. That led to wondering if Mr. B ever felt that way, which made me think about high school. Thinking about that reminded me of Tim's old basement, which reminded me of Mom's basement and the manila envelope with pictures of me she was sending. All of which made me wonder about Sarah, which made me want a whiskey, and that led me right back to worrying about rehearsal again. It was a rough night. I think Evel Knievel might have even made an appearance somewhere in the vicious cycle. So by five thirty, I decided I'd had enough and rolled out of bed.

Noah wasn't pleased.

"Come on, boy. Let's go for a walk. Doc says I need some exercise. And be quiet. I don't want to wake up Mom."

I was still on the fence as to whether Noah could understand English. There was no doubt, however, that he could speak "leash." One jingle of the worn red leash hanging in the front hall closet chased away the yawns and curmudgeonly glare and sent him dancing in a frisky circle. I snapped on the lead, cracked the door open, and he bolted out like a lead dog in the Iditarod.

Noah clearly had done this before.

He dragged me out to the driveway, piddled on the mailbox, and then pulled me down the snow-banked street. We passed by the old house of Mrs. Millwood, who, when I was a kid, insisted that I call her "Millie." She was a sweet old bird. I always could count on her to bring me a matchbox car from her son's old collection to play with while she was at my mom's shop having her hair cut. When I got to high school, Millie came to every night of Camelot to see me play King Arthur. I never met her son, who I found out later had been killed by friendly fire in Vietnam. Looking back, I think Millie sort of latched on to me because of that. Like I said, she was a sweet old bird.

Noah didn't appreciate the nostalgia. He hunched his back and left a steaming pile at the base of her lamppost. Unashamedly, he trotted on down Far Hills Drive, passing the sloping hillside in the Jamisons' yard, where every kid on the block used to learn how to ride a bicycle, and past mean old Mr. Krubb's house. We didn't stop until we reached Joey Barber's place. Joey was my best friend when I was small. He was a scrawny shank of a kid, kind of a Stan to my Ollie. We spent a fair number of summer afternoons in his apple tree, munching on nasty, granite-hard apples and hurling the cores at the big kids who couldn't reach us. Trust me, they deserved it.

Noah dribbled his last in the snow around the mailbox and turned for home. He seemed summarily pleased with himself, almost happy. If I didn't know better, I'd have sworn that he was actually smiling as we cantered back up the street toward home. But when we reached the corner of our yard, he put on the brakes and just stared at me.

"Come on, boy." I yanked on the leash. "Let's go in. It's cold out here."

Noah didn't budge. I yanked on the leash again, this time hard enough to drag him a clawing inch in my direction. "Look, Noah. You've got a couple options here. You can either come along, get strangled, or stay out here by yourself 'cause I'm going in. It's freezing out here."

Noah was nonplussed by my ultimatum, so I tossed down the lead and headed for the driveway.

That was what he had been waiting for. As soon as I let go, he took off like a shot into the yard and toward the front door. The snow was high, nearly knee-high to me and submergible depth for Noah. He didn't care. He bounded through the high snow, cresting and disappearing like a humpbacked whale. And each time he burst above the white line, he was flashing that white-fanged smile of his. Apparently, this was his idea of fun.

For a moment, he stopped to see if I was following. And I'm sort of ashamed to admit it, but the triumphant look in his eyes was too much for me to resist. I hiked up my long coat and plunged in after him.

Noah bounded ahead, and the race was on.

"Slow down, you stupid mutt!" I panted as I thrashed through the yard. Tim was right. I was out of shape. "And wipe that superior grin off your face. Mom loves me more, you know."

Noah reached the porch a good furlong ahead of me, but I didn't care. I was laughing by now, or at least gasping for breath in a chuckling sort of way. Noah struck a winning pose up on the porch, and I just flopped on my back, a submissive loser, and sunk into the strange cocooning warmth of the snow.

The sky was still dark above me. The limbs of the old maple tree were darker still against the school of fading stars. But back over my head, the sun was burning a pink halo into the horizon. It made me feel small, a small kid in a big yard and even bigger world beyond. Lying there, the last of my laughter still tumbling out on ragged breath, life felt big again, big and full of wonder. It hadn't seemed that way for a long time.

For years, I only looked for fun in the bottom of a bottle. Fun had to be complicated and costly. At first, it only cost me a headache in the morning. But then it took away friendships and ruined my jobs. The worst part though, was that it eventually stole my sense of wonder. Looking back, I don't think I had, had genuine fun since the baby died and I left town. Yeah, I think that was it. When I took the money and left town, I gave up on it. Cowards and criminals don't deserve to have fun.

But in Mom's yard, that seemed like a lifetime ago. I was ready to laugh again, even if it took a dog to remind me how. And it gave me a great idea for rehearsal that night.

I made a snow angel, and Noah came over to inspect my work. He climbed up on my chest, still smiling, and gave me a lick up the side of my face. Snow crystals hung from his muzzle. "You know what, boy?" I scrubbed the fur below his ears. "I'm going to try some-thing tonight, and if it works, I'll owe you one. Quit licking me like that. And don't get too excited. You're staying home. I'll decide later whether to put your name in the program credits."

"Sawyer? Is that you?" It was Mom calling from the front door.

"Yeah, Mom. Couldn't sleep, so I took Noah for a walk."

"I should have warned you that he likes to finish by racing across the yard."

"I figured that out. And don't worry, his record is still intact."

"Sawyer?"

"Yes, Mom?"

"Are you laughing?"

"Just a little, Mom. Just a little. But don't tell anyone, okay? It's not good for the tragic image I'm shooting for."

"Well, are you coming in?"

"In a minute. I think I'll make a few more snow angels first."

NINE

"I'm sure you are all wondering what we're doing out here." I scooped up a handful of snow, and most of the sixty cast members nodded their heads. They looked like rows of inmates under the pinkish outdoor lights that lit the school campus, but I tried not to let that deter me. "This show that we are doing, 'Godspell,' is about a group of different people coming together. They have different backgrounds, different ideas, but they come together because of one message. And in some ways, it's just the same for a group of actors. You guys are all different, with different experiences, but we need to come together as a company. It's the message of our show. But the ingredient that speeds it all along, and one that I have unfortunately been letting you miss, is fun. This is supposed to be fun. In fact, when an audience sees you having fun, it allows them to have fun themselves." So far so good.

"But so far, I haven't let you do that. I guess I've been so focused on the blocking and the dialogue and the choreography that I forgot about fun."

"So what are we going to do?" It was Jesus in the back. He was hugging himself, trying to stay warm in his yellow hoodie.

"I'm getting to that, Drew. You might notice that I've set up a couple of sheets of plywood out here in the quadrangle. Those are to use as forts or barricades. Everywhere else"—I stretched out my arms to include the vast limits of the open field that lay adjacent to the auditorium—"is no-man's land."

"Do we pick teams?" Eddie was already catching on.

"No. I'll leave that up to you. But before I turn you loose, I have one important ground rule. Before you can throw a snowball at someone, you first have to say a line or lyric from the show."

"Let me get this straight." It was Donna. She was frowning. "Your strategy for building camaraderie and teamwork is to bring us out here in the freezing night to throw snowballs at each other? You're kidding, right?"

I have to admit, it didn't sound like such a great idea the way she said it. "That's kinda what I was thinking, yeah."

Donna was already turning to head into the warmth of the building. "Come on, kids. We need to rehearse."

But I was already all-in. Heck, I had just spent an hour putting up the plywood barricades and wiring up my other little surprise. This might go down as a colossal failure, but that wouldn't be the first time for me. "Come on. Don't go in." I gave Donna a second to reconsider before packing the snowball a little tighter and hollering, "Okay. Game on. Prepare, ye, Ms. Thewlis!"

My aim couldn't have been better. The snowball glanced against the back of her curly auburn hair and exploded into mist.

She turned slowly, glacially, and glared at me from behind those rectangular glasses. "Oh, you are *so* going to pay for that."

"Don't forget to say a line from the show first!"

I don't think Donna cared much for my directive. She grabbed up a mash of loose snow and barreled toward me. Out of the corner of my eye, I could see the air suddenly populate with a cloud of whizzing snowballs. Over the top of it all, random squeaks of lyrics and dialogue filled the snowy field. And that was about the time that Donna Thewlis crashed into me.

It was a prodigious blow. I feigned a comedic pratfall to the ground, but the truth is, she knocked me over. "I just got back from the hairdresser, you jerk." She arm-plowed a wave of snow over my face. She was breathing heavily, and, for some reason, so was I. For the first time, I could see a few small wrinkles at her temples and the flecks of topaz in her brown eyes. Her hair lay in disheveled ringlets against the dull snow, and the highlights of red betrayed a hint of vanity that I hadn't expected. This Donna Thewlis was more complicated than I thought. I started to say something clever but was quickly stalled when a handful of our Pharisees attacked.

"You know, this is the dumbest idea…" She never finished her insult. I'm sure it would have been a good one, but she got too busy fending off the Pharisees. Off to our right, I could see others in the company taking reconnaissance and moving in to join them.

"They're ganging up on us," Donna had her arms up like a frightened prizefighter as she batted away in incoming snowballs. "This is ridiculous. And you owe me eighty-five bucks for my hair."

"I'm good for it," I lied. "Look, I've got this. You run over behind the plywood fort."

"What?"

"Just get behind the barricade. I'll cover you. Go. I'll be there in a minute."

"You'll cover me?" Donna needled me with a diminishing glare. "What do you think this is, *Band of Brothers?*"

I stood up and proclaimed, "Oh, bless the Lord, my soul!" before bashing three kids with a blistering salvo. I could see Donna scurrying off, and somehow, she didn't seem as mad. Determined, yes. But not really mad.

I drilled a few more chorus kids point-blank, and two others I thumped as they were moving away. I felt a little guilty, but the kids seemed impressed by my skills, and that emboldened me.

By now, the yard looked like a blizzard, but the storm-front was moving steadily toward Donna. The barricade was about forty yards away, and I endured a hail of snowballs as I traversed the span. I could hear the kids still calling out to one another as I ran. It seemed to me that the show lyrics steadily were being replaced by laughter and taunting. It wasn't what I asked for, but I took some consolation knowing they were having fun.

By the time I arrived at the makeshift fort, I could tell that Donna had been getting it in a bad way. Her determined mood had soured distinctly. I hoped that my surprise would be enough to remedy things.

"What took you so long? I thought you were going to 'cover me.'"

"Oh, I've got you covered, Ms. Thewlis. And I happen to know a little about stacking a deck. You and I are about to go all in."

"All in?" she asked. "So now you're a card shark too, huh? I hope this idea of yours is more solid than your metaphors."

She was still feigning hostility, but I could tell she was intrigued. And when I pulled back the piece of plywood her intrigue blossomed into guarded approval. "That's not what I think that is, is it?"

"Torro eighteen-inch twelve-amp electric snowblower with patented snow-auger technology. Powerful enough to plow through patios and sidewalks, but simple enough to be used by anyone, even a theater director."

"Oh, you are a devil, aren't you?" Donna purred.

"And a handy electrician. Although it did take me nearly an hour to run power cords all the way back to the school. But she's fully functional, at least Mom said it was when I took it from the garage. Would you care to do the honors?"

Donna gripped the ignition handle and pushed the Start button. The little dynamo groaned to life and spat out a plume of sugar-white snow that impressed even me. "Okay, this is good," Donna allowed.

"The manual said it would shoot up to thirty feet," I yelled over the motor, but Donna was already off. She cut a mighty swath through the front line of actors, stopping only briefly to fiddle with the hand crank that changed the direction of the spout. "Hey, this thing has got a little directional doo-hickey," she tittered gleefully and sent a spray my way.

"All right, my turn!" I shouted. "Donna? Donna! Hey, don't forget whose snowblower this is!"

"It's your mom's from what I hear!" she yelled back over her shoulder as she tsunamied a batch of chorus girls. Then she was off again, cackling like a mad witch with a brand-new broom.

It may have been a time to take the high road. But this was my idea. Not only that, it was getting cold, and *I was the director* for crying out loud. So I hip-checked Donna off the rig and continued the assault. Surprisingly, she didn't contest me. She just scooped up a few snowballs and galloped along as my wingman, hurling fastballs at the snipers.

"You viper's brood!" I began quoting the first lines of the show. They're John the Baptist's lines, and at the time, I hadn't considered the irony. "Who warned you to escape the coming retribution? Every tree that fails to produce good fruit is cut down. Now I baptize you with water for repentance sake."

I could hear Donna howling at the double meaning and the students were too for that matter. Like I said, I hadn't really thought about the metaphor. I was just quoting the first lines of the show. But, and no blasphemy is intended here, it sort of turned out like a baptism. I guess a better phrasing would be "rite of passage." But whether in singles or small groups, the kids approached the churning plume to be doused by snow. Most inched their way, laughing nervously, shoulder and back leading, then shrieked away as soon as the snow pummeled them. But some of the more daring kids flung themselves spread eagle and took a joyous blast right in the chest and head. But no one was left out regardless of style. Everyone took a hearty splash from the fabulous snow-flinging machine. It was all great fun, kind of like the pure, innocent fun those Bible study kids used to have back in the day. People were whooping and laughing, even the ones that Donna and I had to drive away when they made an attempt to capture our machine. One of our soloists even got a few fingers on the handle grip before Donna pawed them away. The other was repelled when Donna deftly slid a handful of snow down the back of the attacker's sweater.

"Pretty slick, Thewlis! Where did you learn that move? Jackie Chan?"

Donna and I made a formidable team. We were like Sitting Bull against Custer's men.

We made another pass across the field when the snarls and howls of laughter suspiciously abated. Everyone came to a halt, and fearful glances were exchanged.

And then I saw him.

Principal Artie Chambers was standing in the pink glow of a floodlight. His gloved hands were thrust sullenly into his pockets, his long overcoat flapped irritably in the gloomy breeze. And his face? Well, let's just say that I've seen more mirth in a graveyard.

"Would you mind telling me what you are doing out here, Mr. Kent?"

It wasn't an unreasonable question. I should have had a quick answer. But the word *rehearsing* seemed utterly preposterous, and I knew that *bonding* would take too long to explain. It quickly became moot anyway.

Still flush with the fever of the hunt and too immature to realize it had ended, Eddie wound up and screeched, "Hey Mr. C? Turn back, oh man!"

If this had been a movie, the scene would all have been shot in slow motion. The snowball would have left Eddie's hand and slowly arced, silhouetted against the dark sky. I would have stretched out desperate hands and let go a scream that dragged out like a low moan. It would have been dramatic. You know, like the last scene in Rocky II or something. But it didn't happen that way.

It was more like a shutter blink from a "before" to "after" picture. For one moment Artie Chambers was scowling at me, and in the next second, his face was completely slushed over with snow.

Eddie's shot had taken old Chambers right in the temple, covering his forehead, eyes, and nose. Only his mouth and small chin were spared, and across them were straddled his broken glasses.

A terrible silence gripped the yard.

Then with impressive composition, he plucked away his glasses, wiped his face, and pronounced, "Children, tonight's rehearsal is over. Please check the announcements tomorrow for further updates." His tone was dreadful in its evenness, but I could see his face was shaking with rage.

The kids cleared out faster than first class on the Titanic. Chambers waited for them to leave before pulling an envelope from his pocket. He wagged it between pinched fingers and said, "I came here tonight to tell you that the superintendent and school board approved my authority to pay you half your wages up front. They said if I felt comfortable with the progress you were making to go ahead and issue a check." He wagged the envelope a few more times, too angry to find any words. "After what I have seen here tonight, I can't tell them in good conscience that I am comfortable with your....your..." His hand fluttered, gesturing toward the battlefield. "Your progress!" Then he tore the whole thing up right in front of me. He started to throw the torn pieces into the air as one final demonstration but thought better of it. "Your efforts here are no longer required!" He tucked the tattered handful of my fortune back into his pocket and marched away.

If the silence after Eddie's snowball was like the expectant hush before a magic trick, this silence was like the one that follows a burial. It was complete and terminal. I just stood there dumbly and watched Chambers tromp away to his car.

But as the awful consequence of the moment began to take shape in my head, Donna was suddenly there. "You know what you need right now?" she said with a strange buoyancy. "You need to be perked up." I didn't disagree, but I was too stunned to understand what the heck she meant. I followed her like an anesthetized drone to the parking lot. "Follow me," she added blithely. "I'll drive slowly so you don't get lost. It's not far. Just off the square."

As it turns out, Perked Up is a hip coffee shop that specializes in exotic coffees and liqueurs. I was pretty surprised that Hanover had such a place. It looked like it might have been plucked right out of SoHo except for the cluster of men inside the door, all of whom were wearing bib overalls and ratty seed caps.

"Do you remember Sammy Perkins?" Donna led me back to a pair of overstuffed chairs near a retro-looking gas fireplace. "He opened this place after he got back from Afghanistan. After his third tour of duty, he pledged to never lift anything that had more firepower than a double espresso. By the way, the Irish coffee here is Sammy's specialty. But I've found you can't go wrong with the chocolate mocha." I vaguely noticed a burly guy with a white apron drift toward us. "Ed and I liked to come here after tough rehearsals," Donna explained. "Or when we had to make a few of those painful casting decisions. Aside from the sunroom in my house, this is my favorite spot in Hanover."

"Hey, Thewlis!" the burly guy waved and glanced at his watch. "You're early for a school night. What happened? Rough day at the old cheese factory?"

"You could say that, Sammy. Thought we might unwind here for a while."

"Glass of Pinot?"

"No, just some decaf, thanks. But my colleague here might be interested."

"I'll take the Irish coffee," I managed to break out of my trance. The promise of strong coffee laced with whiskey was enough to rouse me from the dead.

"Beans from Columbia, whiskey from Canada, and cream from Wisconsin," Sammy's shaggy beard split with a big toothy smile. "But it's the best *Irish* coffee you've had or double your money back."

I pointed cheerlessly to Donna.

"Oh...Well then, it'll be double Thewlis's money back."

He left with a swirl of apron strings, and Donna and I sat in more silence. There were overhead speakers playing Tony Bennett's "The Way You Look Tonight" a little too loudly, and the seed-cap boys were tapping their work boots. Donna seemed completely content, but I wasn't. So I muttered, "Former."

"What's that?" she said as she accepted a mug from Sammy. He put my Irish coffee on a stained paper coaster and left again.

"Former," I repeated. "You should have told him I'm your 'former' colleague."

She held her cup near the rim with two hands and took a timid sip. "We'll see about that. Artie can be a reactionary. I'll go in and see him in the morning after he's had a chance to cool down and explain things. You may not be off the hook for this show just yet."

My Irish coffee was going down more smoothly than I expected. Sammy hadn't exaggerated. "So at the risk of getting an answer I don't want to hear, why are you being so kind to me all of a sudden?"

"What kind of answer don't you want to hear?"

"I don't know. Like maybe your daughter is having a birthday party and you need someone to dress like a clown or sit in the dunk tank. I just get the feeling I'm going to owe you for something."

She looked surprised by my answer and a little relieved. She put the mug down and settled back in the easy chair. "Okay. Confession time." She drummed her fingers together and chewed on the inside of her cheek before plunging in. "All right. I wasn't happy when Artie told me that you'd be coming here to direct the musical."

"No!"

"You better behave if you want me to have Sammy refill your Irish coffee." She gave me another one of those needling glares that I hoped meant she was teasing. "Anyway, when Artie told me he had e-mailed you, I was ticked. But not for the reason you're thinking."

"And what's the reason I'm thinking, Dr. Phil?"

"It wasn't because I wanted to be the director. Seriously. No lie. I know I'm not qualified to do what you do."

I wondered if I should admit my lack of qualifications. But this was her confession, not mine. And it was pleasant to hear. I figured it was best not to muddy the waters.

"I was content to do my bit with the music," she continued. "You know, work with the kids on the side. And I was fine with adjusting to a new director. Just not you. Well, not someone *like* you anyway."

"Why not me?"

Donna took in a thoughtful breath and leaned forward, elbows on knees. Her mocha now and afterthought cradled in her hands. This was clearly going to be the heart of the confession, and I wasn't sure I was ready for it. I took in a deep breath too.

"I hate it when people get something without working for it," she said. "You know, the lucky ones, or lucky and talented ones like you. I've had to work and scrape for everything I've gotten. Nothing ever came easy for me. Not my job, not music. In fact, the things in life I've loved the most were usually the hardest for me. I doesn't seem right that others should get what they want without trying. And then you whisk in"—she gave a dismissive flip of her hand— "Mr. Broadway Star. And without a single day's work, you jump right to the head of the line. I've seen it before. Back in college. Even here at Hanover when you got all the leads. It just burned me. I suppose some of it is jealously, but most of it is justice. It's not fair." She settled back into the comfort of the chair, shriven and satisfied. "So I guess what I'm saying is that it wasn't so much you I resented but the idea of you."

"But you said resent*ed*. In the past tense." I was hopeful.

"I was in the doorway to the greenroom the other night, sort of eavesdropping." Ah, more confession. "Remember the night Eddie's folks stopped by? You seemed pretty bleak, and I piled on by telling you how little time we had before the show goes up."

"I remember."

"Well, I heard you talking afterwards on the stage. Actually, I heard you talking to Ed when you thought you were alone on the stage. I guess that's when I realized this wasn't as easy for you as I imagined. Part of it is your fault though. You come across as so sure of yourself. But the guy I overheard standing on the stage that night wasn't. I figured I should cut you some slack. What can I say? I've always rooted for the underdog. Here, let me have Sammy refill your drink in case I say too much more."

Sammy was back with a double, and I was glad for it. I wasn't ready for this sudden outpouring of kindness. Not from Donna at least. And she was pretty in the firelight, prettier than I expected, with copper red burning in her tangly hair and her eyes bright with flame. It made me self-conscious. Part of me wanted to reciprocate her generous words. The part holding back quickly became unfettered by the whiskey. I've always been bad with women. "You shouldn't sell yourself so short," I said and hoped the *S*s and Shs didn't slur. "I told you that I was impressed by the way the kids sang. They don't sound like high-schoolers at all. And if teaching them is hard for you, you don't show it either." My praise was running with full head now, and the whiskey didn't know how to rein it in. "I tell you, I've been around my fair share of music directors. Some of them with big names and bigger salaries. And I can tell you that, by comparison, you are really a fine musician, Donna."

"You don't need to patronize me," she snapped, and I was surprised by the sting in her voice.

"I wasn't patronizing. Just telling you what I thought. Sheesh. Regardless of what you've heard, I'm not a complete monster."

Donna stared down into her coffee and swirled it around the inside of the mug. "No, not a monster," she said finally. "Just talented enough to make others insecure."

I really didn't know how to respond, but that didn't stop me from blundering, "You don't need to…um, shouldn't feel that if I…"

"He loved your voice, you know. Ed did." She was still staring into the black mirror of her coffee like it was some kind of movie screen and she was watching scenes from the past. "He said that it was the most pure singing voice he'd ever heard. He never talked about you by name, but he loved to talk about your voice. He'd say, 'That ballad sung by Tony when we did "West Side," now that was as good as it gets,' or 'Remember when our Tommy sang "Almost Like Being in Love"? I can still hear it like it was yesterday. Never heard it performed better. Not Broadway, not even on the West End of London.'" Donna let herself smile at the memory. "I remember one time we were up here," she said, "sitting right by this fireplace. Ed was enjoying a glass of cabernet. You know, when I think about it, Ed didn't so much drink wine as he slow-danced with it. Anyway, we were just unwinding after a lousy rehearsal when all of a sudden he said to me, 'King Arthur sang "How to Handle a Woman" in Act II. You remember the number?' Then Ed takes this long slow sip of his drink and says, 'It still moves me to tears when I think about it, Donna. Such pain and beauty all in one song. I only wish our Arthur had taken that song to heart.'" Donna tapped her rings absently on the side of the mug. "He loved you, Sawyer. He really loved you. You were the special one. Not me. Not any of the other actors he'd worked with over the years. You were it. And it was your voice that kept him from being able to forget you.

"I don't know if you know this, but the reason he never came to see you on Broadway wasn't because he hated you. It was because he couldn't bear to hear you sing. It's true. In fact, once he told me that he hoped that you'd someday sing at his funeral. He said that way, he'd be able to hear it one more time but have the voices of angels to help cushion the blow."

"I don't sing anymore." I couldn't look at her. Those pretty eyes and wistful smile were one thing. But the burden of Ed Bertollini's affection was too much to bear. I stared into the manufactured flames of the gas fireplace. It was my turn to confess. "There are really only two reasons to ever sing. One is for the pure joy of it. The other is for a paycheck."

"And?" Donna seemed genuinely interested.

"I'm out of work now. You know that."

"And?"

I wasn't sure I wanted to speak further. Confessions cost; don't let anyone fool you. And if you don't believe me, just ask Tiger Woods. But I was into my Irish coffee just enough to not care about costs. Heck, Donna was paying for the drinks, so I was already playing with house money. "And I haven't had the joy to sing in years," I admitted. "It's been a long time since I've been happy."

"What happened?"

"Our baby died."

Donna had the grace not to ask further. I'm glad, because I didn't have the faculties to stop myself. We listened while the Tony Bennet CD played itself out. Donna paid the bill, then we both sauntered out to the parking lot and stood between our cars.

"Thanks for the coffee, Donna. I appreciate your trying to cheer me up. But trust me. I've lost jobs before. I'll manage."

"Well, if this is the end of things, I wanted to finish on better terms. I wasn't fair to you early on. I hope you don't hold it against me."

"No worries."

I wanted to say more, something important. But important words had abandoned my mouth. I think I swallowed them with the Irish coffee.

We waited there until the silence grew awkward. Donna put us out of our misery by saying, "Well, it's getting cold, and I need to pick up my daughter from the sitter. Look, I'll talk to Artie tomorrow and let you know what he says. It's worth a shot."

"Thanks, Donna."

She shuffled around to her car door and popped the lock. But then just before she got in, she spied me from over the roof. A mischievous look invaded her face. And what she said filled my stomach with an oily anxiety that I vaguely remembered from adolescence. "But just between you and me, Sawyer," she served up her last confession, "I really hope that this isn't the end of things."

I stayed there in the parking lot and watched her car disappear beyond that last street lamp. My goofy grin felt awkward, but I wore it anyway. I didn't know what to make of it, but I wasn't anxious to chase it away. The grin didn't last long though. The small shelter of hope that I was constructing would come crashing down as soon as I got home. It seemed impossible in that childishly giddy moment but getting fired by Artie Chambers would be the second worst thing that would happen to me that night.

TEN

"What do you mean you didn't get the number?" Mom thought I was angry, but what she heard was fear.

"It only said 'Unavailable' on my caller ID." She was still shaking. "I didn't know who it was, so I answered it."

"Never answer the phone if you don't know who it is, Mom! Never!" But I stopped myself. This wasn't her fault. It was mine, no matter how good it felt to displace the guilt. "And you're sure it was a man's voice, right?"

A timid nod. "With sort of an East Coast accent. What did he mean, Sawyer? What *contract* are you running from?"

"I'm not running." I steadied Mom's shoulders and tried to sound convincing. "Look, Mom, I'll handle this. Don't worry yourself. How Big T found me here so quickly, I don't know. But I'll take care of it."

"This man…This Big T, he sounded very angry. Sawyer, if you need help—"

"I'll handle it, Mom." But my brain was scrambling as to how. "It's been a lousy night. We can talk about it in the morning. But please don't let this worry you. It's Big T's job to sound angry. I'll get it cleared up. Can I borrow your cell phone? Don't think any more about it, Mom. It's all just a simple misunderstanding. You go to bed."

I find it fascinating how quickly bad ideas can leap to mind. They're like dirty jokes. Good ideas, like good jokes, require much more thought. But this bad idea was all I had, so I went with it. Besides, like I told you already, I've stolen money before.

Big T was a guy I sometimes turned to, to loan me money when my worker's comp checks came late. He had a sizeable reputation back in the neighborhood, but I always managed to stay on his "nice list." I was into him for $1500 when I got the letter that the insurance company had kicked me off the dole. I hadn't forgotten Big T, but I'm sure when he got wind that I had left the area, he thought I had. He'd want, at minimum, a token to show my good faith. I knew where to get it.

I dumped the manila envelope on my bed and started counting. Between the ticket and T-shirt money the kids had given me, there was nearly $800 in cash. I parsed out the checks—they would do me no good—and stuffed the remaining wad of bills in my jacket. Noah watched me do it, but I couldn't look at him.

I googled a Fast Cash outlet in East Peoria that wired money and stayed open late. I grabbed Mom's cell phone and keys but made a first stop at the Phillips 66 station to pick up a bottle of Canadian. My Irish coffee was petering out, and I needed to fortify my nerves. It was a night for bad ideas. One deserved another.

The whiskey had its usual way with me. The disaster of the evening soon became clear. My choices became understandable, perhaps even a little noble. Artie Chambers owed me the money. I was only taking what I deserved. What jury would send me to jail for that? And things were getting dicey in Hanover. The whole Donna thing was getting complicated, and I certainly didn't want to run into Sarah after getting dumped from my job. I never thought on that bus ride home that I'd find woman trouble back in Hanover. This was probably all for the best, I agreed with another long draw.

Those old faces on the walls at the high school were right. I didn't belong here. It was time again to quit. In the morning, I'd give Mom some lame excuse. And then I'd...Well, I'd figure that out later.

I took noisy swig when I remembered another morning problem. Tomorrow was Thursday, Bible study day. Tim would be in my driveway at 5:00 a.m. with a goofy smile and expectations. That wouldn't do. I fired off a text and told him I was sick. Yeah, that's a good excuse. I'm sick. The whiskey agreed.

Somehow, I completed the errand, though parts of it I couldn't remember. I slipped into the house through the side door and collapsed on my bed. I lay staring at the textured swirls of ceiling plaster as the room slowly rotated. I tried to imagine it rotating the other direction to cancel the effect. It was going to be a bad night, I knew. Morning would almost certainly be worse. And then I'd start again. Start again by…Well, I didn't really know. In the slow malaise of drunkenness, I didn't care. Maybe I'd started over too many times. Maybe if I had a pistol that worked, I could quit for good. I just couldn't bear Mom seeing it. Or Donna. Or Tim. And please, dear God, don't let Sarah find out.

The bed suddenly lurched, and Noah jumped up. He shoved his wet nose under the hollow of my hand and nuzzled near my side. He questioned me with dark sad eyes. "Sorry, boy. No walk tomorrow. I'm sick." I reached to pet him, but he was gone. I heard him pad across the floor and push the door open with his nose. I don't think he could bear seeing it either. So he left me alone in the half-light, alone and miserable with my thoughts.

The morning burst in diamond-bright, blasting open my eyelids and rattling inside my dull skull. My stiff body ached like I'd played Twister with Momma Cass Elliot all night and won. And I was sure that something—something unnatural and unholy—must have crawled inside my mouth and died. I pulled the blanket over my head.

My head felt like a bucket of glue, that nasty kind that they use to hold boats together. But all of that wasn't half as bad as the shreds of last night's memory that began pasting themselves together in my thrumming brain.

I had gotten fired, hadn't I? Yeah, by that needle-chin Artie Chambers. But Donna had been kind, really kind. She took me to a cool place, and we listened to jazz. And then I stole money. Sonovabuck! I stole school money. Oh, that's right, to pay that loan, and I drove Mom's car. Better check the fenders. How did it fall apart so quickly? What was I thinking? And Tim. I blew him off too. Dear lord, what kind of whiskey did I drink? I hope there's a little left.

I rubbed my eyes and squished it all together.

You know, out of the whole ugly quagmire, there was one part I was glad for. I had blown off Tim. I just couldn't see him after all this. I had let him get his hopes up. That was a mistake. People in my life always got burned when they got their hopes up for me.

I needed to get out. Well, first I needed a drink of water, but then I'd get out. *Crimeny! Someone must have swapped out my tongue for a tube sock in the middle of the night. Okay, I'll get a drink and then walk to the McClugage Bridge and jump off. It's only twenty miles away. I could be there by sunset. Perfect. Darkness to cover it. Drowned corpses are hideous. I know. I watch a lot of cop shows. Good. A plan. A drink of water then the river.*

I pulled back the comforter to get out of bed.

My back had other ideas.

A bolt of hot pain charged down my spine and into my hip. I screamed something that I hoped wasn't profanity and fell back; my whiskey-soaked brain throbbed in applause.

Mom was there immediately with Noah paddling behind. "Sawyer? Sawyer, what is it?"

The look on my face must've told her all she needed to know. "Oh, honey. I know just how you feel." She had no idea how I felt. "Well, sometimes there are setbacks. That's just the way it goes with backs. Here, let me get you some ibuprofen. But don't tell Timothy. He'll never let me hear the end of it."

Before I could protest, she scurried out of the room, and I could hear her dialing. "Yes, I wanted to see if Dr. Kavenaugh had any openings this morning. I've got someone here who really needs to see him." A pause. "Oh, that's right. This is Thursday. And he'll be out of the office all day, right?" Another pause, this time a long one. "Oh no, that's okay. No, don't worry about it. I already have his cell phone number. Thanks. You too. Bye-bye."

She was dialing again. And what she proposed was worse than my pounding head.

"Hello, Timothy, this is Dorothy. Yes, sorry to bother you on your day off, but I've got a son here who I think needs to see you. Sick? Oh, I think he's more hurt than sick. Yes, that's right. I don't think so, but I can ask him." Mom called from the other room, "Sawyer, you think you can get out of bed?"

If I could've gotten out of bed, that infernal phone would've been shattered into a thousand pieces. "Just give me a minute, Mom. I'll be fine." I grunted and reached the edge of the bed. Noah was there but offered no assistance. "Tell Tim to forget it. I'm okay."

"Oh, that's very sweet of you, Timothy. Yes, absolutely. Some ice? Sure, I'll see what we've got. All right. Thanks again, honey. We'll see you soon.

"Great news," she beamed when she popped her head back into the doorway. "Timothy said he'll be here in a half hour."

Tim was there in twenty minutes. He brought with him a portable table that he eased me onto. "This may hurt a little bit." He barely finished his preamble before gouging his thumbs into the small of my back. "That's tender, isn't it? Yep. A little inflamed here too. Well, Finny, I've got bad news."

"I can take it."

"You're going to recover." He pulled on my hip and helped roll me onto my back. He pressed down with his fingers like a spade into my abdomen and fished down deep into the muscles.

"You know my back is on the other side, right?" I winced.

"Just trust me, Finny. I can get to the trigger point easier this way." Then he had me trying to do leg lifts while he pushed back with resistance. I was dubious about the whole operation, but by the time he was finished, I was actually shuffling along better than I expected.

"So how do you feel?"

"Like Boris Karloff."

"Well, those muscles are still little bit jumpy. I've been moving things around a little bit with your treatment. Sometimes, that puts new demands on muscles, and they aren't strong enough for it yet. But I have to say, it's usually not this bad. What were you doing last night? Did you get into an alley fight or something?"

"More like a snowball fight," I admitted.

"That would do it."

"Oh, and I pushed a snowblower all over a field."

"Let's get you back to the clinic. I'd like to get some electric stimulation on that lumbar area. And then you need ice. That's the key, Finny. Ice, ice, ice. I can't promise you'll be back to fighting form, but you'll feel much better, even by tonight."

"I thought you weren't working today."

"Perks of owning the clinic, Finny. I can use it whenever I want." He craned his neck and hollered toward the back stairwell. "Mrs. K? Do you mind if I borrow your son for a while?"

"As long as you need, Timothy. I'll be down here working most of the day anyway," came the distant reply.

Tim looked at me and gave me one of those nitroglycerin smiles. "Don't worry." He tossed his keys up and caught them in the same hand. "I'll drive."

Tim took me to an unoccupied room at the rear of his clinic to do the treatment. I knew something was up. He was odd. The conversation was stilted. The trouble was, I didn't want to deal with it. I knew he was probably upset because I blew them off this morning, but I was at the bottom of the ladder. And I was tired. And the more I thought about it, the more I just wanted it to be over.

All of it.

The only spot of luck was I wouldn't need to walk to the bridge. Mom was going to be busy all day, and I could take her car.

I could tell that Tim was trying to decide what to say. Finally, he led with, "So you had a pretty rough night last night, huh?"

"It shows?"

"Well, you either took a bath in acetone or you were hitting it pretty hard. Because what's coming out of the pores of your skin is pretty high octane. I remember the smell."

"Sorry to stink up your beautiful clinic," I spit back. I had no right to be angry, but I was. And I didn't care what Tim thought about it. I guess that's how men get when they're at their end. "Oh, and so sorry about blowing you off this morning. Yeah, I was drunk. There. Are you happy? I admit it, Tim. I'm a drunk. And I was too ashamed to tell you, so I lied. Yeah, I'm a liar too. And you might as well call me a coward while you're at it." The anger was rolling out deliciously, and I didn't care to check it. That's the great thing about being at the end. There can't be repercussions.

But then Tim said something that cropped my anger. "Actually, I was sort of glad that you blew me off this morning. I didn't want to go either. Dale touched some nerves that I wasn't anxious to talk about again. When the clock went off at four thirty, I didn't want to go. I figured I could always check out the video podcast later. I didn't want to face you with all that stuff being talked about. So if we're counting cowards, there's at least two of us in this room."

"I'm done, Tim." I dropped my eyes. "Not with you...I mean...not this conversation. Well, actually, I do mean you and all this. Everything." I was making a mess of things, but that didn't stop me. "I'm just done with life. I've played out all my cards, and my hand isn't going to get any better." I finally got the nerve to meet his gaze, and I regretted what I saw there. "I got fired last night," I explained. "And then I did something else that could get me arrested. I've screwed everything up. And now the kids and the show are back to square one. I let everyone down. But that's the way it usually goes for me, you know? This act reads just like the one before it and so on down the line. It doesn't seem like it makes any sense to read further."

Tim knew what I meant and tried to cut me off. "You can't just give up now, Finny!"

"Oh, can't I?" The anger was flaming to life again. "Can't I? And just what am I giving up anyway? Have you considered that, Mr. Chamber of Commerce? I've made a wreck of my life and everyone else's life I've encountered. Heck, I even disappoint the nearly dead. I'm like Midas in reverse. Look." I held up my hands and calmed. "It's like this, Tim. I've been near this doorway for a long time. I know every detail of the threshold. And now, it's probably time to step on through."

Tim was unusually quiet. My argument must have been persuasive. But then he asked me a question that I didn't expect. "Would you at least do one thing for me before you do anything final?"

"If it's make out a will, there's nothing much I can leave you."

Tim was untroubled by my attempt at humor. "Would you pray with me, Finny? Just once. Would you do that?"

Remember I told you that I regretted the look in his eyes? This was the look that I regretted the most. Tim's eyes were fiery wet. They held that burning "do or die, man the gates" stare that he got when the team was fourth and one at the goal line. "Pray with me."

"I think God's got bigger fish to fry, at least more deserving fish."

But Tim wouldn't be moved. "You don't really think that's how God works, do you? Finny, God *specializes* in the undeserving. Look, it's like this. I'm a doctor, but I don't insist that my patients get healthier before they come see me. In fact, some of the cases where I've gotten the most satisfaction were the ones where the people were in the worst shape."

"Oh, so now you're God." I was getting angry again.

"Of course not, Finny. Don't be ridiculous. I'm just saying that it kind of works that way. Besides"—Tim's face brightened—"if I were God, the Cubs would've won several World Series by now. Come on. Pray with me."

I knuckled under and told him that I would, but it was a half-lie. I didn't want to quibble prepositions with him, but the truth was this: I was willing to let him pray for me or even right next to me. But he wouldn't be praying *with* me. I was more of a semi-interested spectator when he put his hand on my shoulder, bowed his head, and prayed. "Dear God, thank you for not giving up on me. And thank you for being a God that has a plan and sees much more than we see. Please help Finny to know that you still care. Please let him know that you haven't given up on him either. Show him a little ray of hope to cling to. Could you do that, Lord? Show him a little ray of your hope to cling to. Let him know you still love him and have a plan for him."

"Thanks, Tim," I said as I drew away from his hand on my shoulder.

"You'll call me before you do something rash, right?"

"I'll call you." The lies were getting easy to tell.

"I'm off the rest of the day. You want to grab lunch or something?"

"No, I've got something else to do."

"Where are you going?"

"To make one last apology."

ELEVEN

The bleak sky was spitting sleety rain by the time I pulled up to the hospital. Last night's whiskey bottle was still lying one-third full on the floorboards of the car. I left it there. Some words are better spoken sober.

I didn't find an umbrella, but I didn't care. I was glad for the rain. Not only did the weather match my mood, but it felt like penance. It also thinned out the normal crush of afternoon visitors. The ICU ward was nearly empty when I pushed through the elevator doors and checked in. It was a small grace. I didn't want to make small talk, and I certainly didn't want to answer any questions.

But when I got near Mr. B's room, the door was blocked by two doctors having some sort of a conference. One was a woman, perhaps in her early sixties. She was wearing one of those intimidating white lab coats and had a bulky file trapped beneath her crossed arms. The other doctor was a younger man who looked like he might've just walked out of surgery. He was still wearing his scrubs, but his white mask was pulled down beneath his bearded chin. The woman was talking, and so I ducked over to a water cooler to be unnoticed. I was still close enough to hear what she was saying.

"Yes, that was my concern also." She was nodding but didn't seem pleased that she was correct.

"And of course," the young surgeon responded. "If clots develop, treatment for that can often result in—"

"Proteinuria," she finished his thought for him. "Yes, I'm aware, which is difficult enough on two kidneys, let alone a patient with only one."

"But I still think you're right in recommending surgery. I don't see any better alternatives."

There was a long silence before the woman said, "Well, thank you, Paul. I trust your experience in cases like these. And since you performed the original surgery on Mr. Bertollini, I wanted to consult you first before I contacted the niece."

As the young surgeon shuffled away, she saw me loitering near the water cooler and said graciously, "Oh, are you here to visit Mr. Bertollini?"

"Uh, yeah. I am. But I can come back another time if it's—"

"No, it's fine to go on in. I'm just finishing up making my rounds." She gave me a practiced smile.

"I won't be long," I said. "I just wanted to be sure to see him one last time."

She mistook my meaning, and the practiced smile slipped from her face. It was replaced by a genuine warmth that softened her eyes and released the creases from her forehead. "Now, now, dear. You mustn't think like that. Mr. Bertollini faces a tough road, I won't sugarcoat it. But he's held on this far, and that shows he's tough. And I can assure you that he is in the best possible care."

"Yes, I know that, Doctor..." I searched for her name on her nametag as I shook her hand. "Schaeffer. And I've already met Dr. Stratton. He seems like a very good man. Will he be coming by the room too? I wouldn't want to get in his way."

"Oh, I wouldn't think so. He left for Arizona last week."

I started to ask at that, but a nurse approached her with a question. I used the opportunity to drift away from the conversation and into Mr. Bertollini's room.

It was easier seeing him the second time. The shock of his feebleness no longer blinded me to the subtle hints of his character that were still visible. I could see the familiar shape of his jaw and chin and the laugh lines around the corners of his eyes. The hoses and machines that were keeping him alive faded to mere distractions. I didn't see a half-dead corpse. This was Edward Bertollini, still half alive.

I pulled up a chair, took hold of his soft limp hand, and spoke to my friend and mentor for the first time in nearly fifteen years.

My words weren't rehearsed, but they poured out of my heart like an earnest soliloquy. "I don't know if you can hear me or not, Mr. B, but I hope you can. And even if not, I'm glad I got a chance to see you one last time and tell you what I should've told you a long time ago.

"I'm so sorry. I know those words aren't close to being enough, but they're all I've got. Everything else I've thrown away. I am so terribly sorry. You were so good to me. I never really had a dad, or at least a man that I was proud to call my dad. But you stepped in and sort of filled the void. You encouraged me and believed in me when I needed a father to tell me that I was okay. You showed me that I had talent, and you pointed me toward a future. And yet after all of that, I repaid every one of your kindnesses with hurt.

"You didn't deserve someone like me to come into your life and wreck everything. I know how important family was to you, and losing your only sister must've left you feeling horribly alone. All you had left was Sarah, and I nearly took her away too. Yes, even living as far away as I was, I got word of her suicide attempt. I tried to brush it off as depression brought on by the death of the baby. But the truth is, it was mostly my fault.

"I'm probably going to tell you something that you already know, but I'll feel better knowing that I said it to you anyway. When I left Sarah, I left her in bad straits. You know all the benefit shows, raffles, and potlucks you organized to help raise money for Mrs. Gibson's treatments? Well, you were more successful than you might've thought. The cancer took her so quickly that very little of it got spent. Sarah had over $40,000 in her account when we got married. But it didn't take long for me to grow weary of married life. I wanted to see if I could make it as an actor. I knew that it would take money to set myself up and hire a proper agent. Sarah and I had a joint account, and it was all too easy. I took most of the money the morning I left for New York City. All I left her was enough to make the next rent payment. At the time, I figured I'd repay it all back once I hit it big. But I never did. I took the money, squandered it, and left

Sarah to deal with the fallout. So I guess what I'm saying is, when she tried to hang herself, it was my hands that braided the rope.

"I really didn't mean for it to work out this way. When I married Sarah, I really did love her. At that time, I couldn't imagine ever being capable of hurting her or you like I did. But I also didn't realize how capable I was of loving myself. And when things started to fall apart and then Sarah miscarried so close to term, I saw my chance to escape.

"In some twisted way, I rationalized it. I thought if I could make it big on Broadway, I'd prove you right. I'd be your shining star. Your accomplishment. But again, I was wrong. I was just pushing everyone down so I could reach higher. That's the trouble of loving yourself above everyone else. When it all falls apart, there's no one left to catch you.

"Anyway, once again, I've made this too much about me. This was supposed to be about you. I came here to tell you how proud I am that I once knew you. You did things the right way. You gave of yourself and didn't count the cost. If there's any proof of that, it's that even a jerk like me can't forget how much he loves you. I guess that's really what I came here to say. I'm so sorry, Mr. B. And if you can hear me, please know that I love you."

I don't know where in all of that I started crying, but my face and shirt were soaked with hot cathartic tears by the time I finished. I borrowed a towel from the bathroom to dry up. But just as I was about to leave, I realized I had one last apology to make. "And I'm sorry that I never sang for you again," I said from the crack of the doorway. "I never knew how happy that would have made you. Be happy, Mr. B. Please, be happy. I won't ever sing again. But maybe someday, you'll remember my voice in heaven."

Hearing all that ugliness pour out of my mouth only reinforced how worthless my life had become. The remaining swallows of Canadian Mist confirmed it like the bitter strokes of a gavel. Guilty. Guilty. Guilty.

I drove to the bridge straightaway. There was a dingy, minimart gas station squatting at its foot, and I parked Mom's car there while I finished the letters. One was to Mom. It said what she already knew, but I owed it to her to write it down anyway. The second was to my dad. I hadn't intended to leave him a note, but I guess the speech to Mr. B got me thinking about him. I told him he was selfish for what he did. I told him I could never imagine having a son and then cutting out on his life. I said other things that would be hard for him to read. I used language that would only come out of my mouth when I was drunk. Then I folded the letters and placed them neatly on the dashboard. I tossed the keys under the floor mat and stepped out into the cold drizzle.

It hadn't occurred to me that the river would be frozen. Only a slushy, ice-chunked ribbon broken to accommodate barge traffic snaked through its otherwise smooth white surface. For a moment, I had to consider whether it would be better to be crushed on the ice or drown beneath it.

I chose the latter.

The cars didn't pay me much attention as I marched to the apex of the bridge and stared down at the mud-brown barge lane. Only when I threw the empty whiskey bottle into the water did someone give me a honk and flash me a thumbs-up sign.

I took it as confirmation.

Slowly, I eased myself over the steel railing and stood, heels to bridge, on the narrow ledge.

The river below me was cold and disinterested. What I did here wouldn't matter, and it certainly wouldn't change the course it had been on for thousands of years. I couldn't disagree.

I remember once, I saw a program where two clergymen were debating the consequences of suicide. An audience member asked if an atheist jumped off a bridge and killed himself, was there any hope that he still might go to heaven? One of the clergyman emphatically said no. He said that he could find no place in Scripture where such a man could ever find salvation. The second clergyman, an old skinny English vicar countered that claim. He said he could easily find a place where that man might be saved. When asked where, the old vicar said in a squeaky voice, "Somewhere between the bridge and the water, I should think."

Staring down at the icy river below, the distance appeared more apt for destruction than salvation.

I guess it's human to wonder what people are feeling when they come to the end. I can only tell you that I was overcome by two competing emotions. One was utter despair at the meaninglessness of it all. The other was anger—brutal, carnal anger because that's not the way it was supposed to be. The river was right. Nothing here mattered. And that made me mad.

I was mad at myself. I was mad at theater. I was mad at my gimpy back. I was mad at the empty whiskey bottle. I was mad at the occasional car that honked at me and the wind that fluttered my coat. I was just plain mad. Because something was supposed to matter at the end of it all, and it didn't.

My arms were spread eagle holding the railing behind me. I leaned my body forward, bowed out like an elegant hood ornament. And I made up my mind for certain.

But just as I began to loosen my grip on the railing, a cell phone rang.

I couldn't believe it. But there it was. The tinny electronic tones of Men at Work's "Who Can It Be Now?" piping merrily from somewhere inside the folds of my long coat. Startled, I clutched the railing and twisted back around facing the bridge. As I fumbled for the device still whistling in my pocket, I realized the phone must be Mom's. I had borrowed it last night to call Big T and forgotten to give it back.

"Uh...hello?" I stupidly answered it.

"Oh, good, Sawyer, it *is* you." It was Donna's voice, and she seemed pretty happy. "I called your mom's house, and she wondered if I might be able to reach you at this number. Is this a bad time to talk?"

"Uh...I guess not," I bumbled as I secured my spot along the bridge railing. "What did you want?"

"Well, I went in to see Artie a few minutes ago, but I was too late. Drew, Julia, Eddie, and most of the cast had already been there.

He'd changed his mind by the time I got to his office. The kids really want you back, Sawyer. And I really want you back. On top of that, I have a check from Artie for $1700 hoping he'll get you back. He'll pay you the other half of the wages when we open the show." She hadn't tried to conceal her excitement, but my stunned silence tempered her. "Well, I guess it's not the best, but at least it's a little ray of hope to cling to, don't you think?"

I nearly fell from the bridge when I heard those words. "What did you just say?"

"I said Artie reconsidered and I have a check for you. Can't you hear me? Is this a bad cell?"

"No. You said something else, there at the end. Why did you say that?"

"What?" Donna was starting to get frustrated.

"You said something about a ray of hope. Why did you just say that?"

"Uh…I don't know. I just said it. Look, Sawyer, this is starting to get weird. The deal is this. The kids went in and went to bat for you, and I've got a check for $1700 if you want it. Will you be at rehearsal tonight or what?"

I glanced back down at the river. It was still slogging along just like it had for millennia. What I did here still wouldn't change its course. But this cell phone call was changing mine. "I'll be there," I said. "Tell Artie and the kids I'll be there."

I clambered back over the railing, waving apologetically to a honking Volkswagen. I dialed Tim as I made my way back to the car.

"Finny?" His anxious voice nearly leapt through the phone. "Is that you? Finny, I've been worried to death."

"Well, I promised that I'd call before I decided to do something rash, didn't I?" I said flatly.

"Finny, don't! Just let me know where you are. I'll be right there!"

"It's too late, Tim. I've made my decision. And I know it's rash, but here goes." I took in a long dramatic breath before saying, "I'm coming over to your place tomorrow, and we're going to watch that podcast together. And you know what else? We're going to Bible study next week whether you're a coward or not."

The granite sky was still spitting out sleet like a banshee as I drove home.

I didn't care.

I had money to pay off my debt to the school, and the balance of what I owed Big T. Better still, no one would have to know about last night. I also had people who wanted me. That hadn't been the case in a very long time. But the most important thing I had was the strange new certainty that not only was God real but for some strange reason, he actually cared about me and my circumstances. I didn't know exactly what all that meant at that time. Not even close. But I knew enough to be glad that I had discovered that truth closer to the bridge than the water.

TWELVE

Even though I got to the school twenty minutes early, I was the last one to arrive for rehearsal. When I walked onto the stage, the entire cast was assembled in the house seats and began clapping. It was a slow rhythmic clap that gathered in speed and intensity until it reached an all-out ovation. Over the top, the kids were chanting, "Mis-ter-Kent! Mis-ter-Kent!" I had to turn my back to them to gather myself. The great thing about kids is they still remember how to love big. This group didn't hold back one iota.

"Thank you, guys. Really, thank you." I was able to get them to calm down. "You know, I've been fortunate enough to hear some clapping in my day. But I don't think I'll ever hear a round of applause that will mean as much to me as that one does. Maybe someday I'll write a book. And if I do, I'll write in it that you guys saved my life. Seriously, you'll never know how true that is."

"No problem, Dr. K," Eddie hooted from the front row. "Just buy us all a couple of brewskis, and we'll call it square." The kids all laughed, but Donna batted him with the musical score. "What?" he pleaded. "I was just joking. Alcohol's terrible."

"Okay, we've got plenty of time later to talk about applause and paybacks." I brought the cast back to the task at hand. "For now, we've got a long way to go. So let's get started. Donna? Why don't you warm them up."

The kids began to herd around the piano, but Donna waded through them, a smile on her face and a check in her hand. "Glad to have you back on board, *Dr. K*." Then she pointed to a tall gawky woman who was furiously writing notes on index cards near the front of the stage. "And while I warm the kids up, you should have a chat with our costumer, Ginny Kramer. She wants to go over some of the ideas Bert gave her and see what you think. Good luck, Sawyer." Donna teased me with the mercurial smile, like a joke was being played but only she knew the punch line. "Out of the frying pan and into the fire."

Before I managed two steps toward Mrs. Kramer, she saw me and lit up like Big Bird on amphetamines. She fanned out the index cards in front of me and pulled out a pen from behind her ear. Her voice was high pitched and imperious, like a frantic Julia Childs. "Oh, Mr. Kent, I'm glad we finally got the chance to meet. I've made out a list of questions and put them on index cards that are referenced to each one of the characters. This way, you can just write your answers down and hand them back to me, or you can e-mail me or phone your answers to my voicemail. If you look on the back of each card, you'll see my e-mail address and cell phone number. Now, I'm having trouble with what to put on John the Baptist. Nothing fits. I've pulled some fabric from the costume room…"

Her barrage of questions and suggestions was only matched by her energy, which I swear was sufficient to light up half of Chicago. But it didn't take me but a few minutes to realize that Ginny Kramer was a serious asset. She might strike some as a whirling dervish with a tape measure and sewing pins, but she knew her stuff. And better yet, she knew every kid right down to his hat size.

"I tell you what," I nudged into her rambling. "I'd really like to see the costume accents for scene one. Would that be possible? I think it would help the kids get a feel for the scene when we run it tonight."

"Well…" Ginny Kramer was the kind of person who liked to make a plan and stick with it. I could tell that her mind was racing to catch up with the curveball. "Yes. Yes, I think we do that. I have the hats, ribbons, and bandannas all pooled and in a pillowcase. But I haven't had a chance to assign specific articles to each character. I suppose I could do that tonight if you gave me some time…"

"No need, Mrs. Kramer," I said politely. "Let's just see what gets pulled out of the bag and see if it works. We can make our costuming notes from there."

There was no catching up to that curveball, but to Ginny's credit, she accommodated. "I'll go get the pieces. Do you want the multicolored scarf for Jesus?"

"Absolutely."

I clapped my hands and got the cast reassembled on the stage. "All right, guys, I want to run the first scene through the song "God Save the People." But I want you to understand what we're trying to communicate here. After Jesus is rolled out on the dumpster, you hear his song and slowly approach him and John the Baptist. Eddie? That's your moment. Have the pail and sponge ready. And Eddie? Don't you dare have real water in that pail.

"Now when you approach, I want you to each adopt a different attitude. Some might come full of energy and enthusiasm. Some might be timid at first. For others, maybe there's nothing but relief in your faces. But regardless, there needs to be variety. It's one of the first rules of theater. We always want to give the audience something different to look at. When things all start looking the same, they start reading the program. And that's not good.

"As soon as Eddie wipes you with the sponge, Drew is going to hand you an article of clothing out of the bag. Just take whatever he randomly gives you and put it on in some way. It might be a cap, ribbon, or a bandanna. Each piece is colored to reflect one of the colors that's in Drew's multicolored scarf. See, the idea is that you've heard Jesus's message and now you are already beginning to reflect part of him. That's the point of the show."

We ran to the scene, and the kids executed it with much more energy than they had in previous rehearsals. But when Ginny showed up with Jesus's scarf and the coordinating pieces, the first scene jumped to life. Faces popped with emotion. Body mechanics added variety. And the voices? I couldn't believe that a few dozen kids could pound out such beautiful matured sound. This was all Mr. B's doing. It was his blocking and costume ideas. It gave me chills to witness.

And I knew right then that this show had a chance to be something very special.

We pushed on into Act I and blocked a few new songs and worked on some of the vignettes of dialogue. The kids did a marvelous job. They listened and responded, the two most important qualities you look for in an actor. So I was highly pleased with our work when we wrapped up the rehearsal. I was standing in the center aisle quietly smiling to myself while the kids gathered their coats to leave. But then I heard two words that wholly upended my satisfied mood.

"Hello, Sawyer." The voice came from behind me, and it froze the blood in my veins.

I knew that voice. I didn't need to turn around to identify its source, but I did. And when I saw her there, it was like seeing a ghost. An unnerving mixture of horror and thrill chased through me. It seized visibly in my clenched hands and clamped my chest so tightly that a response barely escaped my throat. "Hi, Sarah," I managed.

She was still beautiful, though she made no obvious attempts to appear that way. She was wearing a plain cotton navy-blue sweatshirt, and her dark hair was pulled into a ponytail that spilled through the back of Nike ball cap. She had on pink running shoes and Levis jeans, and from the way they hugged her shapely hips, it was clear that she was no stranger to the gym. Her olive face looked darker still, shadowed in the brim of her cap. All that just magnified the radiant blue of her eyes that gleamed like neon as she looked back at me.

But there were a few changes. The soft contours of her face were harder now. I wouldn't say hard, just hard*er*. Her posture was more severe. She looked like a woman who had faced cruelty and had learned to remake herself in order to survive in such a world. I guess the best way to describe Sarah was she looked grown-up. She was no longer an innocent girl. And in some selfish way, I found a pity in that.

"So how's it going here?" she asked.

"Actually, the kids are doing a great job in spite of me," I attempted the weak humor but jettisoned it immediately. "We just want to do the best job we can for Mr. B."

"Well, actually, it was because of Uncle Ed that I came to see you tonight. I noticed that you've been up the hospital a couple of times to visit him."

"Look, I didn't mean to presume," I cut in before a wound could be opened further. "I wasn't sure what to do, so I made my visits brief. But if you'd rather that I not go up there, just say the word. I'll stay clear..."

"No. No, it's okay, Sawyer." A small smile actually lifted in the corner of her mouth, and with it, some of her softness returned. "Actually, I was happy that you did go up to see him. I didn't know if you would or not."

"Well, I've been trying to give you your space. I knew you'd be at the hospital a lot and figured you didn't need to bump into me with everything else you had to deal with. And then I met Dr. Stratton, and he told me he thought you were staying out here in Hanover with an old classmate. This place isn't exactly a metropolis, so I've been trying to keep a low profile around town too."

"Oh, you met Jim?" She seemed to be mulling over whether that was a positive development or not. "He didn't tell me he'd seen you. But then again, I suppose I shouldn't be too surprised by that."

"He seems like a sharp doctor and a pretty good guy. But I think he's gone on vacation or something. One of the doctors mentioned he had left the state."

"Yes, I know all about that. But don't worry, Uncle Ed is still in very good hands."

While we were talking, I could see Donna glancing over at us. She was busying herself with some sheets of music to cover her curiosity. But I knew what she was doing. Donna had a terrible poker face.

"We're just finishing up here," I explained. "So...did you want to go get a drink or something?"

With that, the little bit of softness fled her face. "No, I didn't come here for anything like that. I came here tonight, Sawyer, because I felt like I owed it to you to let you be there."

"Be there?"

"Uncle Ed is dying, Sawyer. At least he will die if something isn't done." I knew a little of what she was talking about, but this was her tale to tell, so I didn't interrupt. "He's going in for surgery tomorrow morning. It's tricky. They're making no promises. They need to open up his skull to relieve some of the pressure and hopefully make some small repairs while they're in there. They just won't know what they'll find until they can get in there to see. Anyway, I felt like you should know and that you should be there if you wanted."

"Sure," I responded immediately. "What time?"

"He's scheduled for OR at seven thirty, so I thought I'd get to the hospital around seven."

"That shouldn't be a problem for me. I did tell Tim Kavanaugh that I'd meet him tomorrow, but that can be later in the day. Yeah, seven works great for me."

Her blue eyes flared at that. "Don't say that you're coming, Sawyer, if you're not going to be there."

"I'll be there, Sarah. I promise."

Donna took the ensuing awkward silence to sidle into the conversation. "Hey, Sawyer? I don't want to interrupt, but the kids have all left, and I've finished here too. So just be sure to lock up on your way out. Don't forget to get both doors. And remember, the one on the left is sticky." She favored Sarah with a nod. "Hi."

"Oh, sorry," I picked up my cue. "Donna, this is Sarah. Sarah, this is Donna, our music director. You might remember Donna from high school. She was Donna Myers back then."

"Of course I remember," Sarah took her hand warmly. "Good to see you again, Donna. Uncle Ed always says wonderful things about you and the work you do here with the kids. Sawyer's lucky to have you on staff. Look"—she glanced at her watch—"I really need to be leaving. You go ahead and do your locking up or whatever. But I'll see you in the morning, right, Sawyer?"

"I'll be there with bells on."

"Don't worry so much about the bells. Just be there around seven." And with her ponytail fluttering behind, Sarah was gone.

Donna nodded her approval. "She's still really beautiful, Sawyer."

"Yeah. Yeah, she is."

Donna gave me a moment before saying, "So…how do you feel?"

It was a good question. But I knew exactly how to describe it. "You know how on cartoons Wile E. Coyote will get hit over the head by a mallet and his body turns into an accordion? I feel a lot like that."

"Well, I'll see you tomorrow. Sounds like you should get some sleep. You've got an early appointment in the morning."

She turned to leave, but I stopped her. Too much was happening too quickly. I didn't want to be alone while I sorted it out. "Donna? If you've got time, do you think we could go to that coffee shop for a little bit?"

It didn't take long to mull the question over. "Okay. But this time, you buy. I know you've got the money."

Perked Up was nearly deserted when Sammy greeted us and showed us to the table in the back near the fireplace. "Irish coffee again tonight?"

"No, Sammy. It's tempting, but I think I'll just go with the hot chocolate for tonight."

"Make it two," Donna put in. "And tonight, the bill goes to him."

Sammy left us to the jazzy sounds of the bar, but when he brought our drinks back, Donna started the interrogation. "So when was the last time you saw her?"

I had to do the math, and the answer shocked me. "Almost fifteen years," I admitted. "I can't believe it, but it's been that long. Most of it seems like a lifetime ago. But the last night I was with Sarah seems like only yesterday."

"What happened?" Donna took a sip of her hot chocolate, but her eyes were fastened on me.

I could've decided to say nothing. But strangely, I wanted to tell her. Like scratching an itch until it bleeds, it felt good to let it hurt a little. I wanted Donna to be there when the sting set in. I told her everything. I told her about the distance that set in shortly after our wedding. I told her about the baby and how they let us hold its tiny purple body before taking it to the morgue. I even told her how depressed Sarah became in the weeks that followed. I shamefully told her how I felt relieved.

"So what was bad got even worse," I said over the rim of my mug. "Sarah needed me more than ever, and I just wanted to escape. There was no baby now, and the bonds between us seemed thinner. I think she knew that I was planning to leave, and that last night, her affection was desperate. She wanted all of me that night, and I gave her what I could. But I knew in my heart it wouldn't be enough. I'll never forget her eyes as we lay in bed and I held her. They were sad. So sad. But I felt only pity, not love. That's when I knew it was over. I left for New York City the next morning."

Donna didn't say anything for a long while, and the silence was excruciating. Finally, she said, "That's terrible, Sawyer. That's really terrible."

"And you don't even know all of it. I exhausted most of the bank account before I left. I'll never forgive myself. But maybe now, you can see why I need to wear a flak jacket when I walk down the streets of Hanover."

"No," she countered. "I don't mean that you alone were terrible, I mean that the whole thing was terrible. A baby dying? A wife with depression? I don't mean to excuse your behavior, but twenty-year-old kids can do stupid things in stressful circumstances. And another thing, you need to get over yourself a little bit." Donna's tone was moving from compassion towards preachy, and I wasn't sure I was going to like it. She set down her hot chocolate and said something that I was pretty sure she had rehearsed. "You know what? You make things too much about you. I hate to break it to you, Sawyer, but the world of Hanover does not revolve around your mistakes. We've moved on. Sure, those who were close to Sarah, like Ed or Artie, still remember. But most of us aren't planning our days around how to exact revenge on Sawyer Kent. Honestly, if you needed to feel sorry for something, it should be for how you walk around here like you're number one on everyone's radar screen. We've moved on, so should you."

I was beginning to think that scratching that itch wasn't such a good idea. Donna had a way of silencing me and making me think. But she also tended to put me on the defensive, so I fired back, "Sure. Spoken like someone who doesn't have any skeletons in her closet."

"Oh, I've got skeletons. I've got skeletons, but I just learned to deal with them. Most healthy people do."

I was intrigued. So I let the temporary fire of the moment abate before prying. "Okay, Pirate Thewlis. Let's hear about the bones. You say I make things too much about me. You're probably right. So what's your story?"

"You don't care. You're just being nosy."

The accusation stung me. I cared more than she realized. But as usual, I'd hidden my concern safely behind a joke. "My mistake if I made it sound that way," I amended. "Honestly, I'd like to know. You told me a little. You told me you have a daughter, but I haven't heard anything about Mr. Thewlis."

I wasn't trying to be clever, but my statement knocked on the closet door. Slowly, timidly, Donna let me peek inside.

"My daughter, Stephanie, is twelve, and she's the joy of my life. She's sweet, talented, and fortunately, nothing like her father. I could use words to describe him, but they wouldn't suit a schoolteacher, especially in a public place."

"So if he's such a loser, how did you two get together?"

"We met in college. I was going to Illinois Wesleyan, and he used to show up at parties. He was a mechanic and didn't go to school. But he was good mechanic, I'll admit. He couldn't fix a thing with his brain, but he was good with his hands. So the world of academics had no appeal to him, except for the parties. I'd see him around from time to time, and finally, we were introduced.

"I was young and sheltered. He was older, had tattoos, and was dangerous. I never had, had a real boyfriend before and was shocked that he took notice of me. I just got swept up in all of it. Like I said, twenty-year-olds can do stupid things."

"So a bad boy, huh?" I couldn't help myself. "I wouldn't have expected that of you."

"Why? You've got a problem with bad boys?"

"Sure. Shouldn't everyone?"

"I just find that strange, considering you are one."

"You're kidding me, right? I've earned a few unsavory labels over the years, but I've never been called that before."

"Actually, you're the worst kind. You're a bad boy who doesn't know he's one."

"That's not true. I'm a jerk, and there's a big difference. And besides, I'm trying to reform. Or at least I'm in remission or something. Anyway, this was supposed to be your story."

Donna relented at that and returned to her college days. "Well, the best way to say it was that it was all just dumb. My parents and friends tried to warn me, but I wouldn't listen. They thought I was rebelling. But that wasn't exactly true. I wasn't crazy about his motorcycle or tattoos or drinking. No, for me, the appeal of the bad boy was his confidence. He had this attitude that he didn't care what convention thought. And being an insecure music major, I found it very attractive. Anyway, to make a long story short, within a year, Floyd and I were engaged."

"*Floyd?*" I blurted. "His name was *Floyd?*"

"Yeah, still is. A real beauty, huh? You should've seen the wedding cake. 'Donna and Floyd.' Those two names just look ugly no matter what the color of frosting you use."

"What kind of cake did you serve? Sour cream and onion?"

"Well, I really wanted to use my nickname. But since very few people knew it, we figured it would only confuse the guests."

"Nickname? You *are* full of surprises. You didn't tell me you had a nickname."

"It's my initials actually," she corrected.

"And?"

"It's DJ. All of my family and close friends call me DJ. See, my middle name is Janni. I got it from my mom's best friend. So since I was little, I was called Donna Janni, or DJ for short. I even have a picture of me when I was barely six months old wearing a pair of bloomers that say, 'Donna Janni's Fanny' in pink stitching."

"I'd love to see that one," I told her and meant it. "That would make a great poster for my office." Of course, I didn't have an office. But it sounded good, and she didn't notice.

"Oh no. No one's going to see that picture ever again. It's been locked away in the vault to protect the young and innocent." She laughed at her own joke, and I joined her. We had settled into an easy cadence of conversation, and it was just what I needed. Talking with Donna was a little like river rafting. Some parts were white water, while other sections were serene. But whichever, the journey was pleasing all the same.

"So what should *I* call you?" I dared.

"Hmm, that *is* a good question." She sat back in her chair and rolled over the question for what, I believe, was the first time. The intrigue seemed to delight her. "Well, to be honest, I've gotten used to you calling me Donna. Anything else might sound weird. But…" Her head swayed slowly back and forth as she parsed through the rest of her logic. "Then again, I would like to hear how it sounds when you say it."

"Well, if that's the case, I'll do my best to never speak of it, *DJ.*"

She slapped me on the shoulder with one of the menus and laughed again.

"So whatever happened to Floyd?" I was curious even if it made her stop laughing.

"Well, shortly into our marriage, when I was fat and pregnant, my bad boy did what bad boys do. Apparently, we had very different interpretations of what the words 'till death do us part' mean. Crazy me, I thought that meant until, you know, one of us died. Apparently, Floyd thought it meant until the neighbor lady came over and asked for help with her lawnmower. Like I said, he was always good with his hands. It didn't take long before the divorce papers were signed."

"Do you ever miss him?"

She took a long time before answering. "No, not really. But there are moments with him that I miss."

"I'm guessing holidays are tough." I made my typical mistake and answered for her. "I was lucky. I usually worked holidays and didn't have to think about how alone I was."

"Holidays really aren't so bad. You get used to them. And I got over that 'going to the movies by myself' complex a long time ago. No, it was the little things we used to do that I miss."

"Go on," I coaxed, and even to me, it came out a little creepy.

"You're going to laugh, but Floyd and I used to like to go to garage sales. I know, ridiculous, right? But it was fun. By late March, usually right after the musical closes, the weather is breaking enough that people start having weekend garage sales. Floyd and I would get up on a Saturday morning, have coffee, and start going through the Classified Ads, circling the sales that we wanted to hit. We'd make a plan, pack a cooler, and make a day of it. We kept this ceramic jar in the kitchen that we'd throw loose change and spare bills into. Before leaving, we'd dump it out, and that would be our expense account for the day.

"You'd be surprised how fun it is going through other people's junk looking for little pieces of treasure. And since we didn't have much money, it was cheap entertainment. We only had one main rule. You could buy anything you wanted as long as it wasn't over ten dollars. Anything over that had to be agreed upon by both of us. I remember one time we went toe-to-toe over an eighteen-dollar hammock. You would've thought we were haggling over beachfront property. I finally gave in. I usually did. But I got the last laugh. I got the house in the divorce, and the hammock is still down in the basement somewhere."

"Well, it sounds like you've really come through that strong," I said feebly. She had been talking for quite a while I felt like I should put in something.

"The best part is, I got Stephanie out of the deal. She makes it all worth it. And Floyd may be a jerk, but he keeps his distance. And through my church and a lot of good friends, I've come to terms with everything."

"I've got a question. Does everyone here at Hanover go to church?"

"Only those of us who know how much we need it." She winked. "And speaking of which, don't worry about tomorrow, Sawyer. We'll all be praying for Ed. I can promise you that."

"Thanks, DJ. But I think I'd rather that you pray for me."

THIRTEEN

A small mystery was waiting for me when I got home. There was a Ford Bronco with Wisconsin license plates in the driveway blocking the garage. But the mystery was quickly solved when Mom burst through the side door waving her arms excitedly and calling, "Oh, good Sawyer. You're finally home. There's someone here who's been waiting to see you before she leaves." Then she yelled back in the house, "Andrea! Your brother is here!"

Growing up in the Kent house, or the "Casa de Dysfunction" as I used to joke with my theater friends, was bound to leave a mark. For my older sister Andrea, it pushed her already hard-working nose closer to the grindstone. I think that in our chaotic world, she found that hard work was the one thing she could control. She whizzed through high school with high marks and got a scholarship to the University of Wisconsin-Madison. From there, she went on to dentistry school and met equally hard-working and solid man to marry. Andrea was the practical, no-nonsense rock in our family. Surprise visits usually weren't her forte.

She gave me a perfunctory hug, and we settled into the captain's chairs around Mom's table. Mom was beaming. "Isn't this wonderful? All of us together again around the same table. A few weeks ago, I would've never thought that this would be possible." Then she turned to Andrea, "Honey, are you sure you can't spend the night? It's awfully late, and you never know about the weather this time of the year."

"Mom, we've already been through this. I've got a root canal and a couple of crown preps all scheduled for tomorrow morning. And besides, I don't mind driving at night. I'll have the road myself."

"So what brings you down to Hanover?" I asked. The way my day had gone, no answer would've surprised me.

"Just came down to return a couple of sweaters Mom gave me for Christmas. Seems I'm no longer a size 8, and we don't have the same shop up in Madison. Plus, things have been pretty crazy lately. Jacob's grade-school basketball team made the city playoffs, so we've been running from tournament to tournament almost every weekend. Today, I had a hole open on my schedule, so I thought I'd pop down and take Mom to lunch and get in a little retail therapy. Nothing like power shopping to take the edge off. Oh, and of course, I wanted to see my little brother again."

"Just glad I made the billing somewhere."

We made small talk, and Mom glowed. Andrea kept hinting that she needed to leave. Clearly, there was something left on her agenda, and finally, she bluntly came to it. "Mom, I like to talk to Sawyer alone for a minute. Do you mind?"

"Oh, of course not, sweetheart." And she disappeared into the basement.

Andrea tiptoed to the top of the stairs to make sure Mom wasn't eavesdropping before returning to the table. "I thought I should tell you that Dad's been snooping around lately."

"Dad? You're kidding. Where? When did all this happen?"

"He called me around Christmas time. Must've gotten my number off the Internet. It was all very strange."

"What did he want?"

"He said he just wanted to catch up. He said he was sorry for missing so much of my life and wanted to see how I was doing. I guess he figured Christmas was as good a time as any. He also asked if I knew how to get a hold of you. "

"What did you say?"

"I didn't tell him anything. I wasn't lying. I didn't know where you were. But I didn't tell much about me either. I kept it very brief and very clinical. But then a few weeks ago, he showed up at one of Jacob's basketball games."

"So he lives up by you now?"

"No. He still living here in Illinois, the Bloomington area from what he said. He told me that he was in Wisconsin on business. Actually, he was selling his business and retiring. Just wanted to pop in and say hello. Then he asked me if he could meet Jacob."

"What did you tell him?"

"I told him no. I told him that Jacob was a wonderful boy and he didn't need the confusion. So then Dad asked if he could stay and watch the game. I told that it was a public place and he could do as he liked. But I said if he had any respect for me and my family, he'd watch from the other side of the gymnasium."

"So what happened?"

"He walked to the other side of the court and watched the game. When it was over, he got up quietly and left. I stood by the door of the gymnasium to make sure his car left the parking lot. It did, and I haven't heard from him since."

I let out a low whistle and shook my head. "That is unbelievable. Absolutely unbelievable. I can't believe, after all these years, he showed up again."

"Sound like anyone else you know?" Andrea smirked, but I could tell she was just teasing. "I don't know what Dad's up to, but I thought you should know. And I also want you to keep your eye out for Mom. Today, I managed to get out of her that Dad had contacted her too. She swore up and down that it was just a polite, innocuous conversation. But you know how kind she is. I'm afraid that Dad is up to something and will try to take advantage of her. Sometimes, I think that Mom is little too forgiving for her own good. She could be an easy mark."

"Thanks for telling me. And I'll keep my eyes and ears open."

Andrea angled me with hard eyes and asked plainly, "And what about you, Sawyer? I want you to cut the crap. Are you taking advantage of Mom's good nature, or are you pulling your own load? I just want to know where it stands."

I didn't want to answer her question, or at least not truthfully. But today, I stood with my heels on the bridge and looked at the water. That changes things. "To tell you the truth, Andrea, I came here because I didn't have any place else to go. I had used up everyone I could use, and Mom's door was open. I came back home with debts. And so far, I've earned just enough to pay them back, but nothing more. But I won't use Mom. I know my promise doesn't mean much with you, but you got to believe me. I wouldn't let anything hurt her. And if Dad shows up at that door, he'll have to deal with a guy who has nothing to lose. No man's ready for that kind of fight."

"So what will you do after the show is over? Go back to New York or Boston or Cleveland or wherever?"

"Honestly, I have no idea. I'm just trying to get to the next scene and the next act and the next day."

Andrea accepted my sincerity, and we said our good-byes. It was nearly midnight before I plunged into bed. Noah jumped up and climbed onto my chest. He pressed his cold nose against my forehead and questioned me with his dark soulful eyes. "It's been quite a day, old boy," I told him. "Quite a day. But I'm glad things turned out the way they did. I would've missed you." I scrubbed him behind his velvety ears. "And tomorrow's going to be a busy day. Mr. B's going to have surgery, and I'm going to meet Sarah at the hospital. What do you think of that? Strange events here in Hanover, huh? Now I want you to watch something, boy. You see what I'm doing? I'm setting the alarm clock for early. I don't want any guff out of you when I wake you up for our walk, okay? So you lay down and get some sleep. Yes, thanks for the kisses. You can stop now. Yes, I love you too, Noah.

As I laid my head on the pillow, it occurred to me that for the first time since I could remember, I used the word *love* twice in the same day.

I arrived at the hospital feeling pretty good. Noah and I had, had an invigorating walk, even though he beat me once again in the eleven-meter dash to the porch. I was wearing one of Tim's blue oxford cloth shirts (Sarah always liked me in the color blue). And I was ten minutes early. All in all, I felt I'd done what I could to put my best foot forward.

I found Sarah in the waiting room, nervous, distracted, and alone. There were other people there chatting idly in the banks of chairs or occupying themselves with the insipid daytime network programming that was humming on the flat-screen TV. A mom and a pair of toddlers were in the corner drawing what looked to be dinosaurs on a chalkboard easel. But Sarah wasn't near any of them. She was by herself on the other side of the room skimming a dog-eared paperback and anxiously checking her cell phone.

Someone should've reminded me that I was going to a surgical ward and not on a date.

"Hey, Sarah. Any word on our patient?" I took a seat by a plastic ficus tree that stood adjacent to a wall plaque of the serenity prayer. It was close enough to Sarah that we could converse privately but not so close that she would feel like I was suffocating her.

"No, no word yet. And I wouldn't expect any for some time. The receptionist said they took Uncle Ed into surgery a few minutes ahead of schedule, but it may be hours before we know anything."

"Well, thanks for letting me be here. Can I get anything for you? Coffee? Soda? Last September's issue of *Better Homes & Gardens*?"

"I'm fine, Sawyer. There's nothing we can do except wait. They've got a cool setup here where they send text messages to family members updating a patient's status. So I'll know when Uncle Ed's out of surgery and headed into the recovery room. Why don't you relax and read a magazine or something. They've even got a bookshelf over there if you want to grab something. I'm fine here. I've got my novel, my cell phone, and…well, we just have to be patient."

I've never been a big fan of silence. I get antsy and want to fill the void with something, even if it's meaningless chatter. But I made a decision to follow Sarah's lead this morning, so I plucked up a *National Geographic* magazine and began flipping through it.

I should've expected it would go like this. But I had constructed this crazy fantasy that Sarah and I would spend the hours talking and catching up. Maybe I'd even get a chance to mend some fences. But it didn't go that way.

The time dragged on with excruciating sluggishness. I tried to find interest in a couple of different magazines but kept getting sucked into a ridiculous episode of the *Jerry Springer Show*. "Look at this guy," I attempted small talk with Sarah. "Does he have any other topics on the show besides paternity suits? I mean, how many episodes can you do of 'He's My Baby's Daddy'?"

"I don't know," she offered mildly and then returned to the sanctuary of her book.

I sauntered around the waiting room to stretch my legs and back. I sampled the free coffee and realized right away why the pot was full. Some things are so bad you can't even give it away. Eventually, I found myself back in my seat with my *National Geographic* and using it for cover while I studied Sarah.

I looked for telltale markings on her neck but didn't see any. Her blouse had short sleeves, but they didn't reveal any white hairline scars on her wrists. Sarah had done a lot of healing in the last fifteen years. I was glad for that. But she was a different Sarah, a stronger Sarah, and that I hadn't expected.

There's an old expression that says, "You can never go back home," and that might be true. The Sarah I left all those years ago didn't exist anymore. There was no home to go back to. But I couldn't help wondering if there was enough of the foundation left to start building something new.

Sarah's cell phone finally rang. She studied the screen for only a second before saying, "Well, he's out of surgery. We should know something soon."

We didn't hear anything soon. In fact, it must've been another three-quarters of an hour before a receptionist approached and said, "Sarah? The surgery on your uncle has been completed. If you would please follow me, I'm going to take you back to a separate waiting room. The surgeon will join you there in a moment."

"How is he? My uncle, I mean."

"The surgeon will be in shortly and answer all of your questions."

Sarah looked at me, and her face was as pale as a corpse.

"You want me to go with you?" I asked.

"Please," was all she said, and we followed the receptionist through the double doors and back to get our answers.

We were ushered into a tiny waiting room. It had only four chairs and a table, but we were too nervous to sit. Fortunately, we didn't have to stand long. Dr. Schaeffer was there almost immediately, still clad in her surgical scrubs, bonnet, and shoe coverings.

Suddenly, I felt Sarah's quavering hand push into mine. It was tiny and warm, a precious thing. I cradled it in my hand, wrapping my fingers around it like a treasure.

"The surgery went well," Dr. Schaeffer was saying. "At least, it went as well as could be expected."

I felt Sarah squeeze my hand with relief. I squeezed back but didn't let go.

"Please, would you sit down for a moment," Dr. Schaeffer instructed, and we huddled together around the small laminated table. "Your uncle is resting comfortably, and you'll be able to see him as soon as he is out of recovery and back in his room."

"That's wonderful." Sarah's eyes were bright with tears. "Thank you so much, Dr. Schaeffer, for all you've done."

"But I must caution you, Sarah. We are still a long way from being out of the woods. In cases like these, we always worry about postsurgical infections or even clotting. Either of those developments would create a very serious challenge to your uncle's recovery."

"I understand." Sarah nodded. "But at least he made it through today, and that gives me hope."

Dr. Schaeffer left, and Sarah stood up and threw her arms around me. She buried her face in my chest and began weeping. They were tears of relief, not affection, and I knew the difference. It was an instinctual embrace, the kind shared by people who just survived an ordeal. But all the same, she felt warm and precious in my arms, and I understood the small loss when she let go.

"I'm so happy for you, Sarah. I'm so happy for all of us. And you're right to have hope. You know how your uncle is always full of surprises. I wouldn't be shocked if he was just waiting until the week before the show opens to climb out of that bed and tell us all this was a big joke."

Sarah laughed a little and wiped her eyes. But once again, there was more relief there than anything.

"Hey…look, Sarah…" I stammered. "Maybe sometime soon we could grab lunch together or something. I hear the hospital has a fabulous cafeteria. They say their lime Jell-O here is out of this world."

Sarah just stared at me, her face and eyes inscrutable, for what felt like an eternity. And I thought the wait in the waiting room was agonizing. Finally, she said almost begrudgingly, "Yeah. Yeah, I suppose we could do that. In fact, maybe it's time we should." And then she paused again, like she was turning over a decision behind those incandescent blue eyes. "There something I need to tell you, something you deserve to know. But not here, not now." She wrestled around in her pocket book for a pen and scrap of paper. "Look, I'm going to stay here today and part tomorrow, but then I've got to catch an evening flight back home. I hate it, but there's some business on Sunday that I have to be in Phoenix for."

"Business on a Sunday? Sounds like high stakes."

"It's our big fundraiser for the local American Cancer Society chapter. We throw a big golf outing with area bigwigs and even a few celebrities. I'm one of the organizing administrators, and I have to be there."

"Wow, golf in February," I whistled. "Now that's a concept."

"It'll be nice to feel the sun and heat again. I'd forgotten how cold it gets here in the winter. I can't wait to throw on my swimsuit and splash around in my pool for a while."

A mental picture of just that occurring momentarily distracted me. But then I saw Sarah writing, and she stuck the piece of paper in my hand. "I've been staying with Amy Batson. She's got a nice place over on Torch Lake and has been kind enough to let me bunk up. Here's her address and phone number. I'm guessing that I'll be gone through Wednesday, but I'll stay in touch with Amy, and she'll know. Give me a call after I get back, and maybe we can go try out some of that Jell-O."

The receptionist came in the door and informed us that Mr. B had been transferred to his room in ICU. "Do you want to go up?" Sarah asked.

"No, you go on ahead. I'm supposed to have an early dinner with Tim Kavanaugh and his family, and I'm trying to scrap my reputation of always being late."

"Well then, maybe I'll see you next week sometime. Good-bye, Sawyer. And good luck with the show."

It wasn't lost on me that Sarah left without giving me her personal cell phone number or a hug good-bye.

"Tim, I think I've got a problem."

"Just one?" Tim said over his shoulder as he hooked up the last cord to his new Blu-ray player.

"Okay. So I've got several problems. But I may have one that will keep me from fixing the rest."

A towheaded boy with a popsicle in his hand scurried into the room, "Is it ready yet?"

"I think so, buddy. Here, hand me the DVD. You are going to love *Thomas the Tank Engine* in high definition." Tim popped in the disc, patted the boy on the head, and then I followed him down the hallway to his study.

"By the way," I said, "nice place you got here."

"Aw, it's all Kate's doing. She's the one with the decorative eye. I just make out the mortgage checks."

"And I'm guessing that the polite young boy who greeted me at the door and who is now watching *Thomas the Tank Engine* is your son and not some kind of international slave-labor valet."

Tim chuckled at that as we sat down in a pair of leather chairs he'd situated behind his computer desk. "That's Alex, my youngest. These days, his whole world revolves around trains and cherry popsicles. You'll meet the rest of the brood at dinner. You're okay with pasta, right? 'Cause Kate makes a mean chicken with pesto sauce."

"I'm starving already."

"But first, why don't you tell me about this problem of yours. I'm guessing it has something to do with yesterday? Finny, I was really worried about you. When you left my office, I thought you might be serious about what you said."

"I was serious, Tim. But then something strange happened on the bridge."

"The bridge?"

I told him everything. I told him about the bridge, the cell phone call, Donna's quote, and seeing Sarah and then meeting her again this morning at the hospital. Tim was visibly moved when I got to the end of it.

"Finny, that's phenomenal. I mean that literally. You can't chalk that up to coincidence. That was a phenomenon. It was a God thing. I told you that Christ doesn't give up on us. And then that night you bump into Sarah? That blows me away. Sure, she seemed a little cold to you. Can you blame her? But I don't see any of this as a big problem."

"I think I'm an alcoholic."

My statement silenced Tim. He began to recover and say something, but I cut him off. "Let me finish, Tim. I need to say this aloud. Here's my problem. I think you're right. God's been reaching out to me. I don't think Donna's phone call on the bridge was a coincidence. But I don't want to quit drinking. That's as brutally honest as I can say it, Tim. I like to drink. I want to drink. And a life without drinking seems awfully scary even if it usually leads me to bad places. As crazy as that may sound to you, it's true. And I don't know if I'm ready for God either. I know I'm not ready to sign up for a life where there's a big 'Thou shalt not' list to follow."

Tim let me finish, and then he said something weird. "You used to ride a bike with training wheels, right?"

"Uh...yeah."

"When did you take them off?"

"I don't know, when I was six or seven, I think."

"Why did you take them off?"

"Because chicks don't dig guys with training wheels. Look, Tim, I don't know what this has to do with—"

"Just think about it, Finny," he replied calmly. "Why did you take them off?"

"Because I didn't need them anymore, I guess. Oh, and they slowed me down too. I remember I had a hard time keeping up with the other kids until I got those off."

"So here's the deal, Finny. Following Christ is not about signing up for a big "do not" list. It's about trusting that doing things His way will make you the happiest in the long run. It takes time. It's a process. But trust me, it's true. And someday, you'll look back and won't believe that you once thought you needed alcohol to keep your world up on two wheels. You'll realize how much farther and faster you've been able to travel without it. The idea of going back to those 'training wheels' would be ridiculous. And it's not because they're a 'do not' thing, it's because they're a 'don't want to, I found a better way' thing."

"I can't believe you just came up with that off the top of your head," I chided. "You're not that clever. Where'd you hear that?"

"You'd be surprised how many recovering alcoholics there are out there. You're in good company."

"Like who?" I floated out my question, but the bait caught a different fish.

"Like...well, like Dale Patterson for instance."

"The men's Bible study guy? You gotta be kidding me."

"It just shows you what God can do with broken people. He was completely out of ministry eight years ago. But now he's sober and reaching a lot of men who struggle just like he has. Did you know that our Bible study is simulcast to eight other area churches? There's nearly five hundred men participating with us every Thursday morning. And that didn't happen because Dale said no to drinking. It's because he said yes to God."

"I don't know. That all sounds a little trite. It can't be that easy."

"I never said that it would be easy." Tim logged onto his computer and pulled the workbooks out of his desk drawer. "I said it takes time. It's a process. But it starts with small steps of faith, and you already made the first one."

"When? I don't remember a step of faith."

"On the bridge. You could've jumped, but you answered the phone instead."

We sat and watched the podcast together, jotting down thoughts here and there in our workbooks. But I have to say, it didn't have the same atmosphere of experiencing it live at the church. Maybe it is because I was hungry, but I was glad when Tim's wife knocked on the study door and told us that supper was ready.

Tim had a whole passel of blond-haired kids. They all seemed pretty sweet and bright, but I couldn't keep their names straight. Kate was kind with my mistakes. I could tell right away why Tim married her. She was warm and gracious, and she hugged you like she meant it. There was an easy genuineness about her. She didn't mind laughing at silly things if she thought they were funny. She didn't mind asking a question even if everyone else at the table knew the answer. I liked her right away. And Tim was right; she made a mean chicken with pesto sauce.

It was dark by the time Tim walked me out to the car. "Hey, thanks for coming tonight. And I'll be praying for you, pal."

"I'll need it."

"And just take it one day at a time. Remember, the Bible talks about a 'lamp unto my feet.' Just enough light to take the next step. Don't borrow trouble from down the line."

"Yeah, and a stitch in time saves nine, etcetera, etcetera. Any more words of wisdom before I go, Poor Richard?"

"Just one. I'm proud of you, Finny. Acceptance is the first step to recovery."

I smirked as I fired the car to life. "I'll drink to that," I said. "I'll drink to that."

FOURTEEN

The days began to settle into a natural tempo. I'd get up each morning, take Noah for a walk, help Mom out with her latest project around the house, have lunch, and then spend the afternoon getting ready for rehearsal that night. It was a rewarding rhythm because it felt like I was finally giving and not just taking. Rehearsals at night were progressing well. The scenes were starting to take shape, and the dance numbers didn't look like train wrecks. We still needed to figure out a few costuming details, and not a single wall of the set had been built or painted, but I was pleased with where we were.

The same could not be said for my situation with Sarah or Donna.

I had waited until Friday to call Amy Batson and see if Sarah had returned from Arizona. She told me Sarah had been delayed and wouldn't be getting back until the first of the week. I called again that Tuesday and left a message on the answering machine. Sarah never returned my call.

The funny thing was, my calls to Sarah always made me think about Donna. Somehow, I felt like I was betraying her. It was a stupid notion. I mean, I had no claim to Donna or even to Sarah for that matter. And as far as I could tell, neither one of them had laid any claim to me either. But it all made me feel uneasy. I felt like I was doing something wrong, like I was trading in $200 watch for a $10 lottery ticket.

The more I thought about it, the more I was led to one conclusion. My interest in Sarah was more nostalgia and curiosity than anything else. I wanted to see if we could be right together again because once we were, even if it was brief. I wondered if it could happen again. And I suppose there was a dash of guilt in there too. I wanted to atone. I wanted to fix things. I wanted Sarah's forgiveness.

But with Donna, I just wanted to be with her. I strangely enjoyed her company. She kept me on my toes but made me feel relaxed all at the same time. And there was a persistent steadiness in her that I admired. I felt like I had won something when I made her laugh. I think she felt the same way when she made me think. I guess what I'm saying is, I worried that my interactions with Sarah might somehow ruin all of that.

And there was something else. I had done a good job of staying away from the booze. Tim had been a big help. He advised me to clean out my closet, literally. He told me to clean it right down to the carpet so there'd be no place for me to hide the bottles. My first reaction was that he was crazy. I told him I could always find a place to hide alcohol. But his wisdom was solid. He explained, "Yeah, Finny, but that would mean you'd have to reinvent another first step to your drinking. You'd have to scheme for another way to hide alcohol in your Mom's house. That would require an active effort. Cleaning out your closet won't cure you, but it will eliminate the easy, casual habit."

I tried it, and he was right. But what helped even more was I didn't want to let down Donna. I wanted to prove to her that I wasn't a bad boy, at least not anymore. I wanted her to know that she could count on me. With Sarah, there was a lot of bad ground between us. But that wasn't the case with Donna. And what tillable soil there was between us, I didn't want to pollute with booze.

The kids were another part of the equation. I didn't want to let them down either. Early on, I saw them as sort of a sidecar to Donna Thewlis. I was unprepared for their effect on me. Once I got to know them, they got under my skin, but in a good way. Their untamed laughter, quirky interests, and zest for the future were infectious. They were worming their way into my heart, and I was a willing victim. That was never so apparent as the night when Julia didn't show up for rehearsal.

Julia was one of our main soloists. She was a little more stout than some of our other girls, but she had a pretty face and a voice that rang like crystal. We'd started rehearsing Act II, and when we got to its first big showstopper, "Turn Back, Oh Man," she was nowhere to be found.

"Has anyone seen Julia?" I didn't hide my initial irritation. "Was she at school today? Is she sick?"

"No, she was at school today," Sean, our Judas Iscariot, offered. "She should be here. I saw her in the parking lot."

"Well, does anyone else know where she might've gone?"

There was a murmur among the cast that I couldn't interpret. It seemed to be centered around Sean, at least kids kept looking his way. But no one volunteered anything further.

There's a strange confederation with teenage kids. They'll betray secrets in close confines, but get them in a large public group and they'll maintain a union solidarity to rival Lech Walesa. Fortunately, one of my naïve freshman played the part of scab and crossed the line. "I saw her crying in the hallway, Mr. Kent. She seemed pretty upset."

I was astonished at the flush of paternal concern that surged through me. I crossed over to Donna, my irritation replaced by genuine worry. "DJ, can you run the next couple of production numbers with the cast? I'm going to see if I can find Julia."

"Sure. How long will you be gone?"

"Until I can find her."

I zipped into the hall, but it was empty. I paced through the green room and then the chorus room, but she wasn't there either. Finally, I headed for the parking lot. When the cold air blasted my coatless body, it occurred to me that I didn't know what her car looked like. As it turned out, I didn't have to know.

At the end of a dark row of sedans, trucks, and SUVs, there was a car with its interior light on. Inside, I could see the form of Julia slumped over the wheel and sobbing.

I hustled over and knocked on the window. "Julia? Are you okay?"

When she rolled down the window, I could tell that she wasn't. Her face was red and puffy from crying, and her mascara was streaked down her cheeks. "We just got your big number in Act II. Do you think you can come in and give it a try?"

It was a stupid question. The poor girl was shuddering every time she drew breath. There was no way she was up to performing a musical number.

"I can't, Mr. K," she blubbered. "I can't do it, any of it. I quit. I quit the show."

"Hey now, just calm down," I said gently, but my mind was reeling. "Why don't you come back in? It's freezing out here. If you're going to quit, at least do it where it's warm."

It wasn't very funny quip, but I think Julie was so desperate for any form of levity that she chuckled and sniffed anyway. "I don't want to go back to the auditorium," she insisted. "Not in there."

"Who said anything about the auditorium? I'd be happy with a phone booth at this point. Come on. Let's just get inside, and we can talk about it."

I led her into the cafeteria. It was as bright and cheery of a place as I could think of. Also, there was always a pot of coffee and hot tea brewing for the janitors who worked the night shift.

"Do you like good coffee?" I asked.

Julia had corralled her crying to a mere snivel. "Actually, I do."

"I'm sorry to hear that. Because this coffee is terrible."

I poured us each a Styrofoam cup full, and we sat down at one of the rectangular, municipal tables. "I'm sorry, Mr. K. I know I'm letting you and the show down, but I just can't..." New tears mounted as her voice rose.

"Just settle down, Julia," I said as soothingly as I could. "Don't worry about that just now. I'm more concerned with why you're so upset. Can you tell me what's going on?"

"It's Sean."

"Sean Hodgkins? The guy who plays Judas in the show?"

"Mmm-hmm." She nodded her head solemnly.

"What happened? What did he do to you?"

As a way of an answer, she held out her phone. On it was a text message that read, "Julz. ben thinkn. thnk we shud end r rlationshp. hop u undrstnd. stil frendz tho, rt?"

"He broke up with you with a text message?"

I haven't had many prudent moments in my life, but I had the sense not to make light of her sadness. I've always thought it criminal that adults often expect kids to know what it is to be old, yet they themselves have forgotten what it was to be young. So I let her talk it out, all the while trying to remember what it was like to be sixteen and in love.

She spewed it out in a burst of tear-stained grief. How they'd been dating for seven months. How she'd already been shopping for a prom dress. How she couldn't bear to be in a production where she had to see him night after night.

And it all made sense to me. So I didn't try to argue with her. Instead, I just said, "I'm really sorry, sweetheart. Heartache is the worst. It is, and I know this hurts. But let me just tell you something. Sean didn't break up with you because you're lacking something. It's not because you're not good enough or pretty enough or whatever enough. Good people aren't always good together. So don't make the mistake of thinking you weren't good together because you weren't good enough." I was surprised that the words were coming so easily to me. I guess it was the clarity that comes with having traveled down so many dark roads. Regardless, I still had more to say, and Julia seemed anxious to hear it. "And you need to know, Julia, how special you are. You are sweet and pretty and have a rare talent for singing and acting. Guys with any kind of character will notice that. You're going to be happy again. I know it."

"I'm not pretty."

"Not crying your eyes out, you're not," I teased. "But when you're singing on that stage and in your element...Julia, you're abso-lutely radiant. And here's something else," I kept going as I knew her modesty would want to argue. "Who knows? The next love of your life may be sitting out in the audience opening night. You want to be at your best when you meet him, don't you? So you owe it to that next person, as well as yourself, to heal from all this. It's not easy. I don't mean to make it sound that way. But you deserve it."

She hadn't touched her coffee, and neither had I. It was probably for the best. But she had stopped crying, and her sadness seemed slightly tempered by hope. "And you know, here's something else that I think should help."

"What's that?"

"Sean Hodgkins is kind of zitty. You can do way better."

We went back in, and Julia ended up rehearsing her number that night. I don't think I've ever heard "Turn Back, Oh Man" sung with such smooth, smoky conviction. I think when Sean heard it, he realized he'd made a big mistake.

Donna had told me early on that she thought I had a "nice way" with the kids. At the time, I wasn't sure what she meant. But I found I enjoyed playing the part of both director and counselor. I had another chance a few days later during our costume parade, but this time, it was with Eddie.

Naked theater lights are harsh and blanching. So we fit them with colored material called gels, which help soften and warm their effect. The only problem is, these gels sometimes cause unexpected color changes to the palette of costumes and makeup: purples sometimes become unexpectedly gray, blues look a little green, faces turn orange, and so on. Some directors like to have the cast come out in a costume parade after the lights are gelled but before they've been focused and set.

Mr. B was one of those directors.

In the interest of time, I was going to skip the practice. I felt like I'd had enough experience with costumes and makeup to get by without it. But then Ginny Kramer came whirling out of the costume room, bobby pins and arguments ablazing, and I relented. You can't fight City Hall, and you definitely can't fight Ginny Kramer.

So I scheduled in a costume parade to take place before our Wednesday night rehearsal. The kids filed in one by one, and their makeup and costumes looked about right. Most of the cast were going to wear blue jeans and black T-shirts on stage anyway, so I wasn't really surprised. I was beginning to pay only fleeting attention when I heard a huge whoop of whistles and laughter explode through the auditorium. I looked up to see Eddie standing downstage center wearing nothing but a pair of American Eagle boxer shorts and striking bodybuilder poses with his scrawny arms. Over the top of the caterwauling, he was yapping, "Gun show! Oh, yeah, you know you like it! Gun show, baby!"

"Eddie, what the heck you doing?" I was a little annoyed, and he knew it.

"Sorry, Dr. K, but Mrs. Kramer doesn't have a costume for me yet. I thought we might try this one on for size. What d'you think? John the Baptist with a little American Eagle flavor?"

Before I could say another word, Ginny Kramer burst onto the stage and cornered him. "Edward Parker! Get down to that costume room immediately. You know I have a tunic for you. It's just not hemmed yet. And don't you dare give me that innocent 'I didn't know' face. You knew what you were doing."

Eddie gave me a helpless look. "Looks like I'm wanted in the dungeon," he said. Then he called out to the cast once more, "Sorry, ladies. Looks like the gun show's over. Hope you got your photos while you had the chance."

The kids laughed and hooted, and a few fired off some parting jibes. "Guns? More like pipe cleaners!" someone yelled. "Hey Eddie, nice zero pack!" hollered another. And then a final voice from the back cried, "Yeah, and what's that scar on your stomach? Is that where the mother ship inserted your doofus card?"

Eddie stopped at that and stared out hard into the audience. I have to admit, I hadn't noticed any scar until the comment. But he definitely had a sizable purple scar running vertically up the left side of his abdomen. I didn't think it was any big deal, but Eddie must have. "Shut up, Kyle!" he barked. "You always have to overdo it. Just shut up for once, will ya?" And then little Eddie stalked off the stage.

I didn't have time to ask him about it during the rehearsal that followed, but I found him in the dressing room after most of the kids had cleared out. He was changing into street clothes, and his mood hadn't improved. He was quiet and dejected, an altogether different Eddie.

"You have a ride coming, Eddie?"

"Yeah. Mom's on her way," he mumbled back.

There were stools in the dressing room, so I found one and sat down. "Don't worry about the costume parade or Mrs. Kramer. Actually, I thought it was pretty funny."

"Thanks," came the concise reply.

"I noticed some of the kids were getting on you pretty hard. You know they were only teasing. I hope you didn't take any of that to heart."

Silence. So I pressed further.

"I only say that because you seemed a little upset. You usually take everything in stride, and I just wanted to make sure you were okay. Are you doing all right, Eddie?"

He turned to me, and his face was quivering. "I'm sorry, Dr. K. I just all of a sudden started thinking about Mr. B, and it got to me. It was stupid. I'll do better, I promise."

When I was fourteen, no one told me that being a man didn't mean burying your feelings. I wanted to make sure that Eddie knew it was okay to be sad. "We're all struggling with the fact that Mr. B can't be here," I told him. "There's no crime in that, Eddie. And I know you two were close."

"He's been friends with my folks all my life. Used to come to my soccer games, grade school concerts, all sorts of stuff. This is the first time he's not been around. And…I miss him."

"We all miss him, Eddie." I patted him on his narrow shoulder. "All of us do."

Then Eddie asked me an innocent question that felt like a kick in the gut. "He is going to get better, isn't he, Dr. K? I mean, he's going to come back, isn't he?"

Some truths are harder to tell than others. If it weren't so important, I would've taken the easy road. "I don't know for sure, Eddie," I admitted. "No one does. But you can bet that Mr. B is fighting. And if anyone could find a way out of that hospital, it will be him."

Eddie chewed on that bit of encouragement for a moment before asking me another gut-kicker. "But if he doesn't make it, are you going to stay with us, Dr. K? Or are you going to leave too?"

Usually, I was the one asked to leave, not stay. The question left me skating. "That decision isn't up to me," I hedged. "But if they let me stay, Eddie. I'm going to stay." I should have thought that proclamation through. But it was done. One more promise I'd likely break.

Eddie packed and left. Donna caught me on my way out the dressing room, and my face must've betrayed me. "What's up with you, Sawyer? You look like you've just left a confessional."

"I had a little conversation with Eddie, that's all."

"Yeah, he wasn't himself tonight. What happened?"

"He got to thinking about Mr. B, and it sort of consumed him. But then he asked me if I thought Mr. B was going to die."

"What did you tell him?"

"I told him that I didn't know. What else was I supposed to say?" I ran my hands through my hair, winced, and sighed. "Oh, DJ. There is a whole lot more to this gig than I was expecting."

"That's the way it always goes when working with kids. That's what makes it great."

"And we've only got…how many more weeks until we open?"

"Four."

"*Four* more weeks. And look at this stage, not a set piece built. Nothing. And I still haven't blocked the last two scenes. I'm not even sure what I'm going to do with that. Mr. B's production notes didn't get that far."

"I'm sure you'll come up with something wonderful," she said reassuringly. "It'll all come together, Sawyer. It's looking really good so far. So if you have to feel anything, feel excited. I know the kids are. Tonight, I heard them conspiring about what to get you for an opening-night gift."

"Gift?"

"Of course. The cast always gives flowers and small gifts to the directors and each other on opening night. You can have forgotten that tradition?"

"Yeah, but they shouldn't be spending money on a gift for me. They should save it for each other." I was pleased with how magnanimous that sounded, but then curiosity got the best of me. "So…what were they thinking about getting?"

Donna narrowed her eyes and feigned her displeasure. "I don't know. And even if I did, I wouldn't tell you."

Things with Tim had settled into a natural rhythm as well. Tuesdays and Fridays, he adjusted my back. Friday nights, I usually had dinner with him and his family. And of course, Thursday morning was Bible study.

I was getting pretty comfortable with the guys at the church, and especially the ones that typically sat at our table. Dale Patterson continued to be insightful and ask meaningful questions that took courage to answer. I felt like I was becoming a better man because of it, but I also knew I was still hovering around the edge of a commitment.

Tim tried every approach. He tried being gentle. He tried being a bulldog. He tried to argue with me and at times just understand me. But he knew where I was, and so did I. Despite everything, I was still meandering around the pool deck. Occasionally, I poked my toe in or even splash my face. But I wasn't ready to take the plunge and join the others no matter how fine the water looked.

We were having just one of those discussions after dinner one Friday night when Tim made his position clear. "I'm not going to give up on you, Finny. I'm just not. But it's got to be your choice. No one else can do it for you. And you can't ride on someone else's coat-tails into the kingdom. It's gotta be personal. It's got to be between you and God."

It might sound surprising, but I wasn't annoyed at all by Tim's occasional sermonettes. In fact, I admired him for it. I would've given up on me a long time ago.

"And I'll tell you another thing"—he was gesturing at me with a spatula he was putting away from the dishwasher—"even when Bible study wraps up in a few weeks, I'm still going to—"

"Wait," I interrupted. "Bible study is ending?"

"Yeah, it was only a ten-week deal. We're finishing up with a big all-church extravaganza. Pancake breakfast, the works. That morning, they're going to have video screens to Skype with the other churches that were part of the study. I think some guys from the different churches are even going to speak and talk about how the study impacted their lives. Should I have signed you up as a keynote speaker?"

"Hardly. But I didn't realize that it would be over so soon. I was just starting to get into the swing of things."

"We're only taking the two weeks before and after Easter off. We're starting a new study after that, and it will run all the way into May. It's supposed to build off some of the principles that we covered in the first study. And if you're still here, Finny, I want us to go to that one too."

"Sheesh. I didn't realize that Easter is almost here too. These last weeks have been a blur."

"Don't worry. I'm sure the Easter Bunny can still find you back here in Hanover."

I helped Tim put away the last of the dishes when I realized the time. "I've got to fly, Tim. Mom was going to wait up, and I still need to stop by the video store and drop off some DVDs and get new ones."

"You and your mom still watching that *Star Trek* thing? What is it, Next Generation or something?"

"*Deep Space Nine*," I pretended to be exasperated. "Come on, Tim. If you're going to hang around with me, you have to do a better job of getting your 'nerd' on."

"I can't believe your mom likes that stuff."

"We're already on season three. Thank heavens Video Town has all of them. I think Mom's more hooked than I am. What can I say? The apple doesn't fall far from the tree."

Though most people had made the jump to video streaming, Hanover still had one option for video rentals. It was a small Mom-and-Pop operation on the square called Video Town. It wasn't much of a town, barely even a village. But for a small place, it had an amazing number of movies. Unfortunately, most of them were titles that no one would ever care to watch. Needless to say, they had lots of cheesy science-fiction flicks available.

It was late, near closing, when I hustled through the door and nearly bowled over a patron who was leaving. When I made eye contact to apologize, I realized that it was Sarah.

It was an awkward encounter.

"How are you?" We both said at the same time.

"Fine. Fine." I could've said jinx, but I didn't.

"Look...Sawyer...You're probably wondering..." Sarah struggled for her words. "I didn't *not* return your message because—"

I waved my hand dismissively. "No problem, Sarah. I know you've been busy. You didn't—"

"Actually, things in Phoenix took me longer than I expected. I've only been back for a week. But I was going to call you, Sawyer. I really was. It's just that—"

"No, I never should've put you on the spot by asking you to lunch. It wasn't fair."

But then Sarah seemed to put her mind and words together and said lucidly, "I *wanted* to call you, Sawyer. But I didn't know what I wanted to say. I needed to get my head and heart straight on a few things before I saw you again."

"And..."

"And I know where things stand. It just took me a while to sort it out. So when I get back, let's definitely sit down, give that lime Jell-O a whirl. This time, I'll call you. I promise."

"Where are you going?"

"Back to Phoenix."

"Already?" I blurted and only then realized how needy it sounded. "I just figured you'd be around. You know, with Mr. B still in ICU and not out of the woods and all." For someone who used to deliver lines for living, I had an uncanny inability to deliver a good one when I needed it.

"That was my original plan, but it's just gotten too hard to be in two places at the same time. Work still needs me there."

"Yeah, you were heading off to that big fundraiser," I interrupted. "How did that go anyway?"

"It went fine. Actually, better than fine. We raised a lot of money and, I hope, even more awareness. It was a good weekend."

"Sorry. I got you offtrack. I'm trying to do a better job of not interrupting." I smiled, and I think she understood. "You were talking about being in two places at one time."

"It has been tough," she said, and for the first time, I noticed the weariness in her eyes. She looked tired and wrung out, but she carried it with an elegance that made her even more beautiful. "And now there've been some other developments that I need to be home for to start organizing. I talked to Dr. Schaeffer, and she completely understood. She said that Uncle Ed's condition is stable and it would be impossible to predict any changes whether for better or worse. I found an airline that has a direct flight from Phoenix to Peoria, so if something happens, I can be here in four hours. My plan now is to go home and check back here in a couple of weeks. In fact, I was just dropping off some videos tonight because I catch a flight in the morning."

"I think that's for the best," I said but didn't really mean it. "And I'll keep down the home front here, at least until the show is over."

"How was it coming, Sawyer? I'm sure this hasn't been easy on you either."

"It's coming along. You know how it goes, you're never sure until opening night."

"Well, I can't wait to see it."

"You're coming?" I didn't hide my astonishment well.

"Of course. This was going to be Uncle Ed's last show, and he chose you to finish it. How could I miss it?" She pushed past me and headed for the door. "I'll call you when I get back, Sawyer. See you then."

The door opened and closed with a gust of cold air, and I stood there trying to collect myself. Sarah still had a way of sending my nerves in a tizzy. I think it must've been that. It almost had to be. Because somehow, I never saw the lovely diamond ring sparkling on her finger.

FIFTEEN

"Okay, gang. That was another good week of rehearsal. But we still a long way to go. Next week, I want to block the final scenes and work out the bugs that are still killing us in the production numbers. That'll leave us only two weeks to get used to the microphones, lights, and set while we polish things up."

The kids were gathering their books, coats, and car keys but still doing an admirable job of paying attention. I figured it was a good time to sermonize.

"The show is going to be here before we know it. And remember, we only have three chances to get it right. Three shows—Friday, Saturday, and Sunday. And then it's over. The genie never goes back into the bottle. So let's not have any regrets, okay? Oh, and take care of yourselves. Wear a coat. I don't want anyone showing up opening night sick because they were running around outside in the cold. And make sure you turn your homework in. Remember, if you are on the ineligibility list the week of the show, you're out. All that hard work down the drain. So be accountable to one another. Ms. Thewlis, do you have any last music notes tonight?"

"No, except to stay in your librettos," she instructed. "We're getting a little sloppy with a few of our cut-offs. I want you to especially look at 'Light of the World' over the weekend."

"Okay, now before you go, I know Mrs. Kramer has a few items. You know, in the theater business, there's an old expression that says, 'The *costumer* is always right.' And truer words were never spoken. So I don't want you grousing about what she has you wearing. Got it? Okay Mrs. Kramer, they're all yours."

161

As I walked over to the rehearsal piano, I noticed that Artie Chambers was standing in the back of the house. He had a huge cardboard box in his arms, and he kept trying to peer over the top of it.

"DJ, do you see Chambers back there?"

"How can I miss him, he looks like one of Santa's elves?"

"What's he doing here?"

"Bringing us a cardboard box, I would presume."

While Ginny was going over costuming notes, Artie made his way down the aisle and slid the heavy box on the stage. "T-shirts are in," he explained with a genial nod. "The company left a message in my office, and I saw that the account was square, so I picked them up for you. I know it's great advertising for the show to have the kids out and about wearing them. Figured you'd want them as soon as possible."

"Thanks, Artie," I said. I was so stunned by his jovial demeanor that I used his first name. "I'd almost forgotten about the shirts." I pulled one out to check the artwork. They were cool. *Godspell* was spelled out in stylized letters over the top of our school name and production dates. A rainbow of tie-dyed colors washed through the print.

Donna was admiring it from over my shoulder. "Tell you what, Ginny and I will distribute the T-shirts to the kids. Why don't you and Artie go catch up on old times?" She gave me a wink and left me alone with him.

I didn't have to worry about a stilted conversation for long. Artie was gentlemanly enough to break the ice. "I was looking for an opportunity to pop by and see you, Mr. Kent. I wanted to apologize for my behavior a few weeks ago."

"Please, call me Sawyer."

"Thanks for that. I'm not a big fan of formalities, but I wasn't sure where we stood. Anyway, I'm very pleased that you're here. The kids have all been raving about you, and I think I understand now why old Bert wanted you to step in." He glanced around the empty stage. "So how are things going?"

"I think we'll get there. The kids are working hard, and that's all I can ask."

"How are things coming with the set?"

"You're looking at it." I smirked wryly.

Artie seemed to be weighing it all without passing judgment. "Do you have any help? Have you been able to organize a construction crew or anything?"

"Not yet," I confessed. "I've been more locked in on what's happening *on* the stage rather than what's happening *to* the stage. That's my fault. But I figured I'd bring the cast in next weekend, and we'd get cracking at it."

Artie chuckled, but not in a way that was at my expense. "Have you ever watched a bunch of theater kids who have never held a hammer trying to build a set? It's not their fault, but it's pretty comical. Did Bert draw up any plans?"

"Yeah, pretty precise ones too."

"Let me make you an offer. How about you let me photocopy those drawings? I'll get some guys together, and maybe we can help you with that set. You know, back when I taught vo-tech, I used to help Bert build a lot of his sets. It'll feel a little like old times."

"That would be a huge relief," I told him, and I'm sure he could hear it in my voice.

He took the binder and flipped through it. "Just like old Bert. Detailed and precise." He smiled. "Okay, I'll go ahead and photocopy this in my office. I'll put the binder back on the stage when I'm done, okay?"

"Sounds good. And Artie? Thanks again."

Donna sidled up to me, and I knew I was going to hear it. She didn't disappoint. "So looks like you and Artie are new best friends, huh? Planning cookie baking and sleepovers? Don't stay up all night giggling now, you two."

"Hey, what can I say? I just have a magnetic personality. Maybe after this is over, I'll run for mayor."

I promised myself that I would take the weekend off and not think about the show. It didn't work out that way. I knew I needed to come to terms with the last scene. I was pretty sure what I wanted to do, and it kept eating at me. By Sunday afternoon, I capitulated and went to get the binder to start writing out blocking notes for the finale. It was only then that I realized I'd failed to retrieve it from Artie. So I hopped in the car and made the familiar two-and-a-half-mile trek to the school. I got there just before sundown, and as I approached the auditorium, I heard voices inside.

"Oh, Sawyer, it's you," Artie Chambers said from the stage. He was sitting on its lip, with his legs dangling over the side and trying to hide a thermos behind his back. "I thought it might be Donna or worse, Mrs. Kramer. No food or drink in the auditorium. I was afraid they'd catch me with my contraband." He saluted me with a raise of his thermos cup.

I barely heard what he was saying because behind him rose the walls of a skid row ghetto just as Mr. B had imagined. "You built all this?"

"I had a little bit of help. That's Dick Hirschfield just packing up over there." He nodded to a burly guy in overalls who was snapping shut a toolbox. "See you tomorrow, Dick." Artie waived. "He teaches wood shop and Industrial Arts here at Hanover. And we had a couple other guys give us a hand yesterday. What do you think?"

"What do I think? I think it's fantastic. I could've never gotten this done. You guys built all this in two days?"

"Well, I've had a little experience reading old Bert's blueprints. We had all the materials in the storeroom. It came together pretty quickly. Now, I should tell you, the fleabag hotel and fire escape are plenty sturdy, so are the stairs over there. No problem bearing the weight of your actors. But the rest these walls? Well, don't breathe on them too hard. Some of them aren't held up by much more than furring strips and duct tape." He took a sip from his thermos and looked around. The self-deprecation didn't suit him. He was proud of his work, and he should've been. "Of course, the walls need to be painted. Your cast can do the grunt work and the art department punch up all the specialty stuff. Would you like some hot chocolate? I've got an extra cup."

"Sure," I said and sat down beside him on the stage lip.

"Good, that makes us confederates. Not a word of this to the janitorial staff, got it?" He gave me a toast and leaned back on his hands.

"I don't know what to say. This goes way above the call of duty."

"You're doing a good job, Sawyer. Not just with the theater side of things, but all of it. The kids love you. You know Julia Riley from the show, right?"

"Of course."

"Do you know who her grandmother is?"

"No." I shook my head. "Should I?"

"Her grandmother is the school board president. Julia's folks are divorced, and she spends a lot of time with Grandma Riley. They're close, and they share a lot. Well, a couple of weeks ago, I got a call from Mrs. Riley in my office. She wanted to thank me for hiring such a wonderful director for the show. She said that Julia had been really down, wanted to quit the show. But something you said to her changed all that. She said her granddaughter looks forward to rehearsal every night and that you're a great director to work for. Then Mrs. Riley said that I should be commended for bringing someone in that would hold high the proud tradition of Hanover musicals.

"The conversation made me ashamed of myself. I knew in my heart that I wasn't giving you a chance because I secretly wanted you to fail. But since I couldn't change the past, I figured I could start helping you in the present." He made a sweeping gesture to indicate the set that he had just built. Then Artie put the cap back on his thermos, and he stared out into the dark of the auditorium.

It was quiet in the room, the kind of quiet that makes men philosophical. "I loved her mom," he said. "Sarah's mom. I probably still do, at least the memory of her. Having Ed around made it seem like there was a part of Joanna still here. And I know if we lose him, I'll finally have to bury them both. I think I was wrestling with all of that when you showed up. So"—he shrugged off the deep thoughts and asked—"what brought you up here on a Sunday afternoon?"

"I forgot to get the binder from you Friday night. I've been mulling over the final scenes and wanted to write down my ideas."

"So what *are* you going to do with that?" Artie's question indicated that he knew my dilemma.

"You've seen the show?"

"It's one of my favorites. I've probably seen it seven or eight times, both on and off Broadway. And I probably have seen the last scene staged seven or eight different ways. Everyone has a different idea about what to do with Jesus after the crucifixion. What are you going to do with him?"

"Well, the writers of the show just leave him dead. But they do put in their stage notes that some productions might choose to give a subtle nod to a resurrection. Given everything I've read in Mr. B's binder, I think he was planning a not-so-subtle ending to the show."

"And what do you have planned?"

The more I thought through my idea, the more excited I became. I hopped up and darted upstage to the hotel. "What you think of this—the Pharisees, led by Judas, drag Jesus up the fire escape and crucify him there. All the cast is huddled in small groups downstage except the Pharisees, who stand upstage here nodding their approval. You know how the music goes, right? During the slow movements where Jesus cries out that he's bleeding, I'll have Drew holding a red ribbon in each hand, and when he releases, it will look like stylized blood flowing out of his wrists. But then when the music fires back in, we'll use smoke and lights to suggest lightning and power. You know, real *sturm und drang* stuff. But then the piece retards, Jesus dies, and there is perfect silence on the stage. In that silence, the Pharisees pull his body off the fire escape and then just heave it unceremoniously in the dumpster. You know the part of the music I'm talking about?"

"Absolutely," Artie responded. "That's where the cast starts singing 'Long Live God.' It's beautiful music, very sad."

"Yes," I agreed. "And I'll have the kids pace by the dumpster, touching it solemnly as they walk by. But then the music starts to pick up, remember? It really gathers in tempo and starts to crescendo. Well, as that's happening, I'll have the dumpster start to slowly spin and pick up speed to match the music. And then, in the final two stanzas of the show, with the entire chorus singing 'Prepare ye the way of the Lord,' the dumpster will stop spinning. And as the last powerful notes come blasting off the stage, Jesus rises up out of the dumpster, arm stretched towards heaven, fully alive. What you think about that?"

Artie was thoughtful in his response. "Well, there's a number of things I think about that. The first thing is, I think it's fabulous. The second thing is, we *are* a public high school."

"That was my concern—" I began to interrupt, but Artie continued.

"The third thing I think is, we've done religious shows in the past and didn't cut the religious themes out of them. When we did 'Fiddler on the Roof,' we didn't cut 'Sabbath Prayer.' And when we did 'Once on This Island,' we didn't cut the prayers to the pagan gods." He shrugged. "So why should we now? But the last and most important thing is, you think Bert would've wanted it this way. So do what's in your heart, Sawyer, and let me worry about the nasty phone calls." Artie screwed the cup back onto his thermos. "There something else I want you to consider, Sawyer."

"What's that?"

"I should first warn you that not all the *T*s are crossed and *I*s dotted, but it looks like we're going to create a new position at the school next year. The superintendent told me not to say anything to you until after the show opened, but you're here, and you might as well be thinking about it."

I was intrigued and wanted him to know it. "What kind of position?"

"Nothing grand, but we need someone to monitor the computer lab. The job would pay twelve dollars an hour for thirty-five hours a week. It only lasts the thirty-six weeks we're in school, but we could probably keep you busy over the summer if you want to work with the maintenance staff. And it would include insurance. But the best part is, it would keep you close to the kids. That might be useful next year when it comes time to directing the musical."

I didn't like the implication. "Don't sell Mr. B short. Next year is a long time from now. That should give him plenty of time to recover and get back to work."

"I'm not selling him short. I'm hoping and praying that Bert gets through all of this and makes a complete recovery. But you forget, he's already turned in his resignation. I've got it on my desk. No matter what, I'm going to need a director next year."

I let the significance of that settle on me but still couldn't grasp it. "I can't believe he's going to retire. His job has always been his life."

"I was as stunned as anyone," Artie replied. "But he told me that he accomplished everything he was meant to do here at Hanover, and now, it was time to move on."

"Move on? Where was he going?"

"He's going to keep this house here, but he's bought a small villa in Tuscany. He's going to spend winters and spring there teaching English to children. He's already got a job lined up. He promised he'll come back to Hanover every March to see the musical and planned to stay on through the summer so we could watch baseball. But then he would head back to the old country."

"I guess that makes sense," I said, but it didn't make enough. "I know he was born in Italy and always talked about going back there. But it seems like a drastic change."

"I thought the same thing and told him so myself. But then he said something strange. He said he feared he was getting too attached. I remember he said, 'If the sun draws too close to the flower, the petals may wither.'"

"What exactly did he mean by that?"

"I don't know." Artie shrugged. "I thought it might be Shakespeare or something. Anyway, I'd like you to think about the job. Let me know after the show opens."

"It's a very tempting offer. I don't know that I'll need that long to make up my mind."

Artie's demeanor suddenly turned sheepish. "Well, I think my early characterizations of you colored the superintendent's decision on the matter. He told me I couldn't offer you the job until you've finished this one." Artie was shifting uncomfortably, but then he looked at me and asked, "You will be there opening night, right?"

"And skip out on $1700?" I clowned. "Artie, I may be a cad, but I'm no fool. And I'm a broke fool at that."

SIXTEEN

March came in like a lamb. A warming sun claimed the winter sky and seasoned its breeze with the scents of spring. In the city, March smells like fresh garbage. But in Hanover, the air becomes redolent with farm mud, wet bark, and baby leaves—the perfect aromatherapy for cheering moods.

The show was galloping along. Artie's set helped the kids visualize the physical world we had been creating with dialogue and songs. Once it became painted, rehearsals took on a new life. With things going so well on stage, I was able to turn my attention to the backstage crews. I coached up the makeup and prop people and spent a number of long nights with the tech monkeys hanging lights, creating microphone plots, and programming light cues into our board.

I was pleased, and so was Donna.

We had developed a strong camaraderie that allowed for teasing that our friendship might become more. I was debating about getting her an opening-night gift that might push the boundaries of that, but I hadn't decided yet. I didn't want to spoil what we were constructing. Donna and I worked well together. There was satisfaction in building something worthwhile. That was very new to me. With most women I knew, the closer we got, the more we destroyed. So this was all undiscovered country.

Maybe it was the weather, maybe the good rehearsals, or maybe just Donna, but I was getting used to life going well.

I should've known better.

I don't know where the expression "Waiting for the shoe to fall" comes from. Maybe there was a lot of falling footwear back in the olden days. Regardless, on the morning of our final men's Bible study, a size 13 DDD came thundering out of the blue and whomped me in the butt cheeks, bringing me back to reality.

The morning started well. Tim and I were unusually chatty in the car. When we got to the church, we discovered that a similar mood had infected the crowd. Guys were chattering and laughing while ESPN blared over the large video screens. Coffee pots drained, and pancakes evaporated by the stackful. Then Dale Patterson stepped to the microphone and brought us all back on task.

He favored us with a crooked southern grin and said, "Can you believe it's been ten weeks already? But have no worries, men. We're only taking a few weeks off. Shortly after Easter, we're going to start a new study that springboards off the topics we've covered so far. It's great material, and I hope you can all be a part. But this morning, I don't want to talk about the future. I want to take the next hour and celebrate where we've come. As men, it's important to remember that faith is not a solo sport. Paul had Barnabas, and even Jesus surrounded himself with disciples. Today, we've managed to video link with the other churches who have been partnering in the study with us. Some of the men have agreed to share their stories about what God is doing in their lives. So without any further ado, let's throw it out to Glen from Bethany Bible Church in Lincoln."

For the next forty-five minutes, guys appeared on the video screens and told us their tales. It was pretty good stuff, but I have a short attention span, and some of the stories started sounding a little redundant. One guy realized he needed to invest more of his time with his children. Another was trying to be a better husband. Some guy from Decatur wanted to correct some sketchy business deals he got involved with. Like I said, it was good stuff, but I was getting bored.

There was a whole raft of napkins on my table, and I started doodling more than watching. I got distracted with what was turning out to be a pretty cool-looking mouse in a pirate outfit. I gave him an eye patch, plumed hat, and knee-high boots. It looked pretty good. I wrote the name Petey beside him. But when I drew a curly mustache on him, he looked to me more like a Pierre, so I crossed out Petey and wrote that instead.

Vaguely, I was aware of a guy rambling on one of the video boards. He had a big deep voice, and I think that's what made me take notice. As I doodled, I thought that his voice would be great for cartoons, maybe one featuring a pirate mouse.

I gave Pierre a devilish-looking scimitar while the guy droned on about having thrown away his family in order to build a business. He said about nine months ago, he decided to sell it to retire and, in the process, realized how shallow his life was. He began searching for more, and that was what led him to Christ.

I was putting the final touches on my artwork when I felt Tim's elbow in my ribs. "Finny." I expected him to scold me, but his whisper held astonishment, not reprimand. "Finny, that's not who I think it is, is it?"

I looked up at the screen and saw the speaker.

It was my dad.

I don't remember much of what happened next. I don't even remember leaving the church and getting into Tim's car. I think it was crossing the bridge and seeing the ledge where I stood that shook me from my stupor. "I don't believe it, Tim. I just don't believe it." I tried to hold my hands still, but they were shaking. "I mean, what was he doing there? The guy's a fiend and a creep. He doesn't belong in a church, unless that church in Bloomington is the First Church of Satan or something."

"Maybe he's changed, Finny. Jesus has a way of doing that."

"Not my dad. Not that phony. Trust me, there's got to be some kind of ulterior motive. With Dad, there was always an angle."

Tim had the decency to let me spell it all out. I may have used a few choice words to further describe my thoughts on the matter. Tim didn't flinch. Instead, he calmly said, "Yeah, Finny, but what if there is no angle? What if your dad has changed? What would you do with that?"

I didn't have an answer for him, and it plagued me all day. When I got to rehearsal, Donna could tell that I was still upset.

"What's up with you?" Her words came out harsh, but her eyes were concerned. "You look like you just ran over your pet. Are you okay, Sawyer?"

"I'll be fine." I tried to shrug it off. "I just saw somebody this morning that I didn't want to see."

"Sarah?" There was a hint of hope in her question.

"No, my dad. But Sarah will be back in a few days, and she says there something she needs to tell me. From the sound of it, that's another conversation to dread." I sat down on the stage-left stairs, and Donna joined me. "DJ? How did you get over Floyd? I mean, how did you get over the anger and resentment?"

"Well, there were three ways now that I think about it. They kind of followed in progression. I started by having nightly counseling sessions with my old friend, Pinot Grigio. Let's just say that the results were less than satisfactory."

"Yeah, I've listened to him too. He gives terrible advice."

"But then I had a friend tell me that I wouldn't be truly over Floyd until I felt nothing for him. He needed to become inconsequential to me, and then I would be over it. That advice might have worked if I never had to see Floyd again, but it's impossible in our case. He's still Stephanie's father."

"So what did you do next?"

"I had to do the hardest thing. I had to learn to forgive him."

That seemed out of the question for me, and I told her so. "When you get hurt as a child, it's different. I've hated my dad for twenty-five years."

"I'm not going to tell you how you're supposed to feel, Sawyer. I shudder to think what it would be like to have a parent walk out on you. So, I can only tell you how it worked for me. What allowed me to forgive Floyd was perspective."

"Perspective?"

The kids were trundling into the auditorium, and I knew rehearsal had to start soon. Donna cut to the chase. "I know I haven't been very open with you about my faith, but that's what gave me perspective. It boils down to this—the God of the universe left heaven to come down here, get beaten, mocked, and killed so he could forgive a loser like me. So who am I to hold a grudge? Does that make sense?"

"A little," I said as I flipped through the binder for my rehearsal notes. "But it's a whole lot more fun just to hate him."

"I know it looks terrible. But you have to trust me. It's really good," Sarah encouraged as I placed the enchilada on my orange plastic tray.

"I'll defer to your expertise. You've spent a lot more time in this cafeteria than I have."

"But skip the iced tea," she warned. "It's instant. Nasty stuff."

We found a table near the windows where the afternoon sun was spilling in like a tidal wave. I don't think either one of us knew what to say, but Sarah found an easy opening. "So a big week for you, right?"

"That would be an understatement," I replied as I spread my napkin in my lap. "A full run-through tonight with makeup, tech, everything. Tomorrow, we'll just do a quick sing through and get the kids home early so they can rest. And then Friday is judgment day."

"How do you feel about it? Is everything ready to go?"

"Ask me Saturday," I snickered. "But I think we're ready. At least as ready as we'll ever be."

Sarah took a forkful of her key-lime pie and chewed thoughtfully as she looked out the window. "Funny how life goes. Never in a million years would I have imagined that I'd be back here in Peoria having lunch with you two days before you direct the Hanover high school musical."

"Oh, I've imagined it. But you're not still eating your dessert first, and you usually have an AK-47 in your hands."

"Some habits are hard to break." She popped another bite of pie in her mouth and smiled smugly. "And guns are really not my style. I'm more of a machete girl."

"Well, I count myself lucky that you are even speaking to me. I wouldn't blame you if you still hated me."

She picked at a crouton on her salad and murmured, "Getting over hating you was the easy part, Sawyer."

The statement brought us to the edge of the rabbit hole, and we both knew it. But I wasn't going to plunge into our past unless she was willing. Surprisingly, she jumped right in.

"There's something that I have to know, Sawyer."

"Sure, anything."

"What was it like? Broadway and everything? I mean, did you find what you were looking for? Did you make it like you hoped?"

It wasn't the question I was expecting her to ask, but it wasn't difficult to answer. "I did." I nodded. "I don't mean that to sound vain, but for a while there, I knew I had really made it. It was frightening and wonderful all at the same time. Here I was, this kid from Central Illinois with eyes as big as saucers with my name in the playbill. Early on, I kept thinking someone would find me out. They'd know I didn't belong and they'd send me home. But then one night, I believed it. I knew belonged on Broadway and it was no accident."

"What happened?"

"In the summer of 2002, I was the understudy for Marius in 'Les Mis.' We were playing at the Imperial Theatre in New York. And at the time, only 'A Chorus Line and Cats' had been running longer than us. It was a great production—marvelous director, everything. And then one day, the stage manager comes up and tells me that the actor playing Marius had left the company. His wife was some hot-shot attorney and had taken a job in Toronto, and he went with her. So the role of Marius was mine, at least for the time being.

"It was a Thursday. I remember because Thursday nights are usually the best crowd. It's true. See, weekend crowds come because it's convenient for them. Thursday night crowds come because they are desperate to see the show. They're coming even though they have to scrape themselves up and work in the morning. That's why Thursdays are usually the most enthusiastic and responsive audience all week.

"Anyway, during the first act, I was so nervous that it was all a blur. I was just trying to get to my marks and not forget my lines or screw something up. But by Act II, I'd begun to settle down. You know there's an old theater quote that says, 'You learn your lines so that you can forget them.' And that's kind of the way it goes. Eventually, your dialogue and movement isn't mechanical. It's natural. You're living and responding in the moment to the other people on stage. That's what began to happen to me in Act II. Near the end of the show, Marius has his big solo. It's called 'Empty Chairs at Empty Tables.' Do you know it? It doesn't really matter. But I remember how the song just started pouring out of me. In the show, Marius has lost all of his friends and he doesn't know if it was worth it or not. I could identify. I remember thinking of you when I sang that song."

Sarah had been quiet for a long time. She was staring out the window while I spoke, and I thought that last confession might rouse her. It didn't. It was clear that she had no intention of interrupting, so I finished the story. "Anyway, I ended the song, the lights went black, and the audience broke into applause. At the Imperial, there's a stairwell just off the stage that leads down to costuming and the crossover between stage right and left. I started down to make my change when I realized the crowd was still clapping. I just stood there on the stairs listening to them whistle and applaud for me. And I remember thinking to myself, 'You did it, Sawyer. You made it.'"

All the while, Sarah seemed to be measuring the story like she was weighing each word to determine its worth. Apparently satisfied, she said, "Then I need you to do me a favor, Sawyer."

"Sure. Anything."

"I need you to tell me that it was all worth it."

The old Sawyer would have done just that. But the new Sawyer had stood with his heels on the bridge and genuinely understood the depth of Marius's song. "I wish I could," I confessed. "But it wasn't, Sarah. It wasn't worth it."

Sarah's demeanor changed when I said that. The scale had tipped, and she reluctantly accepted what the story weighed. "Well, the past is probably best left in the past," she said. "We can't change it, and it's too full of landmines to keep walking through it."

She was right, but I didn't want to leave the topic until I finally solved a mystery. "Sarah, this might sound like an odd question, but did my mom send you some pictures of me?"

"No." She blinked with surprise. "Why would she?"

"I don't know. I caught my mom scanning some old pictures of us. And then later, when I saw you at the school and you look so pretty and everything, I just wondered...I guess I hoped..."

"Oh, Sawyer. Let's not go there. We have a past together, but not a future. I've moved forward. I had to. I've got a great career now, and I've met a really terrific man." She paused and then said ironically, "And as it turns out, you have too."

She didn't let me struggle before filling in the gaps. "Remember the doctor you met? Jim Stratton? He and I have been dating for over a year. And a few weeks ago, when I was home, we got engaged."

She flashed me the ring, and I did my best to act pleased. "Congratulations."

"I should probably thank you. Jim and I had been talking about getting engaged, but I think when he met you, he felt a little threatened. When I went back to Phoenix for the fundraiser, he met me at the airport with a ring."

"Should he have felt threatened?" I couldn't help but probe.

"No. He shouldn't have. He's a good man, Sawyer. A solid man. I'm in a good place now. I'm happy."

"Do you love him?"

Her answer could not have been more absolute. "I do."

It was my time to start weighing a story. When I threw it on the scales, it finally added up. "So that's what you needed to tell me."

Sarah's face was perplexed. "Remember, at the video store?" I reminded her. "You said there was something that I should know. It was that you're engaged, right?"

Sarah's perplexed face suddenly colored darkly. She looked down at the table, her eyes unwilling to meet mine. "No," she muttered begrudgingly. "There's something else."

"What?"

"Look, Sawyer, I made a mistake even bringing it up. It doesn't matter anymore. Like I said, the past should best be left in the past. Don't worry about it."

"Don't worry about it? You know my imagination is far worse than reality. If it's something that involves me, I should know."

Sarah's eyes retreated to the window. She knew there was logic in my argument, and she was searching intently for an escape. She was still deep in contemplation when her phone rang.

"Sarah?"

Her eyes snapped back to reality. "Yes?"

"Your purse." I pointed. "It's chirping."

Sarah gladly snapped open her phone. "Hello, this is Sarah." But then worry penetrated her voice. "Actually, Dr. Schaeffer, I'm here at the hospital now. I'm just up in the cafeteria. Yes, I remember where it is. I'm on my way now."

I didn't have to ask. Sarah was already gathering her things and explaining. "It's Uncle Bert. He's taken a turn."

We hurried to the elevators and met Dr. Schaeffer and the small waiting room where we had talked with her before. She was sympathetic but direct with her report.

"Your uncle has had a setback," she said in unnervingly even tones. "He experienced a moderate to severe stroke sometime early this afternoon." Sarah nodded bravely as the doctor continued with more bad news. "Unfortunately, in Mr. Bertollini's weakened condition, immediate treatment is inadvisable. Please know that we will be monitoring his condition round-the-clock, but the next twenty-four to forty-eight hours are critical."

"Thank you, Dr. Schaeffer. I know you're doing the best you can." A tear escaped Sarah's heroic face. "I'd like to stay with him if that's permitted. Just these next couple of days. Can I do that?"

"Of course you can," came the reply. "The reclining chair in his room is quite comfortable, and we'll send up some blankets and a pillow. The cafeteria even has a program that can send your meals to his room if you'd like."

"Thank you. That would be nice."

The doctor left, and Sarah let her tears go.

"Now, Sarah," I tried to comfort her, "the news doesn't sound completely hopeless. If he can just get through these next couple of days—"

Sarah cut me off with a sniff of tears. "Doctors always say those kinds of things when it's bad. I work with doctors, Sawyer. I'm *engaged* to a doctor for crying out loud. I know how they talk."

I couldn't dispute Sarah's insight even though I wanted to. I felt so helpless. "Is there anything I can do, Sarah? Just name it. I want to help."

To my surprise, she said, "Yes, Sawyer. There is one thing you can do."

"What's that?"

"You can pray for a miracle."

"Okay, guys, that was a good rehearsal to go out on. I'm really pleased. If we can sing the show tomorrow just like we did tonight, people will be talking about 'Godspell' for years. Now, it's only seven fifteen. I want you to get home and get some rest. I want you fresh tomorrow night when we open."

"What are the times again?" Julie asked, a pencil poised over her planner book.

"Yes, thanks for reminding me." I nodded. "Makeup call is at five thirty. Microphone check is at six. And I want everyone in the chorus room by six thirty for a final warm-up and last notes. The curtain goes up at seven. Everybody got it? Good. Any other questions?"

An innocent voice chimed in from somewhere in the cast, "Is there any chance Mr. Bertollini will be well enough to see the show?"

The question rocked me. I swear, kids ask the hardest questions. "Mr. B won't be able to see our show in person, if that's what you're asking. But I'm sure some parents will videotape the show and he'll get a chance to see it…one way or another." I could tell by the solemn nods that a few of the cast understood my double meaning. I needed to level with them. These kids had been honest with me since the beginning. It would be criminal not to return the courtesy.

Especially now. "Mr. B is really battling right now. I said without flinching the next twenty-four hours or so are going to be tough. So keep him in your thoughts. Right now, he could use your prayers."

Drew was sitting in the front row, and he turned his bearded face back to his castmates. "Well, gang? Let's do it."

It appeared they had done this before. The whole cast came shambling onto the stage, formed a circle, and held hands. "You too, Mr. K," Drew instructed, and I took a spot between Eddie and one of the chorus girls.

Drew's prayer was powerful in its brevity and eloquence. "Dear Lord, thank you for giving us this show, Mr. K, and each other. But thanks especially for giving us Mr. Bertollini. And we pray, Lord, that you would be especially close to him right now. Please give wisdom and skill to his doctors. And if it be in your will, please give him healing in this life. We know you can do that, Lord, and that's what we're asking. But above all, please let Mr. Bertollini know that as he fights in that hospital bed, that we love him. Amen."Bertollini

"Amen," I intoned because there was nothing more that I could add.

The cast packed up and left. "How about you, DJ?" I asked. "I've got a little preshow jitters I need to work out. Want to grab a hot chocolate or something?"

"I better not, Sawyer. It's going to be a long weekend, and I'd like to spend a couple hours tonight with Stephanie." She gave me a wistful smile. "I hope you understand."

"Of course I do."

"I'll see you tomorrow at five thirty, right?"

"This is where I'll be," I said. But I had no idea that as soon as I got home, I would have every intention of breaking that promise.

SEVENTEEN

"He's called four times this evening already, Sawyer. He seemed very insistent." Mom handed me a yellow Post-it note where she had written a cell phone number.

"Mom, I'm going to use the phone in the basement if you don't mind. I'd like a little privacy." I hoped she didn't notice my hand shaking as I accepted the small piece of paper.

"Who is he? He seemed nice enough, but who is this *Ira Siegel?*"

"He's my agent," I said as I disappeared down the stairs.

I plopped down in Mom's hydraulic beautician's chair and nervously dialed the number. Ira answered midway through the first ring. "Sawyer Kent," his nasally voice blared through the phone. "You are a hard man to track down. I've been trying for over a week. Don't you answer your e-mail anymore?"

"Sorry, Ira. I've been a little busy with a project back here in Illinois and didn't think to check."

"Well, whatever it is, I need to drop it now and catch a flight. I need you out here in Cali yesterday. I checked, and tomorrow, there's a 7:00 a.m. flight from Peoria to Chicago. From there, you can catch a direct and be in LA by midafternoon. I've got the E-tickets all lined up."

"What's going on, Ira? What's all the rush? I've got something here that I'll finish up in only a couple of days. Wouldn't Monday work?"

"Not a chance," came Ira's definitive response. "It's 'McKenna.' You know, the pilot you audition for a while back? Well, A&E Entertainment has found a new producer, and they're pulling the trigger on a pilot and two episodes. They've got Burt Young lined up to play McKenna, and they want you for the librarian."

"Burt Young? As in the Burt Young from the Rocky movies?"

"That's right. Looks like they're actually going to put some resources into this project. Of course, there's no promises. It may all sit in the can and never see the light of day. But it's a chance, Kent. And if you want it, you've gotta be in LA by four tomorrow for the first production meeting. They've got some other hacks lined up for the part, but I convinced them you were perfect and you already know the character."

"Wow," I said stupidly. "This is surprising news."

Ira's bluster was overpowering. "Yeah, it is. So I need you to get your butt on that plane. You'll be there, right?"

There was a large mirror in Mom's beauty shop that sat adjacent to the chair. I could see my shadowy image in the feeble light of the basement. It was hovering there, holding the phone, and looking back at me for an answer. But the question that kept turning over in my head was not whether to board that plane. What I really needed to know was, who am I? As I looked at myself in that mirror, I wondered if I was Old Sawyer or some version of a new one. Old Sawyer would've had no trouble climbing on that plane and leaving everything behind. But this new man that I was trying to become was making it hard. And I wasn't used to hard. New Sawyer had started things. He'd made good promises. He had people believing in him. But New Sawyer was uncomfortable; Old Sawyer was easy.

Like I've said, over the years, I've developed the ability to shut off emotionally, to compartmentalize. I know how to stymie the feelings of the present in order to step into an uncertain future.

That's what I did.

Donna, Mr. B, the kids, Tim, my new job, mom, all of them. I pushed them out of my heart and mind and said, "I'll be there, Ira. You'll pick me up at the airport, right?"

I dashed upstairs, not allowing myself to consider what I had just done. "Mom, I need the car. Don't wait up." I didn't let her answer. I grabbed the keys and motored down the road in search of my old ally, Canadian whiskey. He was waiting for me at the Citgo gas station.

There is a small park on the edge of town, and I drove the car to the back lot near its tiny baseball field. I threw the car into park, twisted the cap off the bottle, and began hammering back the anesthesia.

The whiskey was warm and soothing in my belly, but it failed to stifle the voices of regret that battled like thunder in my head. I drank and drank, trying to chase them away. But the more I drank, the louder the war raged. Images of Donna and Tim and Mr. B were formidable foes. They fired off warnings and compelling arguments. They made my heart flutter with sadness. But as I drank, a new battlefront emerged and dwarfed everything else. I realized that beyond all the ugliness of what I was doing, I was angry with God.

I knew this was no coincidence. I didn't believe in those anymore. God controlled this universe, but I didn't like the job He was doing. I felt like some puppet on a string being bounced from calamity to calamity for His twisted amusement. I thought He was unfair, and I told him so. I thought He was unjust, and I drank to that. I thought that if Hanover was where He was leading my life, that He had another thing coming. I'd show Him. I'd do as I pleased. I'd call the shots. And I swallowed hard believing I was right.

I got drunk. I got lip-slobbering, bleary-eyed drunk. I knew I couldn't drive home, but I could sleep some of it off before heading to the airport in the morning. I closed my eyes and laid the seat back.

That's when the policeman pounded his fist on my window.

"Are you Sawyer Kent?" he demanded.

"Uh, yes, officer," I managed to say.

"May I see some identification?"

I fumbled for my wallet and dropped it twice into the foot well before presenting it through the open window. "What seems to be the matter?" I tried to say.

"Mr. Kent, you're under arrest. I'm taking you into custody—"

"For what?" I blurted.

He took me out of the car and pushed me against the door, snapping cuffs onto my wrists. "You're under arrest for armed robbery. I'm taking you down the station, and you need to know that anything you say from this point on..."

I'm pretty sure he began quoting my Miranda rights, but I couldn't get my pickled brain past the two words "armed robbery." "This is a mistake. I've never robbed anybody! You've got to let me go. I've got a plane to catch." I'm sure I protested further, but somewhere between the patrol car and the Hanover jail, I blacked out.

The jangle of keys and the clanging of a steel door roused me. I sat up and found myself barefoot and sitting on a thin mattress in a cold jail cell. "Looks like he's finally awake," I heard someone say.

A broad-shouldered policeman carrying a cardboard box entered the cell. "I hope you had a good-night sleep. We do apologize for the inconvenience. You're free to go."

"What happened?" I mashed the palms of my hands in my watery eyes.

"Donna Thewlis corroborated your alibi that you were with her at rehearsal Wednesday night and not in New York. And since then, a one..." He referred to a small notepad. "*Ernesto Rodriguez* has come forward and admitted selling your abandoned gun to a known street criminal who matches the description of the robber." He set the cardboard box down beside me. "Your shoes and other effects are in here, Mr. Kent. And there are people waiting to take you home."

For the first time, I noticed Donna and Tim lingering in a hallway adjacent to the short run of cells. I traipsed out to them, box held like a holy relic, still not exactly sure what had happened.

"What are you two doing here?" I sat down on a bench and began putting on my shoes.

"We came to get you, Finny," Tim answered blankly.

"But why you?"

"Probably because we love you." Tim glanced at Donna, who didn't dispute the claim.

Instead, Donna shrugged her shoulders and said, "I can't think of any other reason."

They sat down on either side of me like bookends as I cradled my throbbing head in my hands.

"We were sick to death looking for you last night," Donna was saying. "Your mom was beside herself."

"Wait a minute. Where is Mom? Why didn't she come get me?"

Tim and Donna exchanged a knowing look. Donna made the decision and said, "Because once she found out you were okay, she felt she could be of more help at the high school."

"The high school?" Maybe it was my pulsating head, but Donna was talking in riddles. "What is my mom doing at the high school?"

"She's helping set up refreshment tables for the kids and the grief counselors."

"What grief counselors?" Frustration was kindling to anger.

Donna's flat answer decapitated my temper. "Ed is dead, Sawyer. He died last night."

My two friends afforded me the courtesy of silence while those two statements took root in my heart.

Even though you're expecting it, you can't prepare for finality. It breaks through every battlement you may construct. People may think they're ready for it, but they're not. I thought I was ready for Mr. B's passing. I was wrong. All I had in that soul-cleaving moment was my actor's poise to hold a brave face.

"We've been trying to find you since nine thirty last night," Donna continued. "We need to make some decisions about tonight's show. Artie's leaving it up to us to decide, but we have to know what to tell the cast and parents."

"What time is it?" I asked.

"It's ten fifteen. Why, does it matter?"

"No. Not anymore, I guess." I muttered. There would be no plane to spirit me away from this sadness.

"I know what I think about tonight." Donna touched the back of my arm and made me look at her. "But what do you think?"

My answer actually taught me something. Speaking and hearing truth is strong medicine for grief. Maybe that's why we have eulogies, I don't know. But I knew what the truth was, and it blew a small healing vapor into my heart to say it. "If we want to be selfish and make it about us, then we cancel tonight. But if we want to make it about Mr. B, then there's no doubt we have to do the show."

"That's how I see it too." She offered me a half smile, but there was more relief behind it than it showed. "I'll go tell Artie." She got up to leave.

"DJ? Tell the kids that we'll hold our cast meeting first, at five thirty. I want to see them before they start putting on makeup and costumes."

"Who's DJ?" Tim raised his eyebrow as Donna left.

"It's a long story, Tim." I started digging through the cardboard box. "And thanks for bailing me out...again."

I thought I'd find sympathy in his face, but there was none. He had his hands folded in his lap, and he was irritably tapping his thumbs together. "You know, you cut that pretty close last night," he finally said. "I know the whole gun thing was a mix-up, but they could've arrested you for public intoxication. You're lucky that the police chief's stepdaughter is in the show. He said that the park is a public place, but you were in the privacy of your own car, so he'd let it slide. Why didn't you just call me last night? You could have blown everything. The kids, the show. Everything."

There was no point in bringing up the real reason, so I just said, "I didn't want to, Tim."

That only threw gasoline on his irritation.

"You know what your problem is, Finny?" He flared. "It's you. Every time that decent part of you starts coming to life, *you* get in the way. Here's the truth. You've quit on everything in your life. You even told me so. But the one thing you stick with is *you*. It doesn't make any sense. Maybe it's time to hand over the reins to somebody else. Can't you see it, Finny? You need to finally *quit you* and let God take over and drive. Because so far, you've done a lousy job of it yourself." Tim started to say more, but he just waved his hand in exasperation.

I don't think that anger is usually encouraged with evangelism, but I needed to hear it that way. I needed someone to be brutally honest with me. And like I said, speaking and hearing truth is good for grief.

After Tim drove me home, Noah and I went on a long walk. The sun was shining, and we roved far out of town where the county roads cut through the wet fertile fields. We hiked and hiked, and I poured out my heart about Mr. B, my lost acting job, and the status of my life. Noah listened to it all with a friendly wag of his tail and the occasional cold nose pressed against mine. Noah was a good counselor. He understood that I just needed to talk it out. He never interrupted me once. He wasn't embarrassed when I cried.

But when we got back to the house, the session was over. He splashed two links ahead of me though the sloppy yard and leaped upon the porch. He struck his champion pose, exacting his counselor's fee in full with a toothy grin.

EIGHTEEN

"I'm not going to say something trite like 'the show must go on.' Even though there's some truth in it, those are pretty hollow words at a time like this." I looked at each one in the cast. They were all assembled in the chorus room—red-faced, teary-eyed, arms around each other, and passing Kleenex boxes. "But what I will tell you is if we want to honor Mr. Bertollini, then we'll do a show tonight that he would be proud of. I know it won't be easy, but we all know that's what he'd want."

Donna came alongside me for encouragement, and I needed it. "You know, I've been thinking about it all day, and I suddenly realized something. Mr. B always had impeccable timing. He always knew when to play a line or when to exit a stage. And I think that he was just waiting to make sure that we were ready to go before leaving us to take his front-row seat in heaven. I really believe that." Tears were skirmishing behind my eyes, but I fought them back. "As performers, it's our job to help others come to grips with their feelings. It's one of the things that theater does. It helps people examine their feelings more closely. And I don't know of a show that has a more perfect message for tonight than 'Godspell.' I mean, let me ask you a question. Drew, who dies at the end of the show?"

Drew was startled that I suddenly called him out, but he answered, "Jesus."

"And Julia, who lives again at the end of the show?"

" Jesus," she sniffed and replied.

"And I believe that Mr. B knew that too." I nodded. "You know, it's tradition to give gifts to each other on opening night. You've seen the table backstage full of flowers and packages, right? Well, the more I thought about it today, the more I understood what Mr. B has done. This show was his gift to us. Do you see it? This was the gift that he wanted us to have. So let's not be sad. Mr. B wouldn't want that. But let's go out and return that gift a hundredfold to the audience who's waiting for us out in those seats."

The kids milled out, but I caught Eddie near the door. His face was still slick red with grief. "How are you doing, Eddie?" I said casually. "You ready to go?"

"Oh, yeah. I'll knock 'em dead out there," he replied, but it was bluster, not conviction. He tugged the door open but then let the handle slip through his fingers. He let it fully close before turning to me. "He's in a better place now, isn't he?"

"He is, Eddie. I believe that with my whole heart. His suffering here is finally over."

"But what about you?" he asked.

"No, I'm still suffering." My quip sent Eddie's shoulders bobbing, and he cracked a smile.

"But are you going to stay here with us?"

"That's the way it looks, Eddie. I'm going to be here as long as they'll have me. I think that's what Mr. B was wanting all along."

Eddie tested the logic of my claim before adding. "But even still, I hope you stay because you want to. We all really love you, you know," he asserted plainly and slipped out the door.

Donna was still in the room, and she strayed over to me, her hands behind her back. I could tell she was trying to conceal something. Like I said, she has a terrible poker face. But what she did, I never would have anticipated.

She snaked up close to me, leaned in, and then kissed me on the cheek.

"I didn't think my speech to the cast was that good."

"That was for good luck tonight." Then she reached over and kissed me again on the other cheek. "And that's for my opening-night gift."

"Oh, you found it on the table?"

She nodded. "It was very sweet of you, Sawyer. And, yes, I accept." She gave birth to a full smile as she brought the mason jar from behind her back. Still affixed to it was the note where I had written, 'How 'bout we hit a garage sale or two when this is over?'

I counterfeited a hard glare. "Just know that I've counted that money down to the penny, Thewlis. There's $23.18 in cold hard American currency in there. You better not try to gyp me out of my half."

"You just be sure you check out the table. I think I saw something for you backstage too."

"DJ, you didn't have to—" But she cut me off. She reached up and plunged her lips over my mouth. It was a tender, smooth, warm kiss that wasn't in a hurry to desist. My tense shoulders relaxed, and a delicious languidness coursed down the rest of me. I must have looked like a puppet whose strings had been cut.

"So what was that for?" I stammered as she withdrew.

She shrugged unapologetically. "That was because I wanted to kiss you." She headed for the door. "See you at the curtain."

I drifted in a fog back to the makeup area, a bewildered smile pasted on my face. I'm sure the kids thought I was trying to cheer them. In reality, I was just trying to get my legs back beneath me.

The table of opening-night flowers and gifts wasn't far away, and I hunted through the vases and gift-wrapped boxes until I found a spray of crocuses with my name on the tag. Inside was a gift card to Perked Up and a card that said, 'Here's to All Things New.' Underneath Donna's signature was what I think was supposed to be a drawing of a crocus flower. Donna is a fine musician but a dismal artist.

Shoved to the back of the table was a lonesome package about the size of a cake box. A fat envelope was taped to its top, and my full name, Sawyer Alan Kent, was scripted in green magic marker on the outside. Curiously, I fished it out. As far as I knew, the only person who knew my middle name was Mom, and she had given me a card and vase of roses earlier.

I tore open the thick envelope, but the card inside had a picture of a young boy on its cover and the words "You've Grown up

So Fast." "This must be some mistake," I mumbled. "Probably sent from the office for me to give to one of the boys in the cast."

But when I opened the card, I knew that it was no mistake.

Inside was a bundle of folded papers. Each one contained a computer-scanned picture of me as a boy with my father's image photoshopped into the background. He had written, "I should have been there" at the top of every page, some of which were clearly wrinkled with dried tears. The card itself was blank, save the plea, "Maybe someday we could *catch* up?"

How my father knew, I could only guess. Maybe Old Man Jacobsin at the hardware store told him. But inside the box was a weathered baseball glove. It wasn't the one I threw away, of course. But the sweaty tang of old leather sent my heart barreling back to the hopes of a nine-year-old boy.

I had been holding it together pretty admirably up to that point. But the collision of grief, love, and memory disintegrated my aplomb. Fresh tears burst down my cheeks. I swiped at them, but it was no use. They kept flowing, one wave coaxing out the next until I saw Sarah striding toward me in a fabulous black dress and a flower in hand.

"Sawyer, are you okay?"

I couldn't answer.

"I know it's hard. But Uncle Ed's at rest now. You can—" But then she saw the wad of papers and the baseball glove. Bless her, she understood. "Oh, Sawyer," she whispered sympathetically.

Sarah had some tissue in her purse, and I shamelessly afforded myself. "Thanks for coming," I burbled between snorts and sniffs. "You look wonderful."

"And you look—"

"You don't have to lie." I wiped my eyes with my sleeve. "I know how I look. But this last half-hour has been pretty emotional."

"So your dad wants to reintroduce himself into your life, huh?"

"Guess so."

She strangely brightened. "Well, I think that's great, Sawyer. It's probably time for you and your dad to start fresh. I hope it all works out."

"Start fresh?" I was incredulous. "If you don't remember, he walked out on me and my whole family. What kind of man does that?"

"Like father, like son," I thought she muttered, but I wasn't sure. "I came to give you this and to wish you good luck." She handed me a single daisy. "I took it from one of the arrangements in Uncle Ed's room. I knew I wouldn't have time to stop by a florist, but the more I thought about it, the more appropriate this flower seemed anyway."

"Thanks. It's perfect. I'll wear it tonight." I tucked it through a buttonhole in my shirt. "What do you think?"

"A little goofy, but nice."

"Thanks for the endorsement."

"I'm glad you're going on with the performance, Sawyer. You know what Uncle Ed would have thought about canceling."

"Like an Italian hurricane Katrina, I'd imagine. Plus, it gives us something to focus on to get us through to the funeral. Have you made the arrangements yet?"

"I just left the funeral home a little bit ago." Sarah nodded. "He had many of the details already laid out. You know how he was, organized and prepared at all times. He had a plot already purchased near Mom and Dad's. You remember Oak Trail Cemetery outside of town?"

"Of course."

"Well, the visitation will be Sunday night after your matinee, and the funeral is Monday at noon. Artie Chambers said he'd provide buses for any of the kids that want to attend."

"Good old Artie. You know, for a narrow-chinned weasel, he's a pretty decent guy." I twirled the flower in my buttonhole absently. "So Monday's the funeral. And right after that, I imagine you'll be heading back to Phoenix, huh?"

"Pretty much."

"To marry Jim."

"That's right," she affirmed without the slightest hesitation.

"So I'll have a couple of good-byes to say that day." I met her eyes, and thankfully, there was strength in them. "Be happy, Sarah.

There are so many things that I want to tell you, but I guess 'be happy' says most of it."

"I will." She kissed me one last time, and nothing could have been more definitive. "I will."

"Mr. Kent! Ms. Gibson! I'm so glad to find you together." We wheeled to see David Parker advancing toward us, two large manila envelopes flapping in his hands. "Donna thought I might find you back here."

Sarah was still brushing the surprise away as I made introductions. "Sarah, this is David Parker. His son Eddie is our John the Baptist."

Sarah accepted his outstretched hand.

"David and his wife Cindy were pretty close to your uncle," I informed her.

"I'm so sorry for your loss, Sarah," he said and gave her the same odd appraisal that he gave me that first night. "Your uncle was a great man." He kept looking her up and down before suddenly snapping back to the moment. "Actually, it's because of Ed that I needed to find you."

"If you're wondering about the services, I've just—"

But David cut her off. His voice and demeanor dampened businesslike. "It's not about the services, though you can be sure that we'll attend. No, I have something for you, or rather, your uncle does. You may not know this, but about two years ago, Ed went into the hospital. At the time, he wrote you each a letter. You know Ed. He wanted to be prepared no matter what. Anyway, he left me as custodian of those letters until a time that he couldn't deliver them himself. Unfortunately, that day is today."

He proffered the letters to each of us. I recognized his handwriting on the envelope immediately. "It was a burden he carried for some years. He hoped you'd forgive the way he disclosed it."

I was absorbed with intrigue, but Sarah blanched. Hand shaking, she reluctantly accepted the envelope like it was a snake. She turned it over, examining each side suspiciously before saying hesitantly, "Mr. Parker, I think I may have an idea as to the contents of this letter."

He nodded solemnly. "I would be inclined to agree. But I believe there is more there that he wanted you to know."

Sarah let the cryptic response wash over her. "Well, if it will not be a disappointment, I think I'll open this later. I'm pretty sure it'll be best for me to read it on a plane ride heading home."

"That, of course, is up to you."

"And Sawyer"—she turned to me—"obviously, you can do what you want. But I wish you'd wait too. Until I leave, I mean."

"Sure, Sarah. Whatever you want." I agreed easily but didn't want to. I was as anxious as Pandora after polishing her brand-new box. Everything was so inviting on the outside it seemed a shame not to look inside.

"Well, I'm sure you have a million things to do." Sarah squeezed my hand. "I think I'll go find my seat. It's really starting to fill up in the foyer." She let my hand fall from hers, and she clicked away on exquisite black heels.

"Mr. Parker? Do you know what this is all about?" I held up the eleven-by-nine envelope.

"Most of it, yes."

"Does it have to do with his funeral?"

He hemmed on the answer before shaking his head. "Not really. But I do know that he always hoped you'd sing." He took my hand and pumped it vigorously. "Thank you, Mr. Kent, for all you've done for the kids. Cindy and I are really looking forward to the show." He oddly surveyed me one last time before vanishing up the hallway.

At that moment, I wished I had a million things to do. I needed a distraction. But the truth is a director is nonessential personnel once opening night arrives. I had done everything there was to be done. I had tripped the lead domino. Now I could only watch and hope they fell in the pattern I had planned.

I poked around in the greenroom a bit before checking out the house. With twenty minutes to curtain, it was nearly full. It looked like Mr. B was going to get his sellout after all.

After glad-handing a few of the parents and school board members, I made my way upstairs to the sound and light booth. I kept trying to occupy myself, but my mind insisted on running back to

Donna's kiss, to the baseball glove, to the yellow envelope jiggling in my hand.

I plopped down on a stool in the far corner while my capable crew double-checked the board and nattered over their headphones to the spotlight guys and backstage manager. I bounced the letter on my thigh. *How could Sarah have been so dismissive? Clearly, Mr. B wanted us to open these.*

The envelope felt heavy in my hand. My fingers began to sweat. *Three days isn't that long. I can wait until Monday.*

I didn't want to betray Sarah, but my name on the outside glared at me. I could have sworn that the paper was growing warmer. *Of course, this letter was meant for me, not her. He specifically asked Parker to deliver it.*

I held the envelope to my nose, imagining that I could still detect Mr. B's musky cologne. *Wishes of the dead should be taken seriously. It's really not right for Sarah to delay them.*

I saw the lights in the house go dim and the student on the soundboard cued the preshow announcements. "Welcome to tonight's production of 'Godspell'..."

Why should I wait? I won't see her between now and the funeral anyway.

"We ask that all cell phones be silenced..."

Whatever it is, I can handle it.

"All proceeds benefit Hanover High School Fine Arts."

I spent the last fifteen years tuning him out. And now I have a chance to hear him.

"Hope you enjoy tonight's production of 'Godspell.'"

I clawed open the envelope and plucked out the handwritten letter. There in the soft glow of electronic light, I read Mr. B's last words to me.

> Dearest Sawyer,
>
> Since you are reading this, it is evident that I failed to communicate these thoughts to you while I still had time among the living. I am painfully aware that I shoulder a fair amount of

that shame. It is easy for old men to become set in their ways. They discover too late that their ability to resent is only matched by their capacity to regret. I hope you will excuse the manner in which I tell you these things, but if I were to take these words to my grave, it would be my greatest regret of all.

Shortly after the tragedy of your baby, your sudden departure, and expedited divorce, Sarah discovered that she was pregnant with the issue of your last night together. Mad with grief and her anger toward you, she was determined to abort the child. You might imagine my anguish over this decision. I have always been of the conviction that abortion is tantamount to killing the innocent, but this evoked a personal sadness. The truth be told, I had buried too many family members already and couldn't bear to lose another.

I begged Sarah. I pleaded with her. I applied every pressure and conceit I could devise until finally, she relented. She would put the baby up for adoption, but only under one condition: she wanted nothing to do with the details. I would make all the arrangements, and she would simply sign off on the paperwork.

I was fortunate to have a number of good friends who worked in high places at Catholic Social Services. To this day, I do not know what levers were pulled or rules bent to accommodate us, and I had the dignity to never ask. But after several weeks of pouring through applications, I was able to tell Sarah that we had found the perfect couple.

They were from Roanoke, Virginia, well educated, childless, and in their thirties. The child would grow up in a loving, stable, Christian home. We had even arranged for Sarah to spend the final three months of her pregnancy in Indianapolis. There she could be away from the gossiping mouths of Hanover and under the caring eyes of a friend until the birth.

I was there the day your baby was born. It pains me to tell you this, but by then, Sarah had fallen deep into her depression. She refused even to hold the child.

But I did. And I tell you, Sawyer, I have never held anything more beautiful and precious in all of my life.

But this is where my deceit and litany of lies began.

There never was a couple from Roanoke, Virginia.

Call it the weakness of an old heart, but the idea of your child being raised somewhere else was too much for me.

I had found another couple in the applications. They were decent enough but hardly merited a second consideration, with the exception of one superseding quality. The husband was employed by Caterpillar Tractor Company and had been recently transferred to Peoria. Better yet, they had just bought a house in Hanover, Illinois.

And over the years, I have indulged in the exquisite torment of watching your child grow. He is my secret joy and will never know of our biological connection. But there are ways of being a father to a child, Sawyer. I can only hope that I demonstrated some of these traits to you, and perhaps someday, you can do the same for your son.

There are many things I could tell you about your child, but my hope is that someday, you'll discover these for yourself. Let it suffice to say that he is a loving, talented, and often precocious, young boy, much like his father. His only glaring weakness is that he was born with but a single kidney and that one is now failing.

That is why later this week, I will gladly check myself into a hospital and donate one of mine to your son, Edward Gibson Parker.

There was more—final apologies and salutations—but my eyes couldn't bear them. And at that moment on stage, the opening montage was ending with the startling gunshot blast. The stage fell black. Then out of that perfectly silent darkness came a voice, my son's voice, singing, "Preeeee-pare ye, the way of the Lord. Preeeee-pare ye, the way of the Lord!"

It was all too much for me. My heart was crumbling and couldn't take it in. I stumbled out of the light booth and into the empty hallway. All the while, statements from my last two months tolled like prophetic bells in my mind.

Stuff we have cluttering the middle has to be struck. We need it clear for Jesus to take center stage.

Everyone has a different idea about what to do with Jesus after the crucifixion. What are you going to do with him?

You can't ride someone else's coattails into the kingdom. It's gotta be personal.

Maybe it's time to hand over the reins to somebody else. Can't you see it, Finny? You need to finally quit you and let God take over and drive.

I lurched into the men's bathroom, pushed open the far stall door, and fell to my knees.

It was time. I knew it, and my heart knew it. What I had been keeping at arm's length, I needed to embrace. I couldn't deny what God was doing, and I was ready to say yes.

There on the filthy tiles with my elbows propped on a toilet lid, I finally abandoned the temple of my heart and invited God to come in.

Dear Lord, I need you. Every relationship I've ever touched, I have poisoned with my own selfishness. And now, you've brought into my life two precious souls—Donna and a son I didn't know I had. I'm going to need you, God, for the strength, courage, and wisdom to get this right. I don't know how, and I'm done trying. And I don't know what the future is for me and my dad either. But I give that to you too. I guess what I'm saying is, I quit. Tim was right. It's time for you to take over the reins of my life, and I'm gladly inviting you to do that. I don't know what tomorrow holds, but I pray that I will face it with the risen Savior at the center of my heart. I freely admit that I'm not much of a man. But what I am, I give to you now. Amen.

EPILOGUE

The old man's eyes sputtered open, and he awoke. Dim memories of a painful dream still clung to him. But it had been more than a dream—a reality, a pale reality—that seemed all the thinner now that he was home.

And that's where he was. Home.

Before him towered the gates of a magnificent city. Light of every color clothed its walls, and behind them, he heard voices and laughter and music. Why he'd been away so long, he couldn't say. But none of that mattered now. He was happy; he was complete. He was home.

Suddenly, the gates swung open, and the One to whom this city belonged appeared. His face was radiant with knowing joy. Laughter danced behind his eyes. Then he stretched out his magnificently scarred hands to welcome the old man home.

Edward Bertollini took a step forward when he heard a sound in the distance behind him. He glanced at the Gatekeeper, whose smile encouraged him to linger, to listen for just a moment.

Far behind the old man, echoing from that thin pale dream, came a tone. It was queer and far away but laced with a faint memory. What was it? Was he supposed to remember?

He turned to the Gatekeeper, who nodded once more.

Slowly, Edward Bertollini inclined his ear and listened down the dark path behind him. He heard it again, and this time, he remembered. It was a voice, a voice from that place where he had been. And as he listened, the voice began to gather in strength and conviction.

Edward Bertollini understood why the Gatekeeper wanted him to hear it. The voice explained why he'd been away so long. And its sweetness proved that his journey had been triumphant.

With a cackle, Edward Bertollini hiked up his cloak and sprinted into eternity. And as he entered the gates, he could still hear that sound in his heart. It was the beautiful, magnificent joy that comes from having found something that once was lost.

It was the sound of Sawyer Kent singing.

ABOUT THE AUTHOR

Kevin Hicks teaches history and English at Metamora Township High School in Central Illinois. He has been named "Teacher of the Year" by both his high school and his alma mater, Eureka College. Aside from teaching, Kevin keeps himself busy writing and directing the annual madrigal dinner and directing the school's plays, assemblies, and musicals. In 1992, he met his beautiful wife at a summer stock theater production of Brigadoon. They now are the parents of two teen boys, two cats, and one suspiciously fat dog. When not teaching, directing, or writing, Kevin enjoys kayaking and tirelessly rooting for the Philadelphia Eagles